I0766353

LEAF RUNNER

JOHN C. STROEBEL

ISBN 978-1-80558-513-8 (Paperback)
ISBN 978-1-80558-503-9 (Digital)
ISBN 978-1-80558-514-5 (Hardback)

Printed in the United States of America

Prologue

RUNNING FOR HALF A MILE through briars and underbrush at nearly a full sprint was enough to cause even the fittest athlete to become winded. Jimmy was struck by how a metropolitan region with a population of over four million people could have so many secluded areas. But Rome wasn't like most large cities. The Monte Antenne train station near the edge of the woods should provide him with an escape. If timed correctly, he would only be exposed for a minute or two between leaving the cover of the trees and thicket and boarding the next southbound train before it leaves the station. In the meantime, he had a few minutes to catch his breath.

Jimmy was very good at what he did. Yet it was difficult to explain precisely what he did. It was many things, actually. His particular skills were effective at rooting out and eliminating subversives. Of course, this made him unpopular among certain circles and required him to pay special attention to his surroundings as he went about his business, no matter where his business was.

He'd followed the usual precautions and sensed he'd eluded a pursuer who'd adeptly picked up his trail a couple of hours ago. Although there had been no sign of anyone chasing him for at least thirty minutes, seeing the train station brought him only a small measure of comfort. The problem was that the platform was deserted at this time of night. With no one around, it would be easy for an attacker to strike without fear of witnesses.

This particular mission was unusual for him. Jimmy was chasing down facts and information as himself, rather than chasing down disruptors as someone else, somewhere else in history.

The image on the paper expertly hidden on his person could be a vital piece of a puzzle he'd been trying to complete for months. He wasn't sure because so many questions still awaited answers, but he needed to return to New York soon to see if this new piece fit. The next train was his ticket out, assuming he could shake the person tailing him. Then the real work would begin.

It was time to move. Assuming the train was on schedule, it should arrive in the next minute, giving enough time to board before it left the station. The Viale della Moschea ran between his position in the woods and the train station entrance. A check for traffic revealed that the street was quiet, so he sprinted across it and entered the station. After descending the stairs to the southbound platform, he checked the time. The train should be at the station by now. He peered down the tracks in the direction the train would approach, but there was no sign of it. Jimmy stood alone on the platform.

Branches rustled behind him, and he reeled around to determine the source of the disturbance. Reflexively, he kneeled as if tying his shoe. This movement brought his hand within easy reach of his ankle sheath, and he was ready to attack with the dagger it carried if necessary. Thirty feet away, at the edge of the platform near a thicket, two gray squirrels pattered about, foraging for food. They were unbothered by his presence and went about their business as if he didn't exist. He rose to his feet and walked a few steps in the direction of the playful animals as they chased each other through the underbrush.

A glance at his watch told him it had been at least five minutes since he left the safety of the woods, and there was still no train. It was time to formulate an alternative strategy. He turned back in the direction the missing train was supposed to come from and strode toward the other end of the platform as he pondered other forms of transportation he could employ. The rustling behind him continued.

He was deep in thought as he stared down the train tracks. Then he noticed something had changed. The sound of the squirrels was gone, and all was silent. A creaking sound came from close behind him. He began to turn toward it as gloves grasped him around his throat, squeezing so hard he couldn't breathe. Before he could defend the attack, the strong hands pulled him off balance and whirled his body to the ground. He came to rest lying on his stomach and attempted to raise himself to fend off another attack, but a crushing weight nailed him squarely in the back and forced him flat against the concrete platform.

Jimmy's strength was no match for his assailant. He couldn't reach his knife and couldn't even see his attacker. He'd only let his guard down slightly, yet it was enough to lose any advantage he might've had. A zip tie was secured around his left wrist, and his arms were pulled behind his back. Then another zip tie clenched painfully around his right wrist.

"There's no use resisting," hissed the man kneeling on his tailbone. "As I see it, you have two options: *a*, you agree to join our organization and come with me, or *b*, you die. Walk with us or be trampled. Either way, you'll be out of our way. So which is it?"

"I would never walk with you," Jimmy sneered with righteous indignation.

He squirmed as the man felt his ankle and removed the dagger from its sheath. Jimmy was rolled briskly onto his back with his hands pinned uncomfortably underneath him. He felt a blade against his throat.

"Thanks for making this easy for me. Yours will be a quick death. I prefer it that way," growled the hooded man, his face hidden in the dark of night.

The man lifted the knife and swung his arm. The flash of the blade reflecting the gleam of a distant street light was the final image impressed on the mind of Jimmy Evans as the blood drained from his body.

—————————— 1 ——————————

Consciousness was elusive. I felt only pain, unrecognizable, excruciating pain. Every cell in my body cried out in agony. I could neither see nor hear. Blackness filled me. There was no beginning, no end, and nothing in between. There was only pain and searing heat. This must be hell. It was the only explanation I imagined for what I was experiencing.

Any attempt to move any part of me resulted in throbbing pain and bright flashes in my mind's eye. Each physical effort was met with a pain that generated lightning bolts of various colors that coursed through my mind. Thunder echoed inside my head. I did not know how to make it stop or bring an end to this torment, so I floated there in the stillness for what could have been hours, or it could have been seconds. I had no concept of time.

An icy coolness invaded my suffering and forced away some of the searing heat, if only for a moment. With haste, the flames of pain came back. I heard a gasp. The only other sounds were a gentle voice and a soft crackling nearby. The voice was calm and soothing. It dulled the thunder and dimmed the lightning in my head. The coolness returned, along with a damp gentle touch. For a moment, the pain was manageable.

I had no idea why there was such pain and whose voice floated through the room. My tongue was so dry. Then I could feel the icy coolness again, a cool, damp cloth on my forehead and soft hands touching the sides of my head, with fingers lightly rubbing my temples. My eyelids fluttered open. The lightning flashed, the thunder roared, and the pain returned. The gasp was louder, but

I knew I was making the noise this time. I must be alive to be in such anguish.

A woman's voice hummed quietly. Then words came, as in a lullaby, in a language I had never heard before. She must have been an angel, so heavenly was the sound. The pain began to subside as I tried to open my eyes again, but even the low light in the small room was blinding, and I had to close them once more to regain control of the pain. Curiosity urged me forward, and I cracked one eye open, yearning to see my surroundings. The source of the light and the crackling noise was a small fireplace in the corner of the room, at the foot of the bed I lay upon. I could see someone's arm lying across my chest, and I continued to feel the gentle caress of its hand and fingers rubbing my left temple.

It wasn't easy to see much else in the room, but I was sure it was a place I had never been. The walls were dark coarse wood, and the ceiling appeared to be rough-hewn curved timbers. The colorless room danced and swayed as the flames from the fire shifted. It was as if the room could not stand still, and this dizzying effect only served to reignite the tempest inside my head. I closed my eyes, which gave me time to collect myself until I regained the courage to open them again. As my eyes adjusted, I turned my gaze until I saw a woman's face, framed by long wavy black hair. Middle-aged, she wore a scarf in her hair, and I saw her beautiful green eyes for the first time. Those eyes conveyed both sadness and worry, but there was also an unmistakable look of deep-seated love behind them as if that of a mother to a child. Even in shadow, her eyes sparkled as she sang softly.

She must have realized I was awakening because she stopped singing and brought a metallic cup of liquid to my mouth. I trembled while trying to form my lips to take the drink. Weakness overwhelmed me. Water trickled onto my lips, and I supped it up. The water was cool, and I was certain my thirst would be quenched. Instead, the liquid felt like fire on the back of my throat, and I coughed and sputtered, spraying water out into the room. I could not swallow and could scarcely breathe. I lay there staring off toward the fireplace as dread washed over me. Glancing back at the woman's face, I saw the creases of worry deepen on her brow, her eyes well with tears, and her head slowly shaking from side to side. She gently pulled away from me. I wanted to reach out to her, but I barely had the strength to lift an arm. It was then that I noticed the arm I had moved. The small hand, wrist, and forearm seemed out of place, but that was not what concerned me. I gawked at large red and white blisters covering much of the exposed skin. The rest was purple, and from open sores seeped yellowish pus. As someone sat beside me on the bed, I took my eyes from the arm.

Expecting to see those sparkling green eyes again, I was taken aback when my gaze fell upon a man wearing a dark hood and holding a cross. The cross was wooden and appeared to be carved by hand. The man's eyes were dark, and his mouth formed foreign sounds, words of a language unknown to me. However, some words were familiar, like *Spiritus* and *Christos*. I'd heard them before, in church, at a funeral. This man was praying over me, and a chilling fear crept into me. I wondered if I would die in this strange place among strange people of a strange disease. The pain, which had subsided, roared back.

The priest raised the cross toward me while he spoke and then chanted in a monotone voice while he bowed his head and made the sign of the cross with his other hand. At this gesture, a soft cry emanated from the woman sitting somewhere else in the room. I shifted my gaze to look at her and watched as she rubbed a string of beads in her hand. Unintelligible words passed through her lips as both the woman and the man spoke more fervently. I opened my mouth to say something but could take in only enough air to get a breath. The simple act of breathing took all the strength I had left, so any words I wanted to say remained trapped in the corner of my mind. Each inspiration took more effort and seemed to provide less of what my body critically needed. I could hear my lungs rasping as I drew each breath and bubbles and crackles upon each exhale. The time between breaths grew longer as my brief period of awareness seemed to come to an end. I felt darkness devour me. The flashes of lightning and the claps of thunder became muffled and distant.

Either days or seconds went by; time had no measure to me. I awoke amid the falling rain. I struggled for breath as the bright light of the outdoors made me squint when I opened my eyes. No longer lying on a bed in a small room, I was flat on my back atop a rigid wooden platform. Stiffly, I turned my head to see a crowd of people in strange clothes gathered around. The men wore tunics of muted colors over drab stockings, and the women wore long dark dresses with laced bodices in colors similar to those of the men. There was little else visible, save for a pile of logs and branches lying on the grass between the platform and the people. Raindrops fell upon my face and hands, and the sound of the rain hitting the platform surrounded me, but it wasn't the only sound. The people present began to wail and sob when I turned my head toward them.

The person closest to me was a haggard middle-aged man standing near the platform, holding a fire-lit torch and a small wreath. He spoke loudly so all could hear, saying, "Vim flantin tawd, vim flantin tawd, vi mab tloud reece." The sounds made no sense to me, yet the man continued, repeating them over and over. At times he leaned toward me, making it seem as though he wanted to come closer and reach out to me, to touch me, but something held him back. His eyes were filled with tears, and their pale blue irises stood stark on a canvas of pink. He wore a hat that shielded him from the rain but made no attempt to hide his weeping from those present. Behind him was the woman I had seen previously, wearing a head covering and an outer coat to protect her from the cold rain. Her sobs were louder than the man's, and she heaved visibly as she stood beside a teenage boy. She needed his aid to remain upright because the boy frequently reached out and grasped her to keep her legs from buckling. He was taller than she was but had those same green eyes.

Bryn, the word just took shape in my mind. That was his name. Memories flooded back of Bryn and me running along a small creek, of me falling off a tree branch and being caught by Bryn, of Bryn finding me hiding under a bed and laughing. We always laughed. I loved him so much, like a brother. He was my brother. Other memories appeared from nowhere, memories of Ma and me scrubbing our clothing in a tub, of Da teaching me how to chop wood using an axe whose handle I couldn't get my fingers around. They weren't all happy memories. Memories of sadness were a place I dared not go unless I dropped my guard in a moment of weakness. The family despaired deeply after my sister, Glenys, was born lifeless. Without the anticipated cries of a newborn, the house was quiet for weeks on end.

There was no happiness to be found. I don't recall Da ever striking Ma or even Ma yelling at Da, but I wished one of them would say or do something, showing some grief and emotion at the loss we all experienced. I was broken inside, but they did not address it, unwilling or unable to help me deal with the pain of losing her. Bryn was my refuge during this time. We talked about the loss of Glenys, a sister we would never play with or pester. We didn't know what to say to each other or even how to say it, but we knew how we felt, and that was enough. It had to be enough.

As I watched and listened, the meaning of the words Da was speaking became clear. Somehow, I understood what he was saying. I knew the language now, who and where I was. The words, "My poor child, my poor son, my poor boy, Rhys," shook my soul. My name was Rhys, a ten-year-old boy and brother of Bryn. I lay on a wooden platform in front of my kin and neighbors, minutes away from passing through the veil and dying from the horrible plague that had already taken so many lives.

Not even the children were being spared this time. I saw something like this happen before, after our neighbor's daughter, sweet and beautiful Sara Hughes, whom I took a liking to and had played with since I could walk, broke out in an ugly rash. Even though her farmhouse was several hundred yards away from ours, I sometimes heard her screaming when the wind was just so. It lasted for less than two weeks. I saw her nearly lifeless body placed upon a wooden slab atop a pyre, ready to be lit as soon after her last breath as possible. It was the only way to stop the spread of the scurrilous disease, I was told. I was in awe at how quickly and completely the flames enveloped her. I expected her to jump up and run away from the conflagration, badly wanting her to. She was Sara, whose face I stole glances of a thousand times and whose smile stirred my heart every time I saw it. I wanted to go to her and be with her forever, save her from the fire and run away while holding her hand until we couldn't take another step. My eyes were so full of tears that I couldn't see the rest, nor did I want to. Of course, she did not move, could not move. Now I had my own pyre.

We were gathered on the highest hill on our land, and from atop my pyre above the bowed heads of the dozen or so present, I could see the great Pembroke Castle, stalwart and proud, on the horizon. This was the last image I remember as the sides of a dark tunnel closed in on me, leading me away from the world. I could not turn back; I could only go forward. The pain began to subside but came rushing back with each gasp of breath. Each breath made me pause my journey and held me in place for a moment, for I did not want to travel this path. Alas, there was nowhere else for me to go. I soon began moving again, farther this time, until the next gasp occurred. Farther and farther down the path I went, gasping no longer.

My name was Rhys Alan Turner. On April 2, 1359, I was born to Darren Lewys Turner and Gwyneth Elen (Vaughan) Turner. We farmed near the town of Pembroke, in the county of Pembrokeshire, in the country of Wales. I helped my family work the land and manage the livestock. I came down with the plague in late May of 1369, and on June 2, 1369, I died.

$$2$$

BEAMS OF SUNLIGHT KNIFED THROUGH slits in the curtain and collided with the bedsheet, creating brilliant streaks of white that looked like claw marks made by a great bear. The honking of horns and buzzing of sounds ever-present along Third Avenue filtered up to the cramped room, muffled only slightly by the sole poorly sealed window.

Mercer bolted upright in bed as the nightmare ended, scaring the cat asleep at his feet. The startled animal howled and hissed at him as it scurried under the bed. Beads of sweat dripped from his nose, and his hands were clammy and trembling. He sat for a few seconds, slowly blinking his eyes as he relaxed among the familiar surroundings. A glance down at the mocha-colored skin of his arm, an arm the size and color he had expected and hoped for, continued to ease the anxiety brought on by the nightmare. He was conscious of sounds from the street, which he'd tuned out long ago and almost forgotten. His breathing gradually slowed, and the tensed muscles in his back softened. The sheets on the bed were dampened from the sweat, but they were the same cotton sheets he had slept in a hundred times. Mercer was safe at home.

At times, the fourth-floor East Harlem apartment seemed more like a phone booth than a home to Mercer Evans. He couldn't close the door to the bathroom while sitting on the toilet. The four walls of the single room where he ate, slept, worked, and relaxed sometimes seemed to close in and trap him in a sort of prison. When this happened, nervous energy forced him to leave the apartment and walk the neighborhood streets until the churning feeling in his stomach subsided.

Mercer couldn't remember having a nightmare that rattled him as much as this one. What bothered him most was that he recalled nothing about the dream. He badly wanted to remember its details to identify the fear he felt. Maybe it was one of those falling dreams, or perhaps it was a tornado sucking him out of a house, or maybe he was drowning. Whatever it was, Mercer was shaken, yet he had no idea why. Rolling onto his side brought an empty bottle of bourbon perched on the dresser's edge into view. Moaning, Mercer remembered finishing that one off last night after spending the evening out at Damon's, scoping out the bar-flies, and coming home empty-handed.

A high-pitched bell's diminutive sound pulled him back to the present. The screen on his phone, which sat atop the night-stand, flashed. Its face indicated notifications were pending.

"Shit!" he spat as he reached over and picked up the phone.

The time on the display was 8:34. He should have been at work an hour ago. A quick scan of the list of messages revealed that all were from people in the office, wondering why he wasn't there. The three from his boss showed increasing irritation at his tardiness. Mercer immediately dialed his boss, Winston Chalmers. The call was answered after the first ring.

"Where the hell are you? You'd better either be dead or lying in a hospital bed because if you're not, I'm going to come over there and kick your ass," said the voice at the other end.

Mercer subconsciously ducked as if expecting to be slapped on the back of the head. The words came so fast that it was hard to understand them. But he'd heard this tense voice so often that he knew what was being said. During the brief silence after the man spoke, Mercer envisioned the muscles tensing along Winston's jaw as his teeth clenched and unclenched.

"S… Sir, I… I'm sorry," Mercer said. "I don't know what happened, but I—"

"Mercer," said Winston, the hedge fund portfolio manager, more calmly now. "You're one of my best analysts, and today's a big day. Price is in town, and I need you interfacing with these people from the moment they enter the building until they leave. This one's important, even more important than Lynch was."

"I… I'm really sorry, sir. My… My phone…," Mercer said. He thought about coming up with some lame story about his phone alarm not working, but he'd tried that one before. Instead, he said, "I'll be in the office in an hour."

"See you in forty-five minutes," growled Winston.

When the line clicked off, Mercer knew Winston was angry. He was a gruff and unyielding man. When he flew off the handle at Mercer for being late, which was often, he usually cussed like a sailor. Mercer wondered whether someone else was near Winston during the call because he usually would have brought out the heavy artillery in his arsenal of expletives.

Forty-five minutes to get to work was cutting it close, and Mercer was on a short leash. The employee improvement plan implemented by Winston months before was an attempt to make Mercer more dependable. The next logical career step for Mercer, a senior analyst role, should have been his the prior year. After completing a business degree at Stern, he worked for Highbridge as a junior analyst right out of school. It was clear from the outset that Mercer showed great promise in his chosen career and that he had enough talent to climb the ladder of promotion much faster than his peers. However, excessive tardiness placed a substantial hurdle between Mercer and the more prestigious, higher-paying job. It wasn't because Mercer disliked his work that frequently made him tardy. He was a top-notch employee while on the job. For reasons he couldn't quite put his finger on, simply living life had become a struggle for him.

Mercer crawled out of bed and headed for the shower, tripping on rumpled clothes strewn over the floor. He barely caught his balance as he made his way to the tiny bathroom. After showering, he dried off and wrapped the towel around his waist, brushed his teeth, and left his curly hair to air-dry. The black stubble around his beard could wait another day. He chose to wear the same shirt he had a couple of days before, not yet washed, because it looked to be the least wrinkled of those he owned. He decided the pants he wore yesterday would do for today, so he donned them and then slipped on well-worn loafers. Given the lack of care he used to prepare himself for the day, most men would have looked like they'd slept in their clothes. But Mercer was not like most men. One flash of that beaming smile and anyone could mistake his disheveled appearance for youthful exuberance. The mask of authenticity fit Mercer Evans well, and he knew it.

Unopened mail tumbled to the floor as he gathered up his phone, keys, and wallet from the dining counter. Yesterday, after returning home from work, he picked up the mail from his box in the entryway of the building and dropped it on the counter. He was more interested in going out last night than bothering to look at it and had placed his motorcycle helmet on top of the pile when he returned. One envelope caught his attention as he reached down to pick up the pieces. It was from Uncle Stephen and was addressed in the same scrawling handwriting as the package he received last week.

Last week's package was strange when he'd opened it days before. The box contained a wad of loosely wrapped newspaper, and after unrolling the paper several times, a small jewelry box had spilled out, bounced off the counter, and fallen to the floor. He picked up the jewelry box and turned it over in his hands a few times before opening it. The box seemed quite old. Inside it was, what appeared to be, a tarnished and worn lapel pin. Its greenish patina hinted that it might be made of copper, but its shape and inscriptions were what had caught Mercer's attention. Ornate faded blue and yellow leaves adorned the outer edges, and in the center, a knight's helmet sat above a yellow lion or griffin-like creature which stood in front of a blue background. A yellow scroll along the bottom contained a single word in black letters, *Evans*. The pin was the Evans coat of arms or family crest, but there was no note or letter of explanation. Mercer had no idea why Uncle Stephen had sent him the family crest pin, so he'd shoved it into the nook near the entryway and forgotten about it.

Now Mercer pulled the crest pin from the nook and studied it. With mounting curiosity about whether information about the crest was contained within it, Mercer tore open the envelope from Stephen. It was overstuffed with folded sheets of paper, a strategy often employed by his uncle, so Mercer unfolded the contents and laid the sheets out on the counter. Most of them contained lists of names and printouts from one of those websites that can be used to build a family tree. Uncle Stephen's life was substantially affected years ago after a drunk state senator T-boned his car, nearly taking his life. Since the accident, he hopped between different obsessions like a cricket hops through tall grass. It was clear to Mercer that exploration of their family's ancestry was Stephen's latest obsession.

He glanced at his phone and realized he wouldn't make it to work by the forty-five-minute mark.

"Fuck," Mercer muttered. There would be more explaining to do.

He jogged down three flights of stairs to street level, continued for two blocks to the 116th Street subway station, boarded the first southbound train, and grabbed a stanchion to stand for the half-hour trip to Lower Manhattan.

* * * * *

Lizzy Evans listened intently as the professor paced in front of a large counter on the dais of the theater-style lecture hall.

"And in some cases, the fossa ovalis does not completely close, allowing deoxygenated blood from the right atrium of the heart to mix with oxygenated blood from the left atrium. This is not usually fatal and is, in fact, one of the most common cardiac genetic defects. It often goes undiagnosed or isn't found until a person is in their teens. It's also twice as prevalent in women as in men," said the distinguished-looking woman. She glanced at her watch and continued, "All right, that's it for today. Next time we will discuss defects of the ascending aorta and their related treatments." Then, looking at Lizzy, she said, "Ms. Evans, may I have a word with you, please?"

A few students rolled their eyes while Lizzy slid a tablet computer into her backpack. Then she rose from her seat and slipped her phone into the back pocket of her jeans. Even as the material was getting more in-depth and challenging, she was excited that she'd already waded through all the required prerequisite classes of organic chemistry, calculus, and expository writing and was now getting to the heart of her interests, so to speak. Although she had a couple of years left before earning her bachelor's degree and needed to pass the MCAT to get into med school, her motivation and intellect made it a simple matter of time before she would begin work on her MD.

Lizzy descended the stairs to the front of the room and walked confidently up to the professor.

"Hello, Professor. What's up?" said Lizzy.

"Hi, Lizzy. Thanks for giving me a couple of minutes. So let me get right to it. You've expressed interest in any opportunity to get some exposure to the clinical practice of pediatrics. Well, I think I found one that will get you some hands-on experience much sooner than if you just follow your normal coursework," said the professor gleefully.

"Oh! Professor Mayfield, that's fabulous. Thank you so much!" said Lizzy, gasping for breath.

"So I guess that means you're interested, then?" smiled the professor.

As Lizzy nodded, the professor said, "I'll send you the details. And you are most welcome."

Lizzy gave the professor a quick hug, turned, and bounced excitedly up the aisle steps toward the exit. She entered the hallway, and her pulse quickened even more when she saw the familiar figure leaning against the brick wall across the corridor. He gazed at her intently as she stood in the doorway; a slight smoldering smile emerged on his face. Lizzy grinned like a Cheshire cat as she ran up to him and then stood on her tiptoes to kiss him passionately on the lips. Then she leaned back and stared at him with her deep brown eyes. Connor Walsh had strawberry-blond hair and clear green eyes, his muscular arms bulged under his T-shirt, and he towered over her. Working on his PhD in quantum physics, Connor was several years older than Lizzy.

"Babe, I thought you had lab this afternoon, and I wasn't gonna see you until tonight," she said.

"I switched TA slots with Ahmed today, so here I am." He smiled.

Lizzy could barely hold her excitement as she said, "Sweet, 'cause I'm actually done for the day and don't have much studying to do."

"I know," he said. "That's why I'm here. I figured we'd spend some time together, maybe see a movie or just take a walk. It's up to you what we do, but I have a few ideas." He left it at that, winking at her.

Lizzy laughed while tossing her beautiful long wavy black hair, lightly slapped him on the arm, and said, "Ya big dork. I've got some news I can't wait to tell you." She embraced him and sank the side of her head into his large chest.

* * * * *

As usual, the frequent stops and constant jostling of the train to Brooklyn Bridge-City Hall station lulled Mercer into a trance. Daydreams were a common occurrence for him during commutes, allowing time for his mind to wander and random thoughts to take him on little imaginary journeys. Others would probably have been focused on the Price proposal and the business at hand, but not Mercer. The wandering of his mind while commuting was a welcome way for him to experience his most creative times of the day. This particular commute was composed of sepia images from days of old—of immigrant children standing at the railing of a ship waving to Lady Liberty, of a family piled into a massive boat of a car with Dad driving and Mom wearing cat's-eye sunglasses while snapping instant pictures of Mount Rushmore. Mercer didn't realize he'd forgotten to put down the family crest pin before leaving his apartment as it subconsciously flipped between his fingers over and over.

As Mercer finally entered the Highbridge offices in the World Trade Center complex, he saw Winston in one of his expensive suits chatting amicably with well-dressed men and women and eagerly walked up to them. Winston turned as Mercer approached, not a hair out of place and grinning like a politician as he did with only the most important clients.

"And there he is," Winston said with a hint of sarcasm. "I would like to introduce Mercer Evans. He will be assisting in the management of your accounts here at Highbridge. Mercer is one of our most capable, if not dependable, analysts." As he got to the part about being dependable, Winston lowered his chin and looked at Mercer over the top of his eyeglasses. He turned back toward the team members from Price and said, "He should serve you well."

"Apologies for being late," said Mercer as he greeted each team member with his winning smile.

Ned Lamb, a senior analyst for the past decade, stood at Winston's side and gave Mercer a dull stare. Of course, that was the way Ned always looked. Mercer thought it was one reason Ned rarely got the good accounts. Another was probably because Ned always looked like he was wearing a borrowed suit; they never fit him right. Mercer guessed that Ned would be the lead on this account and wasn't looking forward to working for him. It hadn't gone well in the past when he was on projects with Ned. Mercer felt Ned was incompetent, depending too much on Mercer's skill and strategic mind for critical decisions and then taking the bows for their successes.

Winston said, "Ned, why don't you start the tour for our guests. Mercer will catch up with you in a minute."

Ned led the group away as Winston grabbed Mercer's arm and pulled him aside. Although he kept his voice low, Winston clenched his hands repeatedly and thrust his head forward like a vulture picking on a carcass as he spoke.

"Goddamn it, Mercer. I hate tap dancing with these people. You should've been here prepping for this two hours ago. And I shouldn't need to say it to you, but this is your last chance. If you're late one more fucking time, you're done. Got me?"

"Y… Yes, sir," Mercer stammered. "I… I'll try my best."

"Try your best? Try your fucking best!?" Winston hissed. "That's all you can say? Are you kidding me?"

Winston's face was red, and purple veins popped out on his neck. He paused a few seconds to collect himself.

Winston continued in a more measured voice, "You have such potential, but you're throwing it all away, like yesterday's newspaper. I mean it, kid. This is it. One more MIA, and you're out of here. Now Ned is taking point on this one, but we both know he'll need your A game to pull it off. We can't afford to lose this account, or more than just your head will roll. Do you understand what I'm saying to you?"

Mercer paused and tried to portray a sincere sense of resolve. "I understand, sir. No fucking this one up," he said.

* * * * *

Later that evening, Mercer exited the subway station exhausted. He hadn't gotten enough sleep the night before, and the day's stress had caught up to him, so he ordered some takeout from a Chinese restaurant on the way to his apartment.

"Dinner for one, again?" said the grandmotherly woman behind the counter. "That's the fourth time this week."

"Hmm? Yeah, I guess so," Mercer said absently.

Mercer checked his mailbox when he arrived at the entrance to his building. After taking a quick look at his mail, he tossed all of it into a garbage can and tapped his foot impatiently while he waited in front of the elevator. It was always slow for some reason, but knowing he would soon be eating the contents of the heavenly smelling bag he held momentarily pulled him away from the uncomfortable reality that had become his life.

While devouring the lo mein, Mercer reviewed the pages of ancestry information he had left on the counter. Like an upside-down organizational chart, the pages contained many rectangles connected by lines to other rectangles. There were names and dates inside of each rectangle. He recognized the names of his family and some relatives on the last page, but the rest of the names were unknown to him. Some were names he could barely read, let alone pronounce. The oldest dates were on the first page and went back to the sixteenth century, but there was nothing before 1568.

After spending more than an hour studying his ancestry, Mercer peeked at the clock and decided it was too late to go out. He needed to catch up on some sleep anyway and didn't want to be late for work the next day, so he carelessly tossed the pages onto the counter and settled into his bed. Sleep came almost immediately, and so did the nightmare.

LUMINESCENT THREADS OF COLOR TRAILED through the darkness. Each strand, made of various shades and hues, slowly writhed in the black, sometimes intertwining with other strands. As more threads materialized and the winding accelerated, an image unfolded. Vivid colors filled the darkness, lighter in color toward the top, like leaves in bright sunlight, more muted near the bottom. Each new thread provided more clarity as the image gradually came into focus.

I was standing in the notch of a tree where two large branches came together. I glanced down and felt dizzy; the grass below was a seething mass of movement. The ground was at least thirty feet below me. My hands reached toward the nearest branch to hang on for dear life. The dark-skinned hands and arms in front of me looked nothing like the arms and hands I remembered. I paused as I stared at them but realized that the dizziness remained, and I had a sensation of rocking perilously in the notch. The hands shot out to the branch and grabbed it tightly. The bark was slippery, and I leaned farther toward the branch to wrap my arms around it.

Holding the branch gave me a feeling of stability, which allowed me to relax a bit. I realized that I was facing the branch, with my face pressed against it, so I pushed away slightly and lowered my head to look down. That was a bad idea. The ground was still a death's fall below me, and butterflies filled my stomach. I could not imagine how I had ascended to this height. Standing stone still with eyelids tightly shut, I waited for the butterflies to subside. Finally, I lifted my head and opened my eyes. Spreading before me was a brownish-green landscape. A few tall trees jutted out in places on the horizon, and the land was sculpted in deep steps around the hilly terrain, appearing as if to provide a staircase to the heavens for a giant or a god. I could see such a distance from this vantage point. The dizziness I was feeling began to melt away, and instead, my soul absorbed the splendor of the surrounding land, in all its beauty and glory. I knew that I loved this place, the Merina highlands of Madagascar. It was home.

I observed dots of different sizes moving along the steps in the distance. Some dots resolved into cattle, while others became human. Some of the people were stationary, but others moved slowly, periodically bending down and becoming momentarily hidden among the tall grass while swinging scythes to lop off sections of the plants and then placing them into baskets. Rice harvesters were walking the fields and gathering crops, as they had done for as long as I had breathed and much longer.

"Fana," someone yelled from far below. "Fana, are you well? You started to sway, and I thought you would fall."

Fana? Yes, that was it. That was my name. Images and sounds from my life, significant events such as the births of my daughter Anja and son Haja and memories of the days when people were happy with life and not living in fear poured into me. I remembered that I climbed this tree many times to watch the horizon, to warn the villagers, my brethren, if hostiles approached. Looking up at me was a man wearing lightly colored well-worn work pants and a shirt. It was Raza, kind and wonderful and joy-filled, with a look of concern on his face. He was my best friend, someone I could tell all my secrets to and someone I would trust with my life and the lives of my family. I loved him like a brother.

"Raza," I moaned, loud enough for him to hear. "Raza, I am well. I do not know what malady overcame me, but it was only for a moment. I will be fine, but a drink of water would be welcome. As it is, my waterskin is dry. I will come down now."

"Namana be," said Raza. *Best friend* in Malagasy. I could hear the sounds and understand the words, even though I had never heard them before and didn't know what Malagasy was, but

I knew that was what *I* was. "Are you certain that you can come down safely? I can bring water up to you. Please, let me come to you and give you water so that you may come down without falling."

Raza was right. It would be best if he could bring me water and give me some time to rest before I climbed down. "You are right and true, Raza," I said. "It would be best. Please bring me water."

Raza had already started his climb. Although I had seen him do it often, I was amazed at the speed and skill Raza used to climb the tree. He effortlessly scaled the trunk and used any available branch to launch himself toward me. Faster than it took the sun to reappear after being hidden by a passing cloud, Raza was beside me, handing me his waterskin.

"Thank you, Raza," I said. "You are my closest friend. There is no other man in this world that I could imagine sharing the joys and sorrows of this life. You are good and filled with honor. I love you, brother, and I pray to Jesus Christ that I will be by your side until my last day on this earth."

Raza smiled softly and said, "As do I, Fana." He placed his hand on my head and pulled toward me, lightly kissing my forehead. "As do I," he said again as he released me.

"It is a good and quiet day," I said as the sun continued its trek toward the western horizon. "It would seem Her Majesty's soldiers are not interested in us today."

The scar next to Raza's left eye wrinkled as he smiled broadly at me. "Let us go and see what the women have prepared for the evening meal," he said, and he started to climb down. I watched him descend and followed as soon as the way was clear. It was very odd that I experienced vertigo which almost proved fatal moments before. Now I was shimmying down the tree like a fossa, sliding between branches, and dropping to the ground smoothly.

We walked a couple of miles before arriving at a small village. There was a busyness to it, people hustling between small dwellings made of wood and bamboo along beaten dirt pathways. The air was filled with dust swirls, but the people walking by seemed not to notice. All who lived here were accustomed to the dry conditions, for it was a part of life during this time of year. Raza and I continued to walk until we almost reached the last village houses, then turned down the path leading to my front door. Our families often shared meals, and tonight it was to be at my home. As I entered, I could smell the enticing aromas of cooking tomatoes and onions, then the unmistakable smell of anamalaho.

My eyebrows raised as I said, "Ahh, Raza. Tonight we feast on romazava. We will sleep well." We both laughed, knowing that our mouths would be numb and our speech slurred afterward. We often ate our favorite foods during festival time, and tonight would be no exception.

"A feast tonight and a river swim tomorrow, Fana. I always love festival time," Raza said through a smile of anticipation.

As I always did upon returning to my home, I approached Noro, my wife, embraced her, and kissed her on the cheek three times. She did the same to me.

"Face of my dreams," I said.

"Love of my heart," she replied.

In all our years together, I do not once recall her being too busy, no matter what she was doing, receiving me warmly when I arrived, always with a soft smile and a twinkle in her beautiful dark brown eyes. Her gaze lingered on me for several seconds, as did mine on her. I was reminded of how much I loved this woman and how rare and lucky we were to have such love. There were frequent disagreements with many arranged marriages, sometimes ending in violence and often ending in separation. That was not so for Noro and me; we cherished each other and the family we raised. We loved our lives, and each day, we looked forward to what the day had to offer, thankful for it.

As Christians, we were not appreciated by our monarch, Ranavalona, as we were under her late husband. We knew this put us in some danger, but we also knew the importance of our shared faith. This was one of the reasons why there was always a sentry perched high in a tree, as I was today, to watch for soldiers. Her Majesty's army did not come often, but when they did arrive, there were always one or two of those who, if they were found and did not renounce their faith, would be taken by the soldiers, usually never to be seen in the village again. The placement and constant vigilance of sentries and our communication system usually afforded us enough time to spirit away the believers into hidden caves near the great river, where they would remain until the threat had passed.

"Children, your father cannot move one more step until you come to him and give him a great big hug," I said. Out of the corner of my eye, I saw Anja peaking around the corner of the central support post of our house. As soon as she knew that I saw her, she ducked back behind the post, and I could hear a quiet little giggle. Haja came running up to me and grabbed me around my middle, squeezing me as hard as possible. I squeezed him back, rubbed his head vigorously, and ruffled his hair while he gave a belly laugh.

Meanwhile, Anja stopped giggling and peeked around the corner, looking up at me. She receded when I glanced at her, and I heard the giggles start anew. This repeated a few times as I continued to hug Haja. I quickly turned around to approach Anja from behind and grabbed her in my arms before she could wriggle away. Her infectious laugh, no longer a soft giggle, could be heard throughout the room. As always, she clutched her Marala, a small wooden carving of a ring-tailed lemur made for her by my father when she was born. *Bay*, as the children called him, was taken by soldiers two years ago because he did not renounce his religion. I kissed her and hugged her tightly; she hurried away when I set her back down on the bamboo floor.

After praying, we sat down to eat a wonderful meal. In addition to steaming bowls of romazava alongside cooked rice, we relished fresh carrots and cabbage, and to top it all off, we drank ranonapango. As we ate, we spoke of good things—the birth of a healthy daughter to a neighbor, the sounds of raindrops as they pattered against the roof, and the cool and comfortable weather.

"What a wonderful feast," I said as we finished. "The skill of those who prepared it, the presence of great friends, the energy of children"—I smiled as Anja stood and ran across the room—"all of these are blessed and welcome in this home. I think about each of you every day and am thankful for it. I feel like these words do not get said as often as they should, but this gathering allows me to express my gratitude to all of you. Each day that we avoid being taken by the soldiers, injured in the fields, or starved due to famine, is a gift to be cherished. Now it is time to rest and for children to go to bed." And to Noro, I said, "I will put the children to bed and take care of cleaning up after the meal. Please sit and enjoy a few minutes of peace, my love."

Raza and Voahiran, his wife, said "thank you" and "goodbye" and left for the evening. Noro came to me and, stopping about a foot away, looked into my eyes for a moment. She placed her hands gently on my cheeks and brought her soft brown lips to mine, dwelling there for several seconds and pressing herself into me as we embraced. The warmth of her lips and her closeness brought awareness that all my senses were in tune with her. I could see her tightly curled beautiful black hair while the fragrance of her sweat after a long day of working and preparing the meal elicited flashes of welcome memories from our lives together. I could feel the warmth and softness of her hips as my hands rested upon them and the taste of sweet roses whenever we kissed, which I sensed even after having my mouth numbed by the large bowl of romazava. And I could hear her quiet moans. These things were uniquely her, and I loved her more than anything I had ever loved or ever will.

Noro retired to our room, and I got the children ready for sleep. After a brief bedtime story, they began nodding off, smiling contently as they snuggled into their blankets. I set to work clearing the eating area and washing the dishes. It took much longer than it would have taken Noro because I rarely had the opportunity to clean up and was not very efficient. I was also certain that she would have difficulty finding things when she needed them because I didn't know where anything belonged, so items went where *I* thought they should go instead of where they *should* go. I would apologize to her later.

As I walked the short distance from the cooking area to our room, I felt the fatigue I hadn't noticed earlier. A woman's work takes much more energy than a man gives her credit for, and I was again reminded of how much I take everything Noro did for granted, just knowing she will do it and not realizing how much time and effort is required. I thought she would be sound asleep by this time, as cleaning took much longer than I had expected, but she lay on the floor under our blanket and gazed up at me with a look. I halted for a second, surprised that she was awake.

"Noro, I am sorry," I said. "Did I keep you awake because of the noise I made while cleaning?"

"No," she said. "Come to me, husband, and hush. I would rather the children remain sleeping."

I removed my shirt and pants and slipped beside her under the blanket. She touched my chest and lightly caressed my torso as if creating a beautiful work of art, her fingers the brush and my body the canvas. Her touch ignited something within me, a tingling in the space between my bones and skin which continued to spread until it became embers aflame, and I was consumed with a need for her. I pulled her on top of me, and she straddled me with her legs, pressing against me and moving back and forth along the surface of my skin. We made love until our energy was spent, and then both lay in the afterglow of love's most intimate bond, drifting asleep in each other's arms.

* * * * *

With the morning came a bright cloudless sky. Excited for the day, Haja was up early and said, "Father, you do not need to work today. We go to the river to play and have fun, correct?"

"Yes, Haja," I said. "Today, I have no work. It is a time for us to celebrate with each other and our friends, a time I have looked forward to for many days. Now please ask your mother what she needs help with and do as she says. Run along."

Haja plodded toward the cooking area where Noro was working on breakfast.

I woke Anja, cleaned and dressed her, and brought her to the eating area as we all sat to eat a quick breakfast. As usual, Anja bolted from the eating area in the middle of the meal and disappeared somewhere in the back of the house.

"There she goes again," Noro said, "running off at a whim and causing us to chase after her to the ends of the earth. That girl is going to be the death of us, yet."

"She will grow out of it, Noro," I said. "You remember how Haja was at this age."

"Yes, Father," said Haja. "Now that I see how Anja is, I am sorry for what I did."

"It is all right," I said, chuckling. "It is to be expected of little children. A parent must know this before they have children, or they will find out once they do. We must remain ever vigilant."

After finishing our meal and tidying up the house, we packed up some supplies for the day and strode out into the daylight with me holding Anja in an arm and Haja by the hand. Of course, Anja was clutching Marala. Noro walked ahead of us as we passed several other houses, finally reaching that of Raza and Voahiran. As we approached the door, it opened before Noro could knock, and the pair walked out.

"Hello," I said as Noro greeted them with a hug and a trio of kisses. I did the same. "It is a beautiful day. Let us walk to the river and enjoy ourselves."

With the rain that fell the previous evening, little dust was lifted by our feet as we walked along the path through the hills toward the great river. The sun had barely moved on its daily trek across the sky when we reached the flattened area which led to the riverbank. We set down the packs we carried and dropped to the ground to relax while watching the slowly moving current. We all had been to the river many times to wash and get water, save little Anja. She had been too young to go into the river, and I planned to start working with her today to teach her how to maneuver in the water safely.

Before long, whether it was the heat of the day or the quiet sounds of the flowing water along the bank, I must have drifted to sleep. I was awakened by screams and shouts coming from the direction of the river. I looked to see Haja jump into the water and splash as he was attempting to make his way downriver. I know that the river bottom here can be quite deceiving, especially downriver, because the water deepens quickly the farther from shore, and Haja was heading for the deeper area. Although I was concerned that he was not skilled enough to handle it properly, my heart jumped when I realized he yelled Anja's name. I scanned the area for her and did not see anything. As I leaped to my feet and ran toward the river, I felt Raza running beside me, and I could hear Noro yelling Anja's name behind me.

I jumped into the water and kicked toward Haja. With each stroke, I could see Haja sink deeper and deeper until I could see him no longer. I yelled his name repeatedly as I swam toward where I last saw him with every ounce of strength and speed that I could muster. I looked frantically in all directions and reached the spot but could not find him. Even though I was breathing heavily due to my exertion, the feeling of loss welled up inside me and took my breath away, increasing my panic. Then a piece of cloth broke the water's surface and formed a bubble that was captive on all edges by the river itself. I stroked hard to get to the fabric before it vanished and felt something beneath the surface as I reached it, grabbing at it before it could slip away. Seizing Haja's leg, I drew him toward me but found him harder to move than expected. I continued gripping him and pulled hand over hand until I reached his shoulder. As I lifted his head from the water, Raza got to me from upriver. In that instant, Haja let go of something he was grasping as his body fell limp in my arms. Raza saw what Haja had released and dove for it, breaking the water's surface a moment later, holding the lifeless body of Anja. I called out her name, but there was no response.

Raza and I swam back to the bank as quickly as possible, holding my precious dying children high above us to keep their heads above water. Noro and Voahiran paced the bank as we approached and reached to take the children. They laid the children on the bank and tried to revive them, turning them on their sides and patting their backs to drain the water from their lungs. Raza and I left the water of the river and rendered aid. Haja's chest heaved, and he began to sputter, and, thank God, a moment later, Anja started to cough, causing droplets of water and phlegm to spew out of her mouth. A few seconds more in the water, and both would have died. As I realized that the children were all right, the panic and fear boiling inside me started to cool and drain away. Little Anja was safe and alive, and Haja, brave and heroic Haja, who saved his sister's life by clutching her arm tightly even as he nearly drowned, was also alive.

I sat beside them and started to weep, as did Noro. Then I heard Anja, in a choked and rasping voice, say, "M… Ma… Mara… Marala."

"Anja, I do not know where Marala is," I said.

"Marala, Marala," she cried again, more urgently each time she said the name.

"My sweet girl," I said. "I do not know where Marala is. She may be lost in the river." I thought for a second and said, "How about this? I will make you another as soon as we get home."

"Marala, Marala, Marala!" she cried as loudly as her water-logged voice allowed.

I felt that I must at least look down near the river to see if I could find Marala. I said, "All right then, sweet girl. I will see if I can find Marala for you." By this time, things had calmed down, and we were breathing easier. "Noro," I said. "I will go down to the river and see if I can find Marala. With luck, she may be some-where along the bank."

Noro looked at me, her eyes swollen from crying, and nodded.

I walked back to the bank and scanned the edge, moving slowly to see under every bush and in every crevice. After several paces, I glanced toward the river. My eyes rested upon a stationary log, its tip sticking up a hand's width above the river's surface, and atop it was the carved wooden figurine.

"Ah," I said aloud. "There you are, Marala."

The riverbank was steep here and got higher and steeper as I looked upriver. I thought about going farther downriver to enter, near where I first saw the children but knew it would not be possible to swim such a distance against the more substantial current present in this section of the river. I carefully scaled the riverbank, feeling for hand and footholds as I went, and descended toward the water. As I reached the halfway point, the foothold supporting my weight gave way, and I tumbled down the bank, plunging into the swiftly moving water. Murkiness surrounded me and prevented me from seeing anything underwater. Years of experience taught me to relax and allow my body to right itself. My head broke the surface, and I quickly turned in all directions to get my bearings. The current moved me significantly from where I fell in, so I paddled as fast as possible upriver. I needed to swim as much against the current as across it to make my way toward the log.

After the most fatiguing swim of my life, I finally arrived at the log and grasped its slippery wood. Marala rested comfortably in a small knothole at the crown of the log above the waterline. I took a moment to recover and catch my breath, during which I thought about how much I was willing to give of myself to make my family happy. I realized it was no sacrifice to do so. It was my most profound delight to bring them happiness, and I would give anything I could to hear their laughs and see their smiles. I grinned with the joy of life as I reached to pick up the figurine. The water roiled around me, and the wide-open dripping jaws of a massive crocodile burst from the surface of the muddy river. Before I could move or make a sound, the monster's teeth crashed down around my head and arms. Its crushing weight and clamped jaws immobilized me, and the beast wrenched my body out of the water.

The mortal pain of drowning while being pierced by the knife-like enameled shards, the feeling of utter helplessness and powerlessness, and the knowledge that this was my death caused time to decelerate. I pictured the smiling happy faces of Anja and Haja, never to be seen by my eyes again. An image of Noro fixed itself in my mind as blackness consumed me. Beautiful Noro would have to raise the children without me. Would she be able to recover from the loss of her husband? Only God knew.

My name was Fanantenanirainy. On September 14, 1820, I was born to Beloha and Hanitra. I lived in the Merina Kingdom in the country of Madagascar. On January 5, 1851, after rescuing my two children from a river, I died.

28

4

DIM LIGHT SPARKLED BEFORE HIM like a swarm of buzzing insects, yet his eyes weren't open. The image of crocodile teeth glinting in the sunlight was frozen in his thoughts, and an unpronounceable name, Fanantenanirainy, was branded into his memory. Dizziness and a splitting headache suggested this was no ordinary postbender sickness, and Mercer was concerned he might have fallen out of bed and cracked his skull, or worse. Opening his eyes revealed the darkness of night in his apartment, dimly lit by the pollution of artificial light that perpetually filled the night sky of New York City. He examined his face and the rest of his head with both hands and found no bumps or blood, and nothing was painful to the touch. Groaning, he sluggishly rose and tried to sit upright without wavering. Next to the bed, the stand on which he usually charged his phone was vacant. Inching himself off the bed and dropping to his hands and knees, not yet confident he could stand without passing out, he crawled around the room and searched until he found the phone under papers strewn on the floor near the counter. The screen on the phone showed 4:08 a.m.

He rose to his feet and used a piece of furniture to steady himself against vertigo. Then, cautiously, he felt his way to the bathroom and flipped on the light switch to look in the mirror. The image staring back at him was of a sapped Mercer Evans. His hair was crushed down on one side by the pillow, as was typical after he slept. However, the sunken and tired pale blue eyes were surprising. The man in the mirror appeared old and worn beyond his years, not vibrant and youthful as he had once thought of himself.

29

Still experiencing some wooziness, Mercer moved carefully and deliberately, then rested in the only chair in his apartment to collect himself. As he replayed the events of the nightmare in his mind, he recalled his dream from the previous night. He couldn't remember much about it until now, only that it had occurred, and it rattled him. Now the events of that dream came flooding back—Rhys Turner, the plague, brother Bryn, a funeral pyre. Every detail was etched into his memory as though it had always been there.

Mercer reflected on what was happening to him. His dreams were vivid. It was as if he had become other people who lived in different times and places. It was so real, yet none of it made sense to him. He wondered if these horrifying dreams would happen every time he closed his eyes at night. Living in fear of sleep for the rest of his life frightened Mercer because the struggle he faced getting to places on time would only worsen. He was losing control of his life and on the verge of losing his job. Was he losing his mind, too?

At that moment, Mercer felt a compelling need to reach out to someone he knew—anyone. The problem was that there was no one close to him anymore. Most of his friends had either moved away or started their own families, and he'd lost touch with them. Mercer's father, David, managed the shipping business he'd inherited. Since Mercer's older brother, Jimmy, vanished without a trace, David had expected Mercer to take over the family business. But Mercer chose Highbridge, having no interest in doing so. The two hadn't spoken in the years since. Mercer barely knew his mother, Ellen, who was killed while working in her office on the eighty-fifth floor of the North Tower of the World Trade Center on September 11, 2001. Her remains were never identified. At that time, Mercer's sister, Lizzy, was only a few months old. Although Mercer and Lizzy were inseparable as children, they grew apart as their lives went in different directions. Mercer was alone.

While deep in thought, he stared at the sheets of paper scattered on the floor where he'd found his phone. Somehow, the documents from his uncle had ended up there. He noticed part of a map sticking out from between the sheets and recognized the visible portion as the southern half of Africa, with a large island off the continent's coast encircled in red pen. Mercer reached down to pick up the paper and saw the word "Madagascar" written on the island. His heart thumped like a bass drum, his body pulsing with each beat. The circle on the map was hand-drawn. Could there be something else on the remaining pages related to the island country?

Mercer picked up the documents and began examining their contents, looking for any sign of, or reference to, Madagascar. He scoured page after page of rectangles containing names and dates connected to other rectangles with names and dates, but there were no place names. Starting to lose hope as he leafed through the pages for the third time, he took a closer look at the map. Suddenly, he noticed something he hadn't before, a tiny hand-drawn star next to the word "Madagascar." He rifled through the pages until he found a name with the same symbol next to it. The starred name read "Toavina." It was foreign to him. The dates in the rectangle were 1865 and 1895. There was no name connected before Toavina, but the name after it was Jonah Walters. The other rectangle connected before Jonah Walters was Nathaniel Walters. So Nathaniel and Toavina were Jonah's parents. Walking down the tree toward his name, Mercer determined that Jonah Walters, whose mother must have been from Madagascar, was one of his great-great-grandfathers.

"What?" Mercer said aloud. "I have ancestors from Madagascar? Damn!"

Pieces of a puzzle started locking into place. Dreams of Madagascar, ancestors from there, these things seemed more than coincidence. The problem was that most of the puzzle was missing; the picture contained only a few pieces, enough to see there must be a pattern but not enough to identify what that pattern was. A couple of hours of studying the pages and trying to connect someone in them with the people he knew from his nightmares proved fruitless.

Mercer needed more information and wanted to call his uncle, but he dreaded talking to Stephen, who was about as friendly as a honey badger. However, to dig further, he needed to use the family tree website but couldn't access it without the proper account credentials, which he didn't find in the information sent by his uncle. Great.

Soon, Mercer would have to get ready for work. He couldn't wait any longer. Hoping his uncle would be awake enough at seven in the morning to be approachable, Mercer called him. After Stephen answered, Mercer took on a tone as pleasant as he was capable of and said, "Good morning, Uncle Stephen. This is Mercer. Sorry to bother you."

"Hello, Mercer," said a slow, thin voice. Never one for pleasantries, Stephen said, "You must've gotten the mail I sent."

"Yes, I did. I'd like to talk with you about it. There seems to be a lot of information missing from the family tree, and I need to find out more," Mercer said with a hint of desperation.

"*Need* to find out more?" queried Stephen. Then with the disdain Mercer expected and had hoped to avoid, Stephen said, "Aren't you being a little too dramatic, Mercer?"

Mercer thought it best to skip a direct response and took a different tack. "Um, I received the family crest you sent. Thank you."

"Think of it as a reminder," Stephen said dryly. "It's up to you to carry on the Evans family name, you know. I don't want you to forget that. It's important."

"Okay, I've got it," said Mercer. He continued, "So my problem is that I need more ancestry information, but I don't know how to get it. The pages you sent mostly contain names and dates but no places or other identifying information. Also, the tree isn't complete. Parts of it only go back into the eighteen hundreds, so I think many ancestors are missing."

"Yeah, you can bet there are lots of people missing," Stephen said as though it should be obvious. "I only found nine hundred and sixty-eight so far, but I know of guys who have more than ten thousand on their trees. I captured all I could find without spending a bunch of money on getting access to all of those birth, death, marriage, and immigrant records that you can get. Then there's all of the stuff from overseas. Since you and your dad should be able to afford it, I decided to send you what I had so you can fill out the rest."

Mercer couldn't contain his frustration and, gritting his teeth, said, "Uncle Stephen. You know Dad and I haven't spoken in years. I'm living alone and supporting myself without his help, which suits me fine. So what makes you think I have the money and time to do this?"

In that familiar bullying voice filled with disgust, Stephen quipped, "The apple doesn't fall far from the tree, does it, Mercer? You're both dumbasses. You just told me you *need* this information, so I guess I came to the right place, hmm?"

This discussion was going nowhere fast, and Mercer didn't have time for an argument, so he said, "If you could provide me with the account access, that would be great. That's all I need from you right now." Then a thought came to him, and he said, "By the way, I noticed you circled the country of Madagascar and starred one of the names on the family tree. Do you know if that person, Toavina, was from Madagascar?"

"Yup. The Madagascar connection is on your mother's side. I was surprised, so I marked it. Did you know you had relatives from Madagascar?"

"I had no idea. I was shocked to learn that." Finally, after an uncomfortably long pause, Mercer said, "Anyway, I'm not sure how much I'll be able to dig into all this. I guess I'll let you know when I find out more." Mercer received the account credentials from his uncle and said "thanks" as the line mercifully clicked dead. Thankfully that was over, thought Mercer.

After dressing for work, Mercer stuffed the papers and his computer in his backpack and walked to the train station. To his surprise, he found an open seat and settled into it. Mumbling to himself as the train started rolling, Mercer logged on to the family tree website using his laptop. Next, he explored the site and learned how to access additional ancestry information, for which he reluctantly paid. Soon Mercer was digging through all kinds of documents, deciding to focus on the Walters' branches of the tree. There were death and marriage certificates for Jonah, but his birth register, dated 1895, had very little information. Given Jonah's birth date and Toavina's date of death, Mercer surmised that Toavina must've died during or soon after childbirth. Then he discovered a notation that Jonah's mother was born in Madagascar in the central Merina Kingdom.

An announcement over the intercom called out Mercer's stop, which jarred him away from his research. As the train slowed to a stop, he quickly slid the laptop into his backpack and departed. At a quarter past eight, Mercer arrived at his cube and was startled to see Ned reclining in his office chair.

"Wh… What're you doing here?" stuttered Mercer.

"Late again, huh, Mercer?" taunted Ned.

Mercer snapped back, "I'm here now, aren't I? Don't you have something better to do than just sit here and wait in my office? We've got to put that Price proposal together by the end of the day. I thought you'd have gotten a start on it by now."

"Well, I actually have, sort of," said a sheepish, red-faced Ned. "Take out your computer, and I'll show you."

Mercer pulled his laptop out, placed it on the desk in front of Ned, and opened the lid.

"Whoa!" said Ned. "What's this?"

Mercer had left the browser open on the laptop in his rush to leave the train. It showed sections of his family tree.

"U… Um, it…it's nothing," floundered Mercer. "I was just checking on something during my commute."

Ned panned around Mercer's family tree using the touch screen and said accusingly, "Wow, this is pretty comprehensive. Someone spent a lot of time building this tree."

Mercer slammed the lid down and snapped, "Damn it, Ned. It's none of your business. Can we move on, please?"

"So why the sudden interest in your forefathers, Mercer? Are you getting sentimental in your old age?" chuckled Ned.

Ned had always been a frustrating person, but this probing about Mercer's exploration of his genealogy perturbed Mercer. He involuntarily balled his fist as the urge to punch Ned's puffy countenance overcame him. Instead, Mercer, his face scarlet, hissed, "I was trying to verify something about my ancestry using information from my uncle. Are you happy now? Can we please look at the Price proposal?"

"Hey, sorry," said Ned, with the sincerity of an eight-year-old who ate the last cookie.

* * * * *

After the two reviewed Ned's work, Mercer told Ned he would make some edits, and Ned left the cube. Three hours later, a new proposal replaced the dud Ned had created. So it was no wonder Ned seemed a bit embarrassed when Mercer asked him about it earlier.

It was time for lunch, and Mercer spent the break continuing his research on the family tree. He browsed back to the website and quickly became immersed in his history. After a half hour of figuring out how to spend even more money accessing records from Madagascar, a search of village records from the highlands revealed a bit more information about Toavina. It showed that she had never married and was born to Christian parents; her father's name was Kiady, and her mother was named… Anja.

Mercer sat back in his chair, staring at the name. Short snippets of memories played like an old movie in his head—a baby being born, a toddler crawling across a bamboo floor, a girl playing hide-and-seek while clutching her favorite toy, that same girl sputtering water from her mouth as she lay on the riverbank. The movie stopped abruptly. That was his last memory of Anja.

"Could it be?" he asked himself. A paralyzed feeling overcame him; he was uncertain if he should investigate further, unsure if he wanted to know the answers. Mercer was convinced this wasn't something he'd heard or read when he was younger because he knew nothing of Madagascar. There was no practical explanation for the dream he experienced. If this was Anja, then what? He had to keep pushing, learn more, and take this to its logical conclusion, whatever that might be.

With renewed vigor, he studied more village documents—marriage records, land transfers, death certificates, birth certificates, and everything else he could find. As he analyzed more and more documents, his sleuthing skills improved. He could take a quick look at a record and know whether to scrutinize it or move it aside and check the next one. With the Malagasy names, it was slow going; they were very long, and many of them looked alike. As he scanned another list of marriages, he caught the name Kiady in the left column and paused. To the right were the names of Kiady's parents, then the date of the marriage, then the wife's name, Anja. The names matched those on his family tree, but were they the same people? He scanned the page again, but a connection to Fana wasn't there. The feeling of accomplishment that had welled up inside him was quickly replaced by disappointment as Mercer struggled to find the link. He was about to close the laptop and give up when he noted a scroll bar at the bottom of the webpage and realized he hadn't yet seen the entire document. There was more. He slid the page to the left, and the rest came into view, revealing the names of Anja's parents, Noro and Fanantenanirainy.

The dream was no nightmare; it was real. Mercer was a descendant of Fana and Noro through their daughter, Anja. Somehow, he had gone back in history and lived in the mind of his ancestor for the last twenty-four hours of his life.

So that meant Rhys Turner was also real and probably from somewhere far back in Mercer's ancestry. He was sure that if he dug deep enough, there would be a connection through his family tree from Rhys to himself. Mercer had no idea why he'd relived the last few moments of the lives of two of his ancestors. The next time he slept, another such episode would come. Mercer was sure of it. The facts he'd uncovered meant there was no way he could have dreamt all of it up. Yet there was no way to prove his nightmares were real. Mercer realized he needed help to understand what was happening to him and how to stop it. Unfortunately, he didn't know who to turn to and was sure they would think he'd lost his mind if he talked with someone he knew about his plight.

Since the answer to almost any question was available on the internet, it was an excellent place to start. However, determining which keywords to use in the search was tricky. Ancestry sites were all about, well, ancestry. They didn't describe how to go back in time and *be* one of your ancestors. A search for information about out-of-body experiences produced fascinating results, bringing up all kinds of information from clinical diagnoses, to blogs, to Craigslist ads. But it wasn't helpful. Next, he looked up information on reincarnation and past life regression. These boiled down to using the power of suggestion and false or forgotten memories rather than an actual incarnation of the soul or mind. No help there either.

Half of the afternoon passed, and Mercer hadn't spent any time on actual work. He thought one last search wouldn't take long, so he decided to look up time travel. After sorting through lists of books and movies related to time travel and blogs and videos made by people willing to tell you how to do it, science websites started popping up. There were many theories on time travel and much disagreement between scientists on whether it was even possible. The only thing he could get out of what he read was that someone in the field of physics might have some answers to explain what he experienced.

"Time travel?" boomed Ned's condescending voice from behind Mercer.

Mercer visibly jumped in his chair, then turned to scowl at Ned. "Jesus, you don't walk up behind people like that!"

"Apparently, we're not giving you enough work, Evans," Ned projected so others could easily hear. "I'll have Jason send you half of the month-end data so we can kill two birds with one stone, getting the roll-up performed on time and keeping you busy. I hope you don't have any plans for tonight," sneered Ned. Then he knelt closer to Mercer and whispered, "Oh, and if you need it, the bathroom is down the hall and to the right."

Ned Lamb couldn't contain himself as he roared with laughter.

5

GIDDINESS WAS A NEW FEELING for Lizzy. She'd experienced excitement at various times during her life, but it came during moments of accomplishment, anticipation, or even daring. But this was different, better. There had also been other boyfriends. First, there was the dependable one, then the brilliant one, but the one who made her spine tingle each night they were together was…a jerk.

Connor Walsh was different. Yes, he was older and more mature than other guys she'd dated. But there was something else, confidence, a connection, an intensity—she couldn't quite put her finger on it. All Lizzy knew for sure was how she felt about him, when she was in his arms, when he showed up unexpectedly and surprised her, and when she merely thought about being with him. It made her giddy enough almost to lose her balance when he was near, knees wobbly and legs shaking. Of course, it was way too early in their relationship to let him know how she felt about him. Especially since she wasn't one hundred percent sure she knew herself. Maybe she *did* prefer the strong, silent type. Anyway, this time, she'd promised herself that she would take her time and make sure he was the right one before diving in too far. She didn't want to mess this one up.

Lizzy was settled on the single couch in her apartment while Connor had left the apartment to empty a bag of Chinese takeout containers down the trash chute when she received a text from Mercer. The message was totally out of the blue.

"u no anyone in Physics dept @ NYU," it read.

She hadn't heard from Mercer since the last time she texted him, months ago. It was a simple, "hope ur good," to which he had responded, "gr8." Uncomplicated and infrequent one-line messages reflected their level of communication over the past four years. Why Mercer would suddenly be interested in physics mystified her. But the fact that she was dating a graduate student in the Physics Department at NYU made the message all the more astonishing. Yes, she did happen to know someone.

When Connor returned and saw Lizzy staring at her phone, mouth agape, he said, "What's wrong?"

"Oh… I don't know," she muttered with a far-off stare.

Connor sat quietly in a chair and waited for Lizzy to continue.

After a long pause, as if hypnotized, she said, "It's just that… well… I wonder if he's okay. This is so unlike him."

"Who, Lizzy?" asked Connor sincerely.

Connor's question jarred Lizzy out of her trance.

"Oh, I'm sorry, Connor. It's my brother, Mercer. We rarely talk to each other anymore," she said.

"You have a brother," said Connor. It was more a statement than a question.

"Yes, I have a brother. And his message is strange." She leaned over to Connor and showed him the text.

"Huh," puzzled Connor.

Lizzy thought for a few moments until her demeanor brightened, then said to Connor, "Hey, would you like to meet him?" She looked at her phone and feverishly thumbed the screen.

Connor stammered, "Um…uh. Well, I do have a forty-page paper I need to get done by next week. And I need to do some lab notebook grading. And there's—"

"Awesome, I texted that we can meet him at Damon's at nine," Lizzy chirped.

"Hmm. Well, I guess so. But I'm not sure this is how I would've expected to meet a member of your family."

"Mercer's all right. I think you'll get along fine," she said with a knowing smile that did nothing to ease Connor's apprehension.

Lizzy's phone beeped. She glanced at it, then jumped off the couch and ran to the bathroom, yelling, "I need to get ready!"

* * * * *

Mercer wasn't sure why he'd asked Lizzy that question. Yes, she was a student at NYU, but Lizzy was in premed, and whether she would know someone in the Physics Department was a long shot. Yet Lizzy still wanted to meet him at the restaurant. Maybe she *did* know someone who could help him. It'd been a long day of work, and Mercer was famished, amplified tenfold as he entered the establishment, immediately bombarded by a busy kitchen's pleasing aroma.

Suddenly, someone launched into Mercer and grabbed him around the neck, nearly knocking him off his feet.

"Mercer!" shouted Lizzy as he regained his balance. He hugged her and said flatly, "Hi, sis."

She stepped back and gave Mercer a full once-over. "Oh, it's been so long since I've hugged you. Let me see you. I've missed you. You look…great," she said half-heartedly.

"I'm sorry. I miss you too, sis, and it's been a very long day. I apologize for looking a little worse for the wear tonight," he said. Then Mercer noticed a tall, well-built guy standing behind Lizzy, smiling and glancing at her with anticipation, and said, "So, Lizzy, who's your friend?"

Lizzy turned and seemed to realize that a man was standing behind her. Then she refocused and said, "Yes, Mercer. I'm sorry, I should introduce you two. Connor, this is my brother, Mercer, and, Mercer, my friend, Connor Walsh."

Mercer looked him in the eye as he shook Connor's large hand. Memories of watching all-star wrestling with his dad and brother flooded back as Connor reminded him of some of the mus-clemen he'd seen on the show. Connor wasn't *that* big and was only a couple of inches taller than Mercer, but he carried himself as a champion would. Lizzy beamed at Connor after the hand-shake, and Mercer saw the look in her eyes, a look he knew. Lizzy was head over heels for this guy, and she gushed with joy and contentment. That was how Mercer remembered her and how he always hoped she would be.

After they were seated, Lizzy asked Mercer how he was and what he'd been doing. Connor listened quietly. Mercer put on his best face, but he could tell Lizzy knew he was faking it. After the waitress took their order, Lizzy said, "So you wanted to know if I knew somebody from the Physics Department. Well, it just so happens that Connor is a physics teaching assistant at NYU and is working on his PhD."

"No fucking way," said a stunned Mercer as Connor and Lizzy gave each other a knowing smile. "You're really a physicist?"

"I am," said Connor. "Since I got my master's degree last year, I've been working at the university. I might be able to help you. What is it that you need?"

Mercer was in shock. Here he was, talking to a physicist so soon after thinking he should try to contact one. Connor's direct approach caught Mercer flat-footed, and he didn't feel prepared. He didn't know where to begin.

Mercer took a deep breath and said, "Well, I don't know anything about physics, so I really don't know where to start. I looked out on the internet for some help and just got confused."

"Confused about what?" asked Connor.

"Confused about…well…time travel," Mercer said reluctantly.

"Time travel," exclaimed Lizzy as she looked quizzically at Mercer. "What the hell are you talking about, Mercer?"

Connor sat back in his chair and produced a vexed smile while staring at Mercer. "You don't strike me as a nutcase, Mercer."

"I just want to know if it's even possible. I'm not trying to build a time machine," snapped Mercer.

"Okay, I'm sorry. That was uncalled for." The three sat in uncomfortable silence for a few seconds. Then Connor spoke frankly. "The short answer is that humans can't travel through time. As far as we know, anything bigger than an atom cannot do this."

"Are you sure?" said Mercer.

"Yes. So far, Einstein was right. Of course, I'm not the expert on this, but I doubt you'll find out much more than what I've already told you."

Mercer was pensive, not knowing what to do next.

After a pause, in a more diminutive tone, Connor offered, "I will say this. There has been much work in physics trying to answer this very question. The truth is, we don't really know. We haven't proved it's possible, but we also haven't proved it's not." Then he shrugged with his hands raised.

The siblings' faces both expressed confusion.

Then Lizzy asked, "But why, Mercer? Why do you have to know?"

Mercer needed to come clean; he was sure of that. However, he also knew that, after he told them about his experiences, not only Connor would think him insane.

Mercer tilted his head back and to the side as he said, "I believe it's happened to me."

Stunned, Lizzy said, "What, are you losing your mind?"

"Hmm, maybe. Well, I'm not sure of that, but things have happened to me. Things I can't explain."

"What…things?" said Connor in an uneasy voice.

"I thought they were nightmares at first." Mercer continued with gravitas and emotion, underscoring that what followed was the absolute truth. "In each, I had a vision that I was a different person, living their lives as they would and dying as they did." Lizzy gasped. "Later, I found out that one of them was our ancestor who lived in Madagascar in the mid-eighteen hundreds…" A knot in Mercer's throat forced him to pause before saying, "…and died after saving his children from drowning in a river. I have proof."

"Madagascar?" Lizzy said, struggling to keep up.

"Proof?" queried Connor.

Mercer showed them the website and the updated family tree on his phone that now reached back to Fana and Noro.

"God, Mercer," said Lizzy. "I can't believe this is possible. I just can't."

"You're right to doubt, Lizzy. But Madagascar wasn't the only time this happened to me. The other experience I had was as Rhys Turner, from Wales, who died of the black plague in 1369 at age 10. The tree on the website currently doesn't go back that far, but I'm sure I could trace back to him with time. It's just that I don't want to waste time doing it. I *know* there's a connection. What I need now are answers." He paused, unsure whether he should continue. Then he said, "I'm afraid to sleep at night." His voice was firm yet quiet; his face was stern and determined.

Lizzy took a deep breath, sat back in her chair, and looked away, puzzled.

After a few moments, Connor muttered, "There might be someone."

Mercer's jaw dropped open. "What?" he said.

"Are you kidding?" scoffed Lizzy.

"Professor Giannelli specializes in quantum entanglement. I've heard him lecture on the topic and the possibility that particles can interact over long distances and even through other dimensions. Some say he's a bit on the fringe of the theoretical quantum physics spectrum. Anyway, it might be worth hearing what he says on the matter."

"When can I meet him?" prodded Mercer.

* * * * *

Lizzy was perplexed as she lay in bed that night. It was difficult for her to accept what Mercer claimed was happening. She'd experienced disappointment brought on by him often during her life. Sure, he had a career, but he was a prick to his family. He never showed respect to their father, even in front of others. She wondered if he was attempting to manipulate her in some way. However, the sincerity in his weary eyes and manner was new. Maybe he was desperate. Something told her his words were genuine and that whatever was happening needed to play itself out.

Her face softened, and she dropped, ever so slightly, the defensive shield protecting her from Mercer's previous lapses—missed family gatherings, promises never kept, a multitude of embarrassments.

Connor had promised to send a text to inform them if and when the professor could see them. Lizzy insisted she was present at the meeting, which Mercer had agreed to without hesitation. The message arrived early in the afternoon. They were to meet at the Department of Physics on Broadway at three o'clock. When Lizzy arrived five minutes before the hour, Connor was already waiting for her. She hadn't finished greeting him with a kiss when Mercer jogged up to them, out of breath. He appeared drained, and the bags under his eyes were prominent.

"Mercer, you look horrible. Are you okay?" said Lizzy.

"I didn't sleep last night. I was afraid it would happen again. Anyway, I don't think I could sleep if I tried," said a weary Mercer. "I don't think I can live like this much longer..." His words trailed off as he shook his head.

The three entered the physics building, and Connor led them to a staircase which they descended several flights, ending up in a maze of hallways. The group took so many turns that Lizzy thought they should have dropped some bread crumbs to help them find their way back out later. Finally, Connor stopped in front of a door with a sign that read "Quantum Physics Lab #7." He checked the door handle, and it was locked, so he pressed a button beside the door and waited. Within seconds, the latch clicked, and Connor pushed open the door, then walked into the room, followed by Lizzy and Mercer. Chairs, workbenches, and cabinets filled the laboratory space. Each bench held a variety of electrical instruments sitting on racks above the table surface. Projects in different stages of construction covered some of the bench surfaces. Some projects had many wires haphazardly connecting the pieces on the bench to equipment on the rack. The overhead lights were dim, and a few workbenches provided additional lighting over their surfaces. Most of the benches were unused. Cooling fans from all the running equipment filled the laboratory with white noise.

Connor continued toward the back of the room and stopped in front of an open doorway. Inside was an office with almost no space to move. Sagging bookshelves lining adjacent walls held hundreds of books. Piles of magazines, some of which almost reached the ceiling, covered much of the floor. The desk was barely visible beneath stacks of periodicals and textbooks. The whole area seemed to have a slightly acidic smell, almost like an elder care center.

Reclining in an office chair in front of the desk was a grizzled older man with long salt-and-pepper hair and a full white beard and mustache. Smudged reading glasses perched on the end of his hawklike nose in front of squinting dark eyes and bushy black eyebrows. His plaid button-down shirt, tan and white, was untucked and oversized, as were his khaki-colored cargo pants. As he turned his swivel chair to face them, the chair creaked and groaned.

"Ah, Walsh," said the old man. His voice was soft and quiet but had enough edge to command attention. "What brings you down here this afternoon?" Facing Lizzy, he said, "And who is this young lady?"

"Well, Professor Lazarro Giannelli," said Connor as he placed a hand on Lizzy's shoulder, "this is my friend, Lizzy Evans." Then he gestured toward Mercer and said, "And this is her brother, Mercer." As Mercer and Lizzy shook his hand, the professor's eyes remained uncomfortably fixed on Lizzy. Connor continued, "Mercer is wondering if you could answer some questions for him."

"Lizzy, eh? Must be short for Elizabeth, hmm? Fine young lady. Mason, you say?" asked the professor as he finally shifted his gaze toward Mercer. When Mercer opened his mouth to correct him, the professor resumed, "Which journal are you from? Is this about the measurement of gravitational waves using principles of quantum entanglement? I just finished talking with that woman from *Nature* about the same thing."

"No, Professor," said Connor. "His name's Mercer, and his questions are not nearly as technical. He's not from a journal. His questions are of a more…personal nature."

"Hmph," Giannelli huffed. "I don't have time to talk to every Tom, Dick, and Harry about their personal problems. I have grant proposals to complete, papers to write, articles to review—"

"Speaking of time, is time travel possible?" blurted Mercer.

"Time tr—what? Did you say time travel?" said the professor quizzically.

"Yes, time travel," reiterated Mercer.

"Well, maybe you should check the internet. I'm sure you'll find all sorts of information there," the professor snarled. "Now maybe you could leave so that I—"

Mercer interrupted again and announced, "My mind or my soul, I'm not sure which, traveled back in time…twice. And in both cases, I lived as one of my ancestors until their death."

Lizzy was startled by the conviction in Mercer's voice.

Professor Giannelli sat forward in his chair with an intense look. "Did you say your *mind* traveled back in time?" he asked.

"Yes, or my soul. I was an observer, watching someone else's life unfold before me, seeing every face, hearing every word, reading every thought, feeling every emotion and affliction. *My* mind was in *their* body."

"Mind…mind…mind," Giannelli repeated, staring at the ceiling. He turned around in his chair and scanned the shelves like he was looking for a particular book. Then he stood and walked to the far corner of the room, reached up, and touched the books on the top shelf, one at a time. A few were pulled out and quickly put back. He kept repeating the word *mind*. After pulling one particular book out, he promptly removed the two next to it and reached deep into the shelf. Out came a thick book with a drab green cover and gold lettering. Replacing the other books, he sat back down and laid the tome on top of three other open books lying on his desk. Giannelli stared at it for a few seconds, allowing Lizzy to see the title, *Relationships of Neurological Processes with Quantum Entanglement*. He opened it to the table of contents, glanced at it, flipped to the middle of the book, and then scanned page after page. Lizzy and the others waited quietly and patiently while the professor was absorbed in his search for…something. Finally, he stopped on a page and stared at it intently.

Suddenly Giannelli exclaimed, "Ah, yes, yes. That's it! Warwick, you old fool. You brilliant old fool."

"Well, what did you find?" Lizzy cried out before anyone else could speak.

"What did I find, what did I find," Giannelli repeated excitedly. "Have you ever heard of Zeno's paradoxes?" There was silence. "That figures, there are no philosophers here. First of all, I'm sure you all know that a paradox is a statement that seems self-contradictory but may, through the rigors of science, actually prove to be true. Well, Zeno was a Greek philosopher before Plato and Socrates. He developed a series of paradoxical philosophical problems, attempting to illustrate that motion in time is an illusion.

"One of the most famous was called Achilles and the Tortoise. This paradox states that the two are in a footrace in which the much faster Achilles allows the tortoise a head start. If each racer runs at a constant speed, the faster racer will eventually reach the starting point of the slower one. However, the slower racer has also moved to a new location during this time. Thus, whenever Achilles arrives at a point where the tortoise has been, he still has some distance to go before reaching the tortoise. Although that distance keeps getting shorter and shorter, he will never be able to reach the tortoise. Do you understand?"

Lizzy looked at Mercer and saw his bewildered face. Then she said, "Umm…"

Gianelli plowed on, saying, "On its face, it sounds absurd, but proving this paradox false took centuries. Until quantum physics came along, we were unable to do so quantitatively. Zeno's type of thinking led us to delve deeper into the science and formulate the theories behind quantum entanglement. There is a great deal of science and mathematics behind the entanglement theories that have been developed. We know that quantum particles can interact with each other over great distances and that what happens to one particle can affect another particle, even across a barrier. So far, the science has focused on spatial barriers, but some work has been done on barriers of higher-order dimensions, including the fourth dimension, that of time.

"This brings us to your question, Marvin. 'Is time travel possible?' Well, some have thought so since the dawn of time, but science has so far been reluctant to accept such a bold and unprovable theory. However, some in the science community have spent their lives trying to answer this question. It's the holy grail of science. The one who finds the answer will likely be more famous than Einstein, Newton, Hawking, and Curie. Are you following me?"

Fumbling for words, Mercer said, "I... I think so, Professor. And the name is Mercer. Anyway, you're basically saying we don't know much about time travel, and scientists are studying it right now. So it may be possible."

"Precisely," said Giannelli.

"But how?" pleaded Mercer. "I seem to have no control over these experiences. I'm thrust into an ancestor's mind at some point near the end of their lives and pulled back out when they die. I don't know who will be next or when. I'm afraid to go to bed because it happens when I sleep. Why is this happening to me?"

Lizzy thought Mercer was on the verge of tears.

Giannelli shook his head and said, "As for the how I can't say exactly." Then he continued, "But as to the why, I first have a question for you. When and where were you born?"

"What?" said Mercer blankly.

"You heard me."

"Um, I was born July 15, 1997, at Bellevue Hospital, here in New York."

Excitedly Giannelli said, "So you were, so you were." The lecture continued, "Science is a field with many specialties and subspecialties. There are physicists, like me, there are engineers, chemists, zoologists, and the list goes on and on. But there are also medical doctors: oncologists, epidemiologists, pediatricians, and obstetricians. One such obstetrician practiced at Bellevue for about fifteen years, starting in the mid-1980s. He also had a master's degree in physics and studied quantum entanglement. His name was Amon Warwick. He ran several animal experiments in which he attempted to transfer cognitive processes from one subject to another. Several published papers detail his work, some of which were peer-reviewed and appeared in scientific journals. The problem was that his targeted processes could not translate to human physiology. From a theoretical standpoint, his work was brilliant, but not so from a practical one…" Giannelli trailed off, lost in thought.

"Well," said Lizzy, "what does this have to do with Mercer?"

"Who?" Giannelli said absently.

Mercer raised his hand.

"Oh, yes, Mercer. Well, you see, there was a body of work that Warwick was developing, building a base of evidence to support some new theories and papers he was working on. However, he kept this work very secret during his time at Bellevue. Warwick planned to initiate a large-scale human clinical trial to evaluate these theories, but sadly, he would never complete the work. He died in a scuba diving accident while on vacation in Cape Cod. Such a waste." Again, Giannelli lost himself in thought.

"And?" Lizzy persisted.

"I'm sorry, it's been quite some time since I've thought about all this." He paused, trying to collect himself. "It was rumored that Warwick performed some of his feasibility work on actual human subjects, subjects who had neither the knowledge nor ability to consent to such a dangerous undertaking. The subjects he experimented on were newborn babies."

6

MERCER HAD TO FIND SOMEWHERE to sit or something to lean on. Suddenly his legs felt like limp noodles.

"Newborn babies," Lizzy said, aghast. "What did he do to them?"

"I'm not sure. Presumably, they received a series of injections before leaving the hospital," said Giannelli matter-of-factly.

"They?" Mercer murmured. "Oh god, how many were there?"

"It's difficult to say. Warwick probably started in about 1987, and he died in 2001. I would estimate there are thousands. Of course, not all of them would have the proper genetic sequence to show a response, and the degree of response in each subject would vary."

"And…and the parents had no idea this was happening?" stammered Mercer.

"I don't believe so," said Giannelli.

"What happened to them, the injected babies?" asked Lizzy.

"I don't know," affirmed Giannelli. "I only know what I've told you because I was working in the same laboratory as Warwick for a time, this one. We didn't interact much, but I could see and hear enough to figure out some of what he was planning. You see, research is a special thing to a person. You don't just go traipsing through another scientist's project, asking a bunch of questions. They do their work, and you do yours. You must wait for the paper to be published before you can attempt to understand their experiment. Only then does the work become public knowledge and ripe for criticism."

"What happens after the injections? What are the effects?" asked Mercer.

"As I mentioned earlier, Warwick was trying to transfer cognitive processes from one subject to another. He showed that one rat could induce another rat to perform an action using only its mind. The effects were temporary, and it was thought this could only happen once between two given subjects. I imagine he was expecting similar characteristics between humans. However, since the metaphysical transference ability didn't show effect until after adolescence in the test animals, he likely never got to see the results. None of his human subjects would have reached the proper age by the time he died."

Mercer was ashen. The sandwich he'd eaten for lunch seemed to be urging itself back out of his stomach. "Water," he said. "I need some water, please."

Connor disappeared to find him some water as Mercer sat on the nearest chair he could find.

Lizzy seemed to be getting control of her emotions much better than Mercer was. She said, "So if Warwick was a scientist, where are all of his notes and records? Wouldn't he have recorded every subject's name and date of birth so that he could evaluate them after they reached the proper age?"

"Very astute, young lady," said the professor. "I'm sure he did. But I have no idea where such records would be stored. He never mentioned anything about it around me."

The three were in silent thought as Connor returned with a glass of water for Mercer.

"Thanks," said Mercer, as he sipped slowly. Then he said, "Professor, is there any other information you can provide that might help me?"

"You're welcome to borrow this volume, which contains his published papers. But I'm afraid that's all I have for you." Giannelli handed Mercer the book he'd opened on his desk. His demeanor was solemn as he addressed Mercer, "What I will say is this, if the rumors about Warwick's experiments are true, I think it is plausible that you were one of his neonatal subjects. What you are experiencing might be the result of his work. It may be possible."

With each answer came more questions. Did Warwick discover something no other human had previously observed? Could Mercer be one of his experiments? Mercer thanked the professor, and they left the laboratory in silence. They climbed the stairs to the building lobby and strode toward the main entrance, immersed in their thoughts. Before reaching the revolving door, Mercer stopped and looked at the other two, saying, "Well, I appreciate your help, both of you. I'm just not sure what to do next."

Connor and Lizzy stopped walking and turned to face Mercer. Connor gave him a reassuring look and said, "How about this? If you give me the book, I'll see if I can find anything useful in Dr. Warwick's published papers. Maybe they'll give us some clues. I might have a better idea about what to look for now that we have more insight into what he was up to," offered Connor.

"Good idea," said Lizzy. "Mercer, I have a couple of hours right now if you want to do a little digging regarding Dr. Warwick. Maybe we can find out where he lived or who his family was. If we find someone, they might know where his notes would be. I have the perfect place."

"Lizzy, I can't ask you to do that. I've already wasted enough of your time," Mercer said, shaking his head.

Lizzy exploded, "Mercer Evans, stop that right now! You always do this, pushing family out of your life just when you need us most. You can't keep popping into our lives and then popping out again. If you walk away now, I don't think I could…"

Tears welled in Lizzy's eyes.

"Aw, c'mon, sis," murmured Mercer.

She wiped her eyes and said, "Are you too proud to ask me for help? Mercer, I see your desperation. Now more than ever, you need my help. Please let me help you."

The sincerity in her voice opened floodgates of regret. It was true. He'd pushed her and their father away whenever he felt vulnerable. He was vulnerable now, more than he'd ever been. He risked losing Lizzy forever if he pushed her away this time. He would lose himself in the process.

"You know, you're right, Lizzy. I do need your help, now more than ever," Mercer said in a hoarse whisper. He reached out to her and hugged her, pulling her toward him like he used to when she met him after school. He always waited for her in front of her elementary school so they could walk home together. These were some of his favorite memories.

Mercer finally released Lizzy, and they held each other's gaze for a few seconds. A smile crept onto Lizzy's face, and then Mercer laughed.

Mercer said, "I'm really sorry, sis. I've been an ass. Let's see what we can learn about Warwick. And, Connor, thanks for your help. Let me know if you find anything."

Connor and Mercer exchanged phone numbers, then Connor walked back toward the stairs. Lizzy and Mercer left the physics building and trekked the four blocks to Bobst Library. She found her usual quiet place away from others where they could collaborate. With Lizzy on her laptop and Mercer on his phone, the two went to work to find out what they could about Amon Warwick.

"It looks like Professor Giannelli was right," said Lizzy after a few minutes. "Amon Warwick died on December 20, 2001, in a scuba diving accident while diving off of Cape Cod. Apparently, he was an experienced diver, and there were questions about the circumstances surrounding the incident, but a police investigation turned up nothing, and his death was ruled an accident."

"Interesting," said Mercer. After another couple of minutes, he said, "Here it says that Amon Warwick was an obstetrician on staff at Bellevue Hospital from 1985 until his death. Over the years, a few malpractice lawsuits were brought against the hospital, specifically naming Warwick as a defendant. Settlements were reached in each instance, so none went to trial."

"Hmm…Say, didn't the professor tell us that Warwick got his master's degree in physics from NYU and then received his medical doctorate a few years later?" said Lizzy. "I wonder how many people go from a physics master's to an MD. Do you think that's very common, Mercer?"

"Huh? I dunno, it's probably not unusual."

The gentle clickety-clack of Lizzy's keyboard, the soft, comfy chair he was lounging in, and his state of sleep deprivation combined to lull Mercer into a light snooze. He didn't feel the phone slip from his fingers and fall into his lap, and he didn't know how much time had passed when Lizzy's voice suddenly snapped him out of his catnap.

"I found his obituary. He must have never been married or had kids. The only person listed as surviving him was his sister, Violet. It was twenty years ago, so I wonder if I'll be able to—"

A disoriented Mercer mumbled, "What? Who died?"

"I'm sorry, Mercer, but you really need to rest. Why don't we call it a day?"

Groggily, Mercer said, "No, I'm the one who's sorry, sis. I heard you say something about an obituary. What did you find?"

Lizzy didn't immediately answer, intently tapping on her keyboard and staring at her screen. Then she said triumphantly, "Not what, who. Violet Warwick Vandenberg, Amon Warwick's sister." After a few more taps on her keyboard, Lizzy said, "I have the number for a Violet Vandenberg in Brooklyn."

"I'll give her a call," said Mercer with excitement. This Violet Vandenberg might have the answers he was looking for. He dialed the number, let it ring, waited until it rolled over to voice mail, and left a message.

They searched for another half hour for information on Amon and Violet but didn't find anything. With only a single lead and a sky-high anxiety level, Mercer finally said, "All right, it's time for me to go. I appreciate your help, Lizzy, but I don't know what I'm going to do." He continued with visceral intensity at the point of tears, "I don't think I could take going through that hell one more time. Lizzy, you don't know how scary this is. Imagine watching the last hours of someone's life unfold, not from a distance or through a camera lens but through their own eyes. And there's nothing I can do about it. I'm there, along for the ride, knowing something terrible will happen and not being able to do anything about it. Then as they experience the terror of their death, so do I."

Mercer covered his mouth tightly with his palm as emotions of despair boiled over. While his body shook with sobs, Mercer knew Lizzy was watching him. She stared for a few moments as though she didn't know what to say. Then putting a hand on his forearm, she said compassionately, "I'm sure we'll figure something out. Please hang in there, Mercer. Connor and I will do what we can to help. Give me a call if you need anything, at any time. Okay?"

After the sobs subsided, Mercer was finally able to splutter, "I will, thanks."

Mercer stood, hugged Lizzy, then left her. He didn't have any idea where to go next. If he went home, he would sleep, and he certainly didn't want to do that. He started walking to nowhere in particular and ended up in a subway station. There with the address of Violet Vandenberg repeating in his thoughts, he boarded a train for Brooklyn. Mercer was pondering his predicament, sitting on an uncomfortable subway seat pressed between a large woman speaking on her phone and an older man in tattered clothes who smelled of cheese and alcohol, when his phone buzzed. Excitedly, he looked at the phone, expecting it to be Violet. He was utterly disappointed. It was Ned.

"Yes, Ned. What do you want?" Mercer said sharply.

After a pause, an exasperated Ned said, "Mercer, I noticed you left early today. When were you planning to talk with me about the changes you made to the Price proposal?"

"Ned, I can't discuss this right now," said Mercer.

"We need to have the presentation ready in two days and—"

"Then let's discuss it tomorrow. It's almost at the finish line. Is that all, Ned?"

"Damn it, Mercer. That's cutting it a bit close, and you're in no position to be telling me—"

Mercer ended the call. Ned was a real pain in the ass. As the train came out of the tunnel into the Brooklyn daylight, dark clouds added to Mercer's gloom. The uneasiness inside him continued to build. He had a feeling that finding Dr. Warwick's sister was crucial to helping him uncover the information he needed, information that would help him understand what was happening to him and hopefully allow him to find a way to stop it.

The dimness of evening was upon Mercer when he exited the train in Bath Beach. A drizzle began as he made his way toward Violet's address, and his clothes were drenched when he reached the apartment building he was searching for. The main entrance opened into a small foyer that contained a matrix of mailboxes and a call box. The inner entrance door was locked, so he searched the directory for Violet's name and found it next to apartment 512, as he'd expected. He used the call box to dial her number and waited for someone to answer. The call eventually went to her voice mail, only this time, the system stated that her mailbox was full and couldn't accept more messages. Mercer looked through the inner door while knocking on it in case someone might hear. He waited for a few seconds, then tried again, and after several attempts with no response, he gave up. Mercer had just wasted a couple of hours on a fool's errand. As he opened the door to walk out into the pouring rain, the inner door clicked. He turned to see a hunched old man standing in the doorway.

"Can I help you?" the man said with an East Asian accent.

"Yes," Mercer said, relieved. "I'm looking for someone who lives in this building, but it seems she isn't here. Do you know Violet Vandenberg?"

The man nodded his head, saying, "Ah, Mrs. Vandenberg. So sad. She is no longer here. The Vandenbergs were killed in a car accident while on holiday in Switzerland."

"K… Killed?" uttered Mercer, stunned.

"Yes, three weeks ago. Men came and removed things from their apartment last week. Everything is gone."

"Gone," Mercer said blankly.

"I am so sorry to give you this news. Goodbye," said the man with a slight wave of his hand as he disappeared behind the closing door.

Mercer was frozen in place. That's it. There was nothing else he could learn here. The shadow of night could be seen through the front door. That and the pouring rain. It was how Mercer felt, dark and dreary. He left the building and trudged through the rain back to the train station. There was no one else on the platform as he waited for the next train, so he stood near the edge where the train would pull up, looked fixedly down at the tracks, and let his mind wander. He thought about his life with this new "affliction" and what it would take from him—his job, his apartment, and his mind. Then he thought about what his life was *actually* like—a job he didn't particularly like, working with people he didn't like, spending evenings with friends who weren't really friends, living in a dingy, tiny space, each day pretty much the same as the last. He struggled to identify what was driving him forward and determined he had no idea where he was going and why. His life's direction and purpose were unclear. Many of the goals he'd set for himself when he was a teenager had already been achieved. Sure, like Winston, he would love to become a portfolio manager, but he knew it would ultimately not bring happiness. He didn't know what would, and now he was being forced into a life he couldn't shape by himself, a life that was out of his control. That was what frightened him most, the lack of control. But the reality was that his life had been out of control for some time. He just hadn't realized it.

The sounds of the train coming into the station were distant and muted. The screech of its brakes as it slowed was like any other city noise on any other day, something the conscious mind simply learned to ignore. Mercer stood in a daze, consumed by self-reflection, when he heard a voice yell, "Dude!"

Someone yanked him back from the platform's edge just as the train approached. He'd been leaning forward, unaware of the impending danger.

"Are you trying to kill yourself or something?" a lanky teenage boy in a white sweatshirt and blue jeans with dark curls and a temple fade said to him as he held Mercer's right arm tightly.

Mercer swallowed hard and said, "No. What happened?"

"Dude, are you all right? That train almost hit you, man."

"Um, sorry. Thank you," a dazed Mercer said.

"Man, be safe, all right?"

Mercer nodded as the boy entered the train shaking his head, then boarded the train that had almost killed him. He found a seat and sat in stunned silence as he rode back into Manhattan. Departing the subway near his apartment, he walked wearily through the rain. He hadn't eaten anything since lunch but had no appetite. His feet moved one step at a time, walking in this familiar place with no specific destination until he found himself inside a bar he rarely entered, drinking his usual bourbon Manhattan with some salted cashews. There wasn't anyone he recognized in the place, which was precisely how he wanted it. His sopping wet jacket was hanging on the chair beside him, creating puddles on the floor, and he was soaked to the bone. The alcohol began to dull his senses, and after the third drink, the bartender told him he was cut off. She didn't want to be responsible for his foolishness.

Mercer grumbled as he stood to leave, shoving his hands into the pockets of his jacket so he could snug it around himself. The fingers of his left hand, feeling something flat and rigid in the pocket, pulled out the family crest pin he'd almost forgotten about. He stared at it, turning the pin over several times, then glanced up and saw his reflection in the etched mirror behind the bar. A crack in the mirror split the image down the middle of his face and made it distort like a Picasso painting. Mercer barely recognized the man staring back. He looked back down at the crest. *What is this good for?* He palmed the pin, plunked it onto the polished wood bar, and left.

Mercer's apartment was only a couple of blocks away. Given his state of intoxication, which resulted in a few wrong turns, it took almost twice as long to get home as it should have. By the time he reached the entrance to his building, the rain had reduced to a light sprinkle.

He dropped onto the corner of his bed, still wearing his waterlogged jacket, and tried using his alcohol-infused brain to plan his next move. Sleep was not an option, although his body and mind were thoroughly exhausted. One thought kept bubbling up to the surface. Was there a way to escape this situation, a way out, a way to fix what was happening to him, to bring an end to it?

As he often did, he decided to seek refuge in the one place he knew of where his mind was at its most creative. The roof of his apartment building was a place of solitude for Mercer, a place where he could allow his mind to process a problem, create solutions, and plan. If ever there was a need for such a place, it was now.

The service access stairwell was familiar to him. He'd climbed it many times to get to his place of peace, where he could think and be by himself while soaking in the beauty of the city skyline surrounding him. He crossed the rooftop, which looked like a swimming pool, and approached the ledge overlooking Third Avenue. As he usually did, he gazed southward along the street. Through the mist, he was able to make out the silhouettes of skyscrapers jutting out along the landscape of Lower Manhattan. He thought of his mother and relived some of the few fleeting memories. The rain picked up as he turned and leaned forward to peer over the edge. The movement of his head immediately made him dizzy and gave him the urge to retch. He closed his eyes.

7

A HIGH-PITCHED WHINE CAREENED THROUGH the back of my head, ricocheting off the inside of my skull as though my ears were ringing. The pitch of the sound began to vary, shortening in duration, and resolved to a specific area outside of my body. Rhythmically, the noise gained familiarity, like the squeaking of a bat when searching in the dark for food. Something rustled on my chest and then ran across the fabric of my shirt, rousing me. Opening my eyes revealed a dim room. Two dark round eyes stared at my face behind quivering whiskers and a vibrating pointed nose. My arm swept over my chest with the speed of a diving falcon, flinging the black animal through the air and across the room, causing it to shriek before it made a thud against the door as it struck. The only light came through a narrow slit under the door, and the hobbling rat cast dancing shadows around the room as it scurried away.

The room was unfamiliar. I lifted my head as I noticed several strange sensations—the ache of hunger in my stomach, the stiffness and immobility of my back and shoulders, the feeling and stench of the film of days without a bath, the dull but gnawing pain coming from my right foot, a deep thirst making my tongue and lips crack. A pang of fear welled up inside me as I sat upright on the cot where I was lying and tried to take in more of my surroundings. There wasn't much to see, nor was there much to hear, save for the periodic sound of dripping water coming from somewhere and the distant groans of men. There was no one in the space with me, and there was no way to see out because the room had no windows. I needed to get out of this miserable place, so I stood to walk

60

toward the door when the gnawing pain in my foot felt like it was going to chew through my toes. I stumbled and nearly fell to the floor, catching myself on the cot's edge. I quickly sat back down, moaning and grabbing at my foot, when I realized something was missing. Bandaged stumps, still seeping blood, were where the smallest two toes should have been. The discovery of missing toes unleashed a torrent of pain, and I cried out. I yelled for a few moments, hoping someone would hear and come to my aid.

After an indeterminate amount of time without help arriving, I decided to try to stand again. I was much more careful this time, favoring my right foot to prevent the stabbing pain I felt earlier. I regained my footing and swayed while trying to find my balance, slightly stooping for fear of bumping my head on the low ceiling. Though the room was small, the few steps it took to reach the door took more than a minute for me to complete. I felt around the door for a handle to open it, but there was none. I pushed against it and then tried to throw what weight I could against it, but nothing happened. I banged on the door with my fists and yelled for help, but still nothing. I wasn't going to stop until someone responded or opened the door for me, so I kept pounding and howling. As I was leaning against the door, it opened suddenly, dumping me onto the hard floor outside the room. A bright light blinded me, and a swiftly moving shadow crashed into the side of my head. All went dark.

* * * * *

As I awoke, I could feel a hand pulling my hair and holding my head back, forcing me to look up toward the ceiling of a dingy room lit by a single bulb. The hand released its grip, and my head fell forward. There were two chairs in the room; I was in the one facing the closed door, and the other chair faced me and was occupied by a small man in a military uniform with a dark scowl on his face. He wore a drab green jacket and pants and a hat of the same color with a bill in front and a pin placed front and center on the crown, a red five-pointed star circumscribed by a thick golden circle.

"So the glorious teachings the People's Army has provided you do not yet find their way into your heart," said the man in broken English. "Do they not, John Freeman?"

Memories began flooding into me. I was US Army Corporal John Freeman from Bridgeport, Connecticut. My father was a fisherman, and I had a younger brother and sister. I enlisted in the army as soon as I graduated high school, feeling called to serve my country and honor the brave soldiers who fought and died in World War II a few years earlier. As part of the Second Infantry Division, I was sent to Korea when the hostilities started as part of a UN effort to stop the North Korean offensive. I was captured in a battle near the Naktong River as my platoon leader desperately tried to shepherd us out of enemy territory. I was taken prisoner, uninjured, and made to march for so many days I lost count, pummeled with stones thrown by civilians along the way, and eventually ended up in this hellhole.

I said nothing.

"Life would have improved for you, you know," said my captor. "Ankle Biter" was how I thought of him, like a Chihuahua constantly nipping at me. "If only you would have embraced the enlightened ways of communism. I fear it is getting too late for you, however. You continue to resist and attempt to bring other more reasonable men who accept these ways under your misguided influence. Do you still choose to resist?" He waited for a moment, giving me a chance to capitulate, which I had previously decided I would never let happen. I gave no reaction.

"Hmm, it is too bad," he said as he bowed his head slightly. Someone behind me grabbed my right forearm roughly and locked his hands around it, causing my hand to start tingling almost immediately in the viselike grip. Even if I had my usual strength, I don't believe I could have moved.

"There is a point of no return," said Ankle Biter. "You are nearly at that point, John Freeman."

He rose as he pulled a pair of wire cutters from his coat pocket. I had seen this tool before, being used on each of my toes. It still had crusted blood staining its cutting edges. He walked toward me, flexing his fingers to open and close the blades.

"You may survive the day, but it will cost you." He placed the cutter blades on either side of my little finger and started to squeeze. The pressure was already unbearable, yet the finger barely bled. The pressure, the pain, and the blood continued to increase slowly, the torture unceasing. In this instance, he took his time cutting off the digit. The toes were done quickly, more humanely.

As I had done on previous occasions of extreme pain or delirium induced during days of confinement in the sweatbox, I allowed my mind to return to a place of comfort, a place of safety. My mind was the only thing left that I could control and they could not. The only way I could tolerate the agony was to retreat from it, to disconnect the mental from the physical. It was so difficult. It never got easier, not like riding a bicycle or driving a car. And now it was worse than ever before.

I placed myself on a bench near the beach at Seaside Park, staring out toward the break wall that was resolutely guarding and protecting the entrance of Bridgeport Harbor in the distance. Seagulls were noisily going about their business, floating on wind currents while searching for food scraps in the water and on the sand. I could hear the whooshing sounds of waves crawling up the shoreline and then retreating while others roiled over them to take their place. The smell of sprays of water stirred memories of growing up within sight of the ocean while catching the scents of the sea in the breeze.

The cracking sound I heard was not of a branch falling from the tree near the bench. It was of a bone in my pinkie finger being snapped in half. The physical world tried to come rushing back, torment and all, but I fought as hard as possible to keep it at bay.

Something wrapped itself around my neck and choked me. Being unable to breathe, I felt myself losing awareness.

* * * * *

It was happening again, Mercer knew. As Corporal Freeman lost consciousness, Mercer's essence was pulled into a place in John's mind between waking and sleeping. John's conscious mind was replaced by that of Mercer. With all the physical senses of John's body shutting down, Mercer sought the refuge of his subconscious. In this disoriented state, he recalled a memory from childhood where he was quietly playing in the living room of the family's apartment. He was working to build the tallest tower he could out of building blocks while his favorite cartoon played on television. Jenna, the babysitter, was on the couch talking on the cordless phone like she always did. In the background, he could hear Lizzy crying in her bedroom, as babies tend to do when left alone in their cribs for too long. The tower was getting taller, and, as often happened, the wailing of sirens rising from the street could be heard through the closed windows of the apartment. This time the wail didn't seem to go away, there were a few pauses, but more sirens continued to pass by.

The big puppy and his best friend were making huge sandwiches on television. Both were opening their mouths to take bites when the screen changed to a serious man in a suit holding a microphone. Behind the man, in the distance, were the two tallest buildings in the city, one of which had smoke coming from it. The man talked, so Mercer returned to his work and placed another block on the tower.

Jenna said, "What happened?"

With Lizzy still crying and the sirens going by, Jenna sat unmoving, watching the television as Mercer put another block on his tower. The tower teetered and fell to the floor as he started placing the next block, making Mercer slump to his knees. He sat back for a moment and watched the television as an airplane came from the right side of the screen and smashed into the tower that was not smoking.

"Oh my god," Jenna said quietly. The phone in her hand was at her side. Then she said, "Wait, Ellen?"

"Momma?" Mercer said quietly.

"Oh my god! *Oh my god!*" Jenna's voice rose to a scream. Mercer turned to look at Jenna and watched as tears streamed down her cheeks. "Oh no, Ellen. Why did you go to work today? Oh my god, no, Ellen." Jenna choked as she said the last words.

"Momma!" Mercer screamed. "Get out, Momma! Get out of the building, Momma! No! No! *No!*"

The memory was vivid. Mercer recalled every detail of that moment. Then as suddenly as it had begun, Mercer's essence was forced out of John's consciousness.

* * * * *

The discomforting heat I felt was tempered by the cold hard surface pressed against the side of my face. As I gathered my bearings, I noted the sweat dripping from my nose and figured the stabbing pain in my hand made me sweat. I was lying on the floor face down, in shock. A pair of hands hoisted me up and into a chair, the chair in which I had already been tortured repeatedly. The other chair was empty, so I waited impatiently.

The problem was that I was unsettled; I hadn't been so on edge since arriving in this godforsaken place. Something wasn't right. I felt like a piece of me was not missing but different. I was able to control my emotions and fear up to this point. But now, was I starting to break? A new fear rose inside of me, seeping up out of the depths, invading the areas of my mind which allowed me to separate mental from physical. I became aware of every bump on my head, bruise on my body, and nick on my skin, let alone the searing areas of pain on my foot and hand—the urge to cry out and give in overwhelmed me. I had to redouble my efforts to gain control.

I was concentrating on regaining my composure when Ankle Biter entered the room and sat in the empty chair. "When my work is particularly effective, interesting things come to light, John Freeman," he said. "My superiors were very curious about the information I obtained from you. I apologize for making you wait, but, in light of this information, several things needed to be set in motion so we can improve our understanding."

"In…information," I asked in a rasping voice. It felt like it was days since I'd spoken a word.

"Yes, John Freeman, information that you provided to us. I think we had what you would call a breakthrough. I am told not to prod further until our guest arrives."

"Guest?"

"Yes, guest. My, you are talkative today. I am wondering if I should have started with the fingers. We would have made progress much more rapidly."

I could think of little else but wondering what information I might have provided, which excited Ankle Biter. I also didn't understand how the silent treatment I was skilled at for so long was easily stripped away. It was time for me to fight whatever demons surfaced and restore the stoicism I'd portrayed all these months; I couldn't give up now. Summoning my resolve, I sat stone-still, planning to not acknowledge anyone or anything for as long as possible.

Ankle Biter stood and paced around the room but was otherwise quiet. I ignored him, but he seemed both excited and apprehensive when he did happen to cross my field of view. He always showed excitement while torturing me, so this was no surprise, but the concern expressed on his face and his manner were new. I wasn't sure whether this would be good or bad for me, so I continued to wait. Ankle Biter was not a patient man, so he and his pacing grew more agitated every minute someone didn't come through that door.

The interrogation room door eventually opened, and in walked a tall man in civilian clothing. He was clean-shaven, with black hair and pale skin. He wore rimless glasses with thick lenses and a fedora that matched everything else he wore, including his shoes, all of which were ecru. That was all I could determine without moving my eyes to look at him directly. He closed the door and swaggered across the room toward me.

Before reaching me, Ankle Biter said, "We still have nine fingers to work with, so I—"

The tall man's hand shot into the air, palm flat, halting Ankle Biter's words.

"I'll take it from here," he said with an unmistakable East Coast accent.

"But, Sir Lutomir, I believe we can—" started Ankle Biter.

The man turned and glared at Ankle Biter, who flashed a look of fear and exited the room.

"It's just us now," he said as he bent down in front of me until we were eye to eye. "Well, you've got a bunch of people all hot and bothered, son. Let's find out if it's just all a wet dream, heh?" He chuckled as he stood and slowly walked around me. When he was in front of me again, he picked up my right hand, examining the bandage. He then took a closer look at the bandages on my right foot.

"Tsk, tsk, tsk. Amateurs. Well, I don't believe you'll need to be losing any more digits, my friend," he said with a wry smile.

I deliberately prevented myself from turning to face him, wondering whether he would stop this nonsense.

"'We cannot escape history,'" he said. "Do you know who said that?"

I didn't move.

"Abraham Lincoln did. It means that we all have an impact on history and that we can't escape this fact. What do you think your impact will be, Corporal?"

I didn't blink.

"Tell me, what is this World Trade Center you were talking about?"

I had never heard these words and had no idea what a World Trade Center was. I didn't recall ever saying anything about such a place. I made no reply.

"Yes, I thought so. I didn't think you would know anything."

I started to feel relieved that maybe I would at least get taken back to my cell and left alone for a while.

Then he said, "But I do know a way to get what I'm looking for."

He snapped his fingers, and the door opened. Some men walked in with a large wooden box, metal cans, and towels, closing the door behind them. They set the box on the floor and laid me on top of it, strapping my arms and legs to the fasteners on the box. Someone covered my face with a towel as I struggled to free myself, stopping after realizing the effort was fruitless. The room became silent. Then I heard the metal ting of one of the cans being lifted and brought closer to me. My face became wet, and I could not breathe, so I fought to pull away from the deluge that filled my nose and mouth, but it was useless. I was drowning in this room on top of a wooden box. I jerked, trying to avoid the water or disrupt its flow, but it kept coming, smothering me, and I coughed and sputtered. The water did not stop.

"Almost there," said the deceitful man dressed in white.

My lungs burned for air, and I was at the point of passing out. The unsettled subconscious I had so far been able to contain came roaring back into the fore. At that moment, I realized there was another presence in my mind, a presence which I had neither control nor knowledge of. But I was still John Freeman, the man being subjected to the physical agony and torture of the present day. The intermixing of thoughts, emotions, memories, and sensations overwhelmed me.

As I was slipping into oblivion, I heard the man, the Deceiver, say close to my ear, loud enough for me to hear, "I know what you are. You are in the now and also in the future. You are John Freeman, but who else are you? That's what I'm going to find out, little by little, each time I bring you near death, Leaf Runner."

8

THE BURNING IN MERCER'S LUNGS forced him into fits of coughing, but he could get air into them and expel the water, gasp by precious gasp. The grim reality of his situation came into focus as he felt the bindings on his ankles and wrists, unable to move, but the towel covering his face was no longer present. Lutomir and the other men, still in the room, stared at him.

Lutomir, with a look of satisfaction on his face, said, "Well, it's a start. I already knew the part about New York City and the destruction that will occur there, but I'm sure we can get more out of you next time. Given that I know some information about this man, John Freeman, I'm sure I can narrow down who you are in a couple more sessions. I'll let you rest a bit before we try again."

Mercer didn't think even *he* could narrow down who he was at that moment. There were so many mixed emotions and memories; it was all a great jumble. But there was also more clarity. There was another presence in his thoughts, a presence he knew existed, a presence that had been there since he entered this mind. What was interesting was that it didn't frighten him. Instead, he got comfort from the knowledge that he existed in this body, at this time, alongside a stranger. The stranger was distant and muted, for Mercer was in the here and now, in control of another's body and suffering the physical pain and fatigue afflicting that body. He had never experienced so much pain. He could feel the throbbing wounds of John's toes and finger and a level of exhaustion beyond understanding. As much as possible, he tried to use the respite to allow himself to relax, which was difficult given the assault on his senses. The realization that he was not in his own body overwhelmed him, pushing his afflictions aside, but it was also familiar to him. The impossibility of his predicament struck him, yet he couldn't deny how real it was. The torment he felt could not be imagined, he knew.

His thoughts finally caught up to the statements of his captor. Replaying the words in his head brought him to the conclusion that things would continue this way; the near-drowning would be repeated again and again. Even if he were to divulge the information Lutomir was seeking, namely that he was Mercer Evans, he felt the only ending possible was death for John's body. Either Lutomir would kill John to try to kill Mercer, or John would die of exhaustion. The sooner, the better for them both, he hated to admit, but he had to figure out how to prevent Lutomir from learning who he was.

There wasn't much time left for him to think before the next round of torture commenced. He decided to use the time to figure out what aspects of the body he could control. He exercised his mind on physical control and found he could manipulate its remaining toes and fingers and move its limbs within the limitations of the restraints. He could control the body's breathing when he wanted to, so all motor control felt similar to his own body. The pain he felt was through the sensory nerves in the body, so those were also working. So far, all seemed normal.

Next, he explored his thoughts and attempted to learn more about the presence he felt there. Probing with his mind, he tried to enter the area where the presence existed, but it was closed off. An impenetrable barrier stood between him and what he presumed to be John Freeman's soul. Although they both occupied the same mind, they occupied different spaces, kept apart by an invisible shield. At present, however, he was the one with direct access to the outside world through the body's senses, able to see a dim light through its closed eyes and hear quiet voices through its ears. He wondered if he could change places with John, giving him back control and find his way out and back home. He didn't know how to do this, so he just tried pushing himself outward to see if he could leave as easily as that. The effect was to enhance his senses and sharpen his control of the physical. Although potentially useful, it was not particularly helpful at the moment.

He had to try something else, so he retreated, backing himself into the deeper recesses of his mind as if plunging himself into a pool of deep water. The physical seemed to become more distant, the senses duller, as he had experienced after receiving gas while having a tooth pulled at the dentist's office. Only, this time he was able to control that state and not continue to drift deeper. He came back above the pool's surface and regained the senses and motor control he had just receded from. He took a few more dips into and out of that pool and appreciated that he could slip in and out so easily. Each time he vacated, he felt the other presence filling the gaps. That presence seemed unable to force its way to the fore, while Mercer could come and go as he wished.

As Mercer was about to move forward to the place where he could control the body, he sensed a tapping on its forehead. Mercer dove back into the pool to hide from the torment he expected was to come, leaving John to face the next assault. The body's eyes opened, and Mercer could see what John saw, but John had control.

* * * * *

I opened my eyes to see the Deceiver staring down at me. I had no idea how long I slept, a restless, fitful, uncomfortable sleep. I blinked a few times as the Deceiver smiled.

"It looks like we're ready to continue," he said.

The towel, still wet, covered my face. The tinging of the metal can sounded again, and then the deluge of water began. I fought it as hard as possible with some renewed strength, but it was no use. I was restrained too tightly. I sputtered and coughed, gasping for air. I tried gulping the water to see if I could beat it and make them pause so I could get some air. This almost worked, except the soaked towel allowed no air to pass before the next water pour hit it. Again I could feel myself starting to pass out as I backed away from the situation around me and slid into oblivion.

* * * * *

Mercer could feel himself being yanked from the pool, being forced back into the place of control as John's presence receded from it. The water stopped, and the towel was pulled away. Under Mercer's control, the body coughed until the air could fill its lungs. It took several deep breaths until he was able to breathe normally again.

Then Lutomir spoke. "So tell me, Leaf Runner, what is your name?"

"H… How?" Mercer asked.

"Ah, you are wondering how I know what you are. Well, I might get to that after you answer my question, so I'll ask you again. Who are you?"

"M… M… M…"

"C'mon now. You can do it. Mmmm, what?"

"M… Motherfucker," Mercer spluttered.

"Tsk, tsk, tsk," Lutomir said, waggling his index finger. Lutomir finally dropped the Mr. Nice Guy routine. "That's not very nice. One thing I know, you filthy parasite, is that I'm not talking to your host, Corporal Freeman. He wouldn't be blabbing like you are, you stupid patsy."

Mercer tried to jerk himself out of the restraints and spit at Lutomir. His anger boiled as he fought to defend his honor.

"That's it," Lutomir said, taking on a tone of encouragement. "It seems I've gotten your attention. I'll bet somebody you knew died in that tower, hmm?"

Mercer fought as the other men watched and waited. "Damn you," he screamed.

"Now we're getting somewhere. Was it someone close to you? Someone you loved? How old were you?"

Mercer finally realized what was happening, that Lutomir was goading him to get him to talk, to divulge his identity. Up to this point, it was working perfectly because Mercer, who had never been in a situation like this, didn't know how to recognize it and what to do to stop it. It was clear to Mercer that he didn't have anywhere near John's ability to resist interrogation. It was time for him to escape. Mercer knew that he would eventually cave, which would be bad; although he didn't understand why it would be bad, he felt it. He dove for the pool, trying to get below the surface as quickly as possible. However, John's presence was slow to fill the void left by Mercer, so he couldn't pull away before hearing Lutomir once again.

"Who died in the World Trade Center?" he asked and waited for an answer. "Damn, we're losing him again. This could take longer than I thought."

* * * * *

As I awoke, the Deceiver was yelling at the men in Korean. They ran to the door as the Deceiver stood over me. He stared at me with a perplexed look, looking directly at my eyes. When I turned away, he grabbed my chin and made me face him. He wouldn't let me close my eyes, holding both of the lids open with his thumbs. He was very impatient and glanced between me and the door, swearing periodically. I guessed he wanted the men to return with something to continue my torture. They weren't gone for very long, and I knew my hunch was correct when they returned carrying the metal cans. They must have refilled them.

The towel and the deluge came quickly, and I slipped back before long.

* * * * *

Mercer was aware John was receding and creating the void which had drawn him out of the pool earlier. He was determined not to be pulled toward it but was uncertain how it could be avoided. He attempted to grab on to the pool's edge with his mind, but nothing was there to hold. He couldn't get his mind to attach to anything and continued being sucked into the vacuum of the void until he was at the place of control, opening the body's eyes.

"Stop," said Lutomir. Then with a note of triumph, he said, "There you are. Since you're starting to figure out how this works, I think I need to speed things up a bit to get from you what I came for. How about we start with John Freeman. What relation is he to you?" Mercer must have been noticeably surprised because Lutomir said, "Yes, that's right. I know he must be someone from your family tree, probably a grandfather or granduncle. Either you are a Freeman, or you know the family name. Who has the name Freeman, your mother or your father?"

Ellen Freeman, Mercer's mother, was a niece to John Freeman, the very John Freeman whose body Mercer now occupied. Ellen's father, James, after whom Mercer's brother was named, was John's little brother. Lutomir was getting too close.

Panic set in as he frantically tried to figure out what to do, but his mother was all he could think about. Mercer found the empty spot he'd carried with him all these years, a place he'd avoided and almost forgotten about since before he was a teenager. Yet it was right there, as it had been all along. He sped past it, trampled over it, ran around it, and plain ignored it for so long, but it had always been there. All he needed to do was seek it, which he did.

He saw his mother's face, smiling and happy, looking at him as he held her hand and skipped along beside her. She loved him so much, and he loved her back. He loved her still but had pushed those feelings away when she left him at such a young age. There were so many questions he would never be able to ask her. He wished to his core she was still alive so he could know her as an adult. But he knew now that she was with him and had always been. The empty spot was now filled.

Mercer next thought about John, wondering if there was any way he could save him. If he told Lutomir everything, it might be possible John would be spared, but there was no guarantee. It also would put Mercer, and possibly his family, in jeopardy, a risk he was unwilling to take. John would have to be left alone, and Mercer hoped that, whatever happened, he would be at peace.

Mercer didn't recall much ever being said about John by any family members, so he guessed John must never have made it out of Korea.

"C'mon, boy," prodded Lutomir. "You don't have much time. You're looking pretty ragged, so I suspect you might not survive another dousing. As for me, I could sit here and do this all day. Well, what do you say?"

Mercer wanted to say something and lay into this beast, but he also knew John wouldn't have said anything, would have stood firm. For once, Mercer did the same. John had, without knowing Mercer existed, given Mercer a gift. He'd shown Mercer how much suffering the human body and mind could endure. It was beyond anything Mercer could have dreamed possible. John also taught Mercer about purpose. John was willing to give his life for people he would never know, people with a future of possibilities he would never experience. John's sense of purpose was beyond admirable.

Mercer had to go *now*. Sorrow filled him—sorrow for John's suffering and, likely, the imminent loss of his life. But Mercer knew he could provide neither help nor comfort to John. Mercer drew upon his newfound hope, the hope his mother had placed in him as a child, the hope that had always been there, the hope which would give him the courage to explore his true purpose, and used it to make his way back to the body of Mercer Evans.

He dove into the pool and went down, down, down, finally reaching a place where time stood still and where he was but a speck on a leaf attached to a massive branch of a colossal ghostly tree. Above him, the branch was divided into smaller branches. The smaller branches held any number of leaves and split into even smaller branches. The branching continued past a height that was beyond his capability to perceive such enormity. The translucent tree was boundless, far more extensive than any tree on Earth.

The leaf Mercer rested upon contained an inscription saying "John Clarence Freeman." Below the name was two dates, like on a tombstone, which read, "August 8, 1929–November 11, 1951." He looked at a leaf nearby and read his grandfather's name, James

Herald Freeman. For the first time since arriving here, he looked down. Below him, the trunk filled his view. He observed a second huge branch some distance away, coming together at a notch with the branch he occupied and sharing the same trunk.

Like a cat, Mercer moved down the branch toward the tree's trunk, passing the leaf which contained his mother's name, and found his name carved on the trunk near the tree's base. He touched the letters of his name, thereby entering another pool, then kicked himself toward its surface, going up, up, up.

* * * * *

As I came back into consciousness, the Deceiver loomed over me. His anger boiled as he stormed around the room. Then I heard Ankle Biter's voice drowned out as the Deceiver berated him.

"We're done here," said the Deceiver. "Kill him."

Ankle Biter leaned over me, bent down, and glared into my eyes. I heard a click near my left ear just before the world exploded.

My name was John Clarence Freeman. On August 8, 1929, I was born to Elias George Freeman and Gertrude Ann (nee Wassermann) Freeman. I grew up in Bridgeport, Connecticut, in the United States of America. I enlisted in the United States Army and was posthumously awarded the Medal of Honor. Sometime during November of 1951, I was killed in action.

* * * * *

The pattering sensation on his head felt like little fingers gently tapping. Drips of water rolled down his face, tickling his cheeks as they passed over them, and fell from the bottom of his chin. Mercer opened his eyes to see a cityscape sprawling before him, dulled by millions of transparent raindrops from a heavy downpour. He looked down and was immediately faint; sixty feet below him lay the street. His body swayed slightly, and the world spun around him as he fell.

9

THE HARD SURFACE OF THE building roof knocked the air out of Mercer's lungs as he landed flat on his back. Hard rain pelted his face and mouth, making it more difficult for him to regain the full breaths he needed. Although he struggled to breathe, relief filled Mercer. Not because he'd just barely avoided a fatal fall, but because he was back. Mercer was back in the present, in his own body. And he was alive.

He pushed himself up to a sitting position, allowing his face a respite from the rain that battered it and giving himself a few moments to process what had happened. After the experience of being John Freeman, of seeing the impact of a resolute purpose in life, of gaining some control over his affliction, and of finding the well of hope he'd forgotten since his mother's death, Mercer felt profoundly grateful. He *did* have hope. He felt hope for the future. Filled was a hollowness inside him, a hole he was unaware existed, which had prevented him from considering a future of happiness and joy. He no longer lacked control over the genesis of his nightmares; he could tame the menace. A smile started to break out on his face, and from somewhere deep inside, joy bubbled up, breaking through the surface into laughter. Unrestrained, genuine, cathartic laughter flowed from Mercer as he embraced life anew. Had anyone seen him like this, they would have thought him mad.

The buzzing phone in his pants pocket tugged him back to reality, and the laughter subsided. It was an unknown caller, so Mercer immediately declined it. These calls were usually scams, anyway. He'd already slid the phone back into his pocket before his mind registered the time on its face. He quickly pulled it back out to verify he'd seen it correctly. Only about five minutes had passed since he arrived on the roof. How was that possible? Although he had no way to keep track of time while in John Freeman's body, he was sure he must have been there for several hours, yet only a few minutes had passed for Mercer Evans. Amazing!

It was time to get out of this rain and into some dry clothes. Surprisingly, the intoxication provided by the alcohol earlier had receded almost entirely. Mercer rose to his feet, left the roof, descended the service stairs, and entered his apartment.

Again his phone buzzed, and again it was an unknown number. With annoyance, he set his phone to block all anonymous calls. Before putting it down, he rattled off a quick text to Lizzy. It said, "happened again, Im ok."

He needed a hot shower, so he peeled off his wet clothes and entered the small bathtub shower. It could've been a Roman bath for how good the hot water felt on his skin, so he took his time and enjoyed the soothing warmth of the water cascading over his body.

After enough time had passed that the water was lukewarm, Mercer realized his relaxing spa time was over and turned off the shower. When the sound of the falling water finally ceased, it was replaced by the buzzing of the intercom. Although it was late, someone was at the building entrance, desperately trying to get his attention. He ran over to the intercom and mashed the button with his thumb.

"Hello?" he said.

"Mercer, Mercer, this is Lizzy. Are you okay? Can you let me come up, please?" she said, agitated.

"Yes, I'm fine, sis," he said as he buzzed her in.

Before he could pull on a mostly clean pair of pants, she knocked on the door. He unlocked then opened it and barely had time to brace himself as she ran and jumped toward him, hugging him tightly.

As she backed away, a confused Mercer said, "What's the matter, Lizzy? Is everything okay?"

"Well, you tell me. You were so concerned about it happening again. When you texted that it did, I was sure you told me you were okay just to keep me from worrying. Then you didn't answer my texts and calls. I buzzed you for ten minutes with no answer. Well, I'm worried," she spouted frantically.

"Please have a seat, sis," he said comfortingly, patting a spot on the mattress next to him as he sat on the end of the bed. While she took a seat, he said, "It's been a long day, and I had a few drinks earlier, so please be patient with me. Sorry, I was in the shower when you tried reaching me, but I really needed that."

Lizzy listened intently, her eyes unblinking and fixed on his face as he told her about his unsuccessful trip to Brooklyn and how he ended up on the roof.

"Anyway, I was up on the roof, standing near the ledge, and when I looked down at the street, a wave of dizziness and nausea passed over me. I closed my eyes. You know, until then, I thought that it was sleep that brought them on, the nightmares. But after I closed my eyes, I was pulled into John Freeman. It wasn't a nightmare. I was wide awake when it happened. At first, it was terrifying."

Mercer recounted his experience in John Freeman's body.

"Oh my god," Lizzy said. "How horrible. So John was Mom's uncle?"

"Yes. He was an amazing young man. He went through torture worse than I could've ever imagined, worse than death, and he did so without complaint. I've never met someone like John Freeman." Mercer paused for a few seconds, lost in emotion. "But there's more. I learned some control over this…ability, as the professor called it. So far, I've thought of it as an affliction. It's not. It's something I can do, like a hidden talent. I also learned there are others with this ability. This Lutomir must also be a Leaf Runner, he called it. I'm scared, Lizzy."

"Scared about what?" she asked.

"Scared that someone is now looking for me. He was trying to identify me, and knowing I'm related to John Freeman would make his job much easier. Lutomir's descendant is likely alive today. Someone I've never met might be searching for me, and I have no idea who they are. I don't know what he wants with me."

"I'll stay here with you tonight, Mercer," said Lizzy, with a concerned look. "You shouldn't be alone."

"Sis, I promise you, I'll be fine. And this place is cramped, anyway."

"But wouldn't it be easier for you to go through this with some help? You don't have to do this on your own. Please, Mercer. I want to help."

Mercer thought for a few moments and said, "All right, I guess you can stay the night. I'll sleep on the floor."

The two chatted about life, memories, and family, and Mercer realized he'd been missing this piece of his life. For so long, distancing himself from his family had isolated him from those who loved him most. A basic need was being met as they talked, like having air to breathe or water to drink.

Even though it was after midnight, neither felt the desire to sleep, so they hopped onto the family tree website and researched their ancestors. They found more information about John Freeman, how his remains eventually did return to the United States, and he was given a proper military burial. After a couple of hours, they connected back to Rhys Turner. Rhys's brother, Bryn, was the genetic link to Mercer and Lizzy. The size of the tree had grown to over three thousand and showed no signs of stopping.

Fatigue finally caught up with them, and they said their good nights, Lizzy taking the bed and Mercer the floor. Mercer slept soundly except for one point during the night when he felt himself being pulled back into the ancestry pool. This was how the nightmares started. He allowed the process to continue, wanting to experiment with his control and see who and when he was being pulled to. The leaf he stopped at on the ancestral tree showed the name "Corbin Hugo LaCroix" and a birth date of 1784. He allowed himself to float toward the surface. However, wanting to know if he could stop the process, he forced himself back to the bottom of the pool and moved down the branch to his name on the tree's trunk, back to the present. Learning that he had the control needed to keep from being thrust into the body of one of his ancestors, he rested peacefully until morning came.

Mercer awoke to bright sunlight streaming through the sheer curtains of his apartment and bathing his face in its glow. The heavy clouds and rain of the night before had passed, and the sky opened to a beautiful morning in which he was thankful to be alive. Lizzy had already made coffee and sat on the bed looking at her laptop.

"Do you have anything to eat in this place?" she asked.

"No, sorry," said Mercer. "I'll run down to the bakery and grab some Danishes or something. Does that work for you?"

"You bet. I'll be waiting," she said with a smile.

"See you in twenty-five minutes," he said over his shoulder as he jogged out the door, grabbing the baseball cap that was wedged under his motorcycle helmet to cover his mussed hair and throwing on his light green jacket. The bakery was a few blocks away, but it had the best cinnamon rolls, so it was worth the walk. Several minutes later, he entered the bakery and made his purchase, hugging the warm bag of goodies. As he exited, a bald man sitting in a car across the street turned his head to look away from Mercer, as if the man didn't want to be seen observing him.

Mercer continued walking and tried not to look at the car. As he rounded a corner, he casually glanced back toward the car, but the space it had occupied was empty. Strolling at his usual pace, he found himself alert, catching every sound and identifying every vehicle in his field of view, especially if it was a dark blue car. Other than its color, the sedan the man was driving was nondescript. It could have been any car owned by anyone. Mercer felt that everyone was looking at him. Anyone who glanced at him might be watching to see where he'd go or what he'd do next. His imagination took over, and adrenaline-induced paranoia made his heart race.

The walk back to his apartment seemed to take forever, but he noticed nothing else out of the ordinary until he was fifty feet from the main entrance of his building. The same car he saw earlier was down the street in front of him, barreling toward him. He turned to flee and noticed two men running on the sidewalk to cut him off. Trapped from in front and behind and by the building to his side, he dropped the bag he carried and ran into the street. The squeal of tires and a horn blowing startled him as a large delivery truck swerved to avoid him. The truck slammed into a parked car next to Mercer, missing him by inches.

Mercer stood, paralyzed with fear, staring at the crumpled vehicle underneath the truck. He looked up to see the angry face of the truck driver, who was trying to open his door to get out. Screeching tire sounds came from behind him, and as he turned to protect himself, an opening car door knocked him off his feet, and he tumbled to the ground.

"Shit!" he heard someone yell.

Someone grabbed a dazed Mercer under the arms and lifted him. Then he was dragged to a car and pushed into the back seat. A man slid in beside him and closed the door. The car accelerated.

"What's going on?" Mercer yelled as full panic set in. "Who are you? Where are you taking me?"

"Quiet!" a gruff voice barked from the front seat. "Damn it, that's not how this was supposed to go."

Swinging his fists at the men on either side of him, Mercer cried out, "But you can't do this. Where are you taking—"

Something hard smashed into the side of his head, and the world went black.

* * * * *

Lizzy was in the middle of a scientific paper about pediatric oncology care when she heard a loud crash outside. It must have been pretty big if she could hear the sound so easily from this high up with the window closed, so she went to the window to look. There was a great deal of commotion on the street below, but it was difficult to see much else, so she grabbed a spare set of apartment keys and headed for the elevator. The elevator doors opened to reveal a crowd gathered outside the building on the sidewalk. A box truck sat atop a crushed car, and people stood around, pointing and talking. Lizzy's emergency medical training kicked in, and she began to assess the scene.

"Is anyone trapped?" she asked several people. Most shrugged their shoulders and said they didn't know. She heard sirens in the distance as she walked around the crumpled vehicles and found a man sitting on the sidewalk with his face in his hands. She knelt beside him.

"Are you okay? I have medical training," she said.

The man looked up and said, "I… I thought the guy was trying to kill himself or something. I just missed him. My boss is gonna be pissed."

"Are you okay?" she asked again.

"Yes, I'm fine. Just a little shook up, that's all… They grabbed him and took him. Just like that, he was gone."

"Who was gone?" asked Lizzy.

"The guy on the road with the baseball cap, wearing a green jacket. They took him."

Lizzy's heart jumped as she realized Mercer was wearing his green jacket when he left to get breakfast. Panic filled her while she stood and backed away from the scene. She immediately pulled out her phone and called Mercer. The call went right to his voice mail, indicating that either his phone was turned off or it was destroyed. Mercer was gone.

She walked back to where the truck driver was sitting, now talking with emergency responders. He told them the same story about Mercer jumping in front of him. When he got to the part about Mercer being taken, one of the police officers asked, "Can you describe the vehicle that took the man?"

"Yes, it was a dark blue Malibu, no more than three years old. I couldn't scc the driver, but a man wearing blue jeans and a black jacket grabbed the guy and shoved him into the back of the car, then the car sped off."

"Was there anything more you can remember about the car or the man in the black jacket? Do you think you could identify him?" asked the officer.

"I didn't get a good look at their faces, so no. I also don't remember anything else about the car. I didn't get the license plate."

"My brother," Lizzy muttered.

"Sorry, ma'am?" said another officer standing near Lizzy.

"My brother. I think they took my brother," she said in shock.

"What is your name, ma'am?" the officer asked.

"Lizzy. Sorry, Elizabeth Evans."

"Lizzy, can you come with me so we can talk somewhere a little less…crowded?"

"Okay," she said, dazed.

The officer led Lizzy to her cruiser, opened the front passenger door, motioned for Lizzy to get in, and gently closed the door behind her. Then she walked around the vehicle and slid into the driver's seat, closing her door.

"Lizzy, I'm Officer Holloway. Is it okay if I ask you a few questions?"

Lizzy consented. Officer Holloway asked Lizzy to describe Mercer and what he was wearing and took notes as Lizzy spoke.

Officer Holloway asked, "Do you know where Mercer was going this morning?"

"Yes, he ran out to grab some breakfast for us. This is his apartment building," stated Lizzy as she pointed over her shoulder.

"Did you arrive before he left, or was he already gone when you got here?"

Lizzy paused for a second, then offered, "Mercer's been going through a lot lately. Last night, before midnight, I got a text from him that made me worry. He didn't reply to my texts, and his phone went to voice mail when I tried calling him, so I rushed over here."

Last night Lizzy had experienced despair, thinking she might have lost Mercer, and then joy, seeing that he was okay. Now he was lost again, but this time he'd been taken. Mercer was right. Someone was looking for him; only this wasn't the work of just one person. This was a coordinated kidnapping done in broad daylight.

She continued, "Mercer mentioned that he thinks somebody's looking for him."

"Somebody's looking for him? Did he say who it was or why they're looking for him?" asked the officer.

Lizzy didn't know how to answer the officer's questions without making her and Mercer seem crazy. The truth was too unbelievable. As she struggled for something to say, the emotions of the last twelve hours finally erupted, and Lizzy sobbed, "I don't know who it is or why they want him. All I know is that he's scared."

The officer put her hand on Lizzy's shoulder. "Is Mercer in danger?"

With a slight nod, Lizzy gulped and said, "Yes, I think so."

— 10 —

THE SLAPPING SOUNDS OF WIND buffeting plastic sheeting like a ship's sails roused Mercer to wakefulness. Slowly regaining his bearings, he tried to identify his surroundings. Concrete made up the floors, pillars, and ceilings. It wasn't possible to see through the translucent plastic sheeting attached where an outside wall or window should be. Mercer was inside a building under construction. Sitting tied to a chair with a gag in his mouth, he could neither free himself nor make much sound. Four men sat in chairs facing him like points on a compass, staring at him. They reminded him of those burly guys who played heavies in the movies, stone-faced sentinels.

He sat for a few minutes, taking everything in and noticing every detail. Sounds came from the street, which seemed far away, so he presumed he was at some height. They were the sounds of a city, probably New York City, but everything around New York City was also "city," so that wasn't very helpful. On the concrete behind him, he heard footsteps made by hard-soled shoes. Only, these didn't sound like any shoes he'd ever worn. The gait was quick, and the steps were light, giving Mercer the impression that it was a woman who approached, a woman with purpose.

"Why is he still gagged?" said a female voice. "Please remove it. This isn't a gulag, and he will not be treated like some sort of prisoner."

She walked past him, and he caught the scent of her perfume. A twenty-something woman in heels, wearing a white blouse and a gray jacket with a matching pencil skirt, stood in front of him.

Her black hair was pulled into a twisted updo, and her striking deep green eyes glowed against rich caramel skin.

"I apologize for the overexuberance of these men, Mr. Evans," she said in a businesslike tone as the gag was removed. "We've no intention of harming you, but we need to talk with you immediately. Since we could not contact you in a timely manner, we had to take…extraordinary measures. Have you been hurt?"

Mercer sat quietly without expression. If there was one thing he learned from John Freeman, it was how to behave under duress.

"Mr. Evans, we're not here to bring harm to you. We merely want to discuss your…ability. You see, you're not the only person with such a gift. The members of our group have a similar ability, and we would like to help you understand it and learn how to use it."

Her manner shifted from businesslike to spirited as she continued, "I, too, was frightened when strange things began to happen to me. I didn't know where to turn. But I, luckily, was found before I did something to harm myself to escape what I didn't understand. I was educated about my talent and have embraced it as a special and unique gift. This is what we hope for you, Mr. Evans. We want to help you."

Maybe it was her words, words that echoed familiar feelings and experiences. Or perhaps it was her demeanor. She was firm and factual, yet Mercer detected an undercurrent of sincerity and authenticity. This was different than what John experienced under the torment of Lutomir. His guard eroding slightly, Mercer muttered, "Who are you?"

"Ah, good," she said. "My name is Aniyah Wright." She motioned for one of the men to untie Mercer. "I want you to know that you're welcome here, and we don't intend to keep you against your will. We would merely like the opportunity to show you a bit of who we are and what we know to help you utilize your ability to the fullest. Assisting others like us is what we do."

"Assisting others, huh? More like kidnapping others," chided Mercer as his hands became free.

"I apologize for all this cloak-and-dagger nonsense, but first contacts often go sideways, so we've developed procedures which allow us to maintain a certain level of…control over the situation."

Rubbing the goose egg on his head, Mercer fumed. "You call causing an accident and almost getting me killed, then knocking me out 'control'?"

"We're still refining," said Aniyah. "Please follow me. Also, until we become more well-acquainted, some of my men will be present if things get…out of hand."

Aniyah turned away and walked as Mercer stood and followed her with two of the lapdogs in tow. They descended several flights of stairs before reaching a closed door. She knocked and waited. The door opened, but there was no one there. Aniyah walked through it, and Mercer followed into a dim hallway, through another door, and into a darkened office area filled with cubicles in various states of construction. Executive offices were placed along the outer walls of the building, from which the only available natural light entered the large room. Trailing Aniyah as she walked toward the light, Mercer struggled to remain focused and alert, distracted by her silhouette. She entered a corner office and motioned Mercer to follow, which he did. One of the men closed the door behind them, and the lapdogs remained outside. The office was large and well furnished, almost as luxurious as Winston's office at Highbridge, and smelled of flooring adhesive. Although there were windows from floor to ceiling on two adjacent walls, all shades were drawn. A distinguished-looking older man with salt-and-pepper hair parted to the side and a stubble beard sat in a high-backed leather chair behind an imposing mahogany desk. In his expensive-looking tailored suit, the man radiated confidence and intellect.

"Mercer Evans," he said in a refined English accent as he rose from his chair. "It is a pleasure to meet you. I am sorry for the calamity surrounding our first contact with you. As a rather nascent organization, we have made strides in learning how to prevent such episodes. However, each situation presents its own unique challenges." He walked toward Mercer, extending his hand. "My name is Nigel Trowbridge."

Mercer stood with his hands at his sides, his face emotionless.

"Please, Mr. Evans. I very much hope we don't start things off on the wrong foot. I did apologize, and I can promise you that we shan't need to take such drastic measures again. We attempted to call you several times. Our need was pressing." He kept his hand extended and waited.

Remembering the unknown calls he'd received, Mercer needled, "You know people don't answer unknown callers, right?"

"An oversight on my part. My head of security can be over-zealous at times. We will be bringing a new highly secure communication system online shortly, which will avoid this problem, among others."

Mercer was torn. On the one hand, he knew of at least one ruthless Leaf Runner, so trusting anyone associated with Leaf Runners would be challenging. On the other hand, the words and manner of both Aniyah and Nigel did not raise red flags. If he asked to leave, would they let him? It was at least worth letting this play out for a while to see what the catch was. Mercer warily reached for Nigel's hand and shook it.

"Excellent," said Nigel. "Shall we sit?" He extended his hand toward the guest chairs in front of the desk. "I would offer you something to drink, but as you can see, our accommodations are not yet completed. I beg your forgiveness."

As Mercer sat with his back to the entrance door, he noted a built-in wet bar in one corner of the room devoid of stock and glassware.

Nigel reclined in the desk chair, clasping his fingers. He reminded Mercer of an expensive lawyer. Nigel said, "I'm sure you are wondering why you've been brought here today. Obviously, it has something to do with your ability. It's referred to as 'metaphysical transference' and allows you to join your ancestors' minds, but there is more. I represent a select group of individuals who demonstrate this transference ability. These people, who call themselves Leaf Runners, understand the privileges and obligations associated with such a talent. Its impacts cannot be underestimated, nor can it be treated in a cavalier manner. Am I clear so far, Mr. Evans?"

"Yes, I believe so," said Mercer. "Does this mean I'm not *actually* a Leaf Runner until I agree to join your group?"

Nigel leaned forward and said, "That is correct. The Leaf Runners have all agreed to a sort of covenant. Like yourself, we know many people who are only now discovering their abilities. However, accepting everyone into the fold would be a recipe for disaster. Without knowing each individual, without each person agreeing to certain rules which they must understand and to which they must abide, there would be chaos."

Mercer was puzzled. Based on Nigel's statement, he'd incorrectly concluded anyone with abilities like his was referred to as a Leaf Runner. Yet Lutomir had assumed Mercer was one.

Sensing Mercer's confusion, Nigel reached for the intercom on the desk, punched a button, and said, "Please send him in." After releasing the button, Nigel sat back in his chair and waited.

Mercer heard the entrance door open, then close. He didn't turn to see who had entered, but he immediately recognized the voice and whipped his head around in shock as the person spoke.

"Good morning, Mr. Trowbridge, Ms. Wright, Mercer," said Ned Lamb as he walked to a bookshelf beside the main desk and sat on its corner. Mercer's eyes were riveted on Ned.

"Hello, Mr. Lamb. Thank you for coming," said Nigel. He shifted his focus to Mercer, saying, "Mr. Lamb was kind enough to bring you to our attention. It appears we almost got to you too late. That stunt you pulled last night would have made this opportunity moot. Fortunately, you came to your senses. What led you to retreat from such a dreadful course of action?"

Mercer looked at Ned, dumbfounded. He pointed at Nigel and said, "Are you with them?"

Ned said, "Yes, Mercer, I'm a Leaf Runner."

The bombshell that Ned was a Leaf Runner blew Mercer's mind. Therefore, it took him a few seconds to realize Nigel had spoken. Most of Nigel's words escaped Mercer, but he did remember…

"Dreadful course of action?" Mercer sounded bewildered as he said the words.

"Why, of course. Last night, you nearly jumped off your apartment building roof. What changed your mind?" said Nigel.

Disoriented, Mercer uttered, "Jumped? No, I didn't jump." As the events on his roof the previous night replayed in his mind, he realized how it might have looked to an observer. "No, no. I didn't jump. I transferred as I was leaning over the ledge. I was lucky it didn't make me fall to my death."

The room fell into an uneasy silence. Finally, Nigel said, "I truly apologize, Mr. Evans. I mistakenly assumed you were planning to take your own life. There have been a few Leaf Runners who we discovered after a failed suicide attempt." Nigel casually looked at Aniyah and gave her a slight nod. "Often, without a plausible explanation for such experiences, the human mind cannot constructively process these episodes of transference. The mind is fragile, and traumatic events can lead to dire consequences. Because we presumed this reasoning applied in your case…well, you can appreciate our desire for urgency."

By the time Nigel finished, Mercer had recovered from the shock of seeing Ned and said, "Ned, how did you know?"

A smug look broke out on Ned's face as he said, "Well, it could have been the sudden interest in your family tree. Maybe it was your fascination with time travel. Or maybe it was that you're even less dependable than usual. Anyway, as a Leaf Runner myself, the pattern was obvious." Motioning to Nigel, he said, "So I alerted Nigel here."

"Jesus, Ned. You had them kidnap me?" shouted Mercer as he stood. Aniyah placed herself between Mercer and Ned.

"Come now, Mr. Evans," said Nigel. "Mr. Lamb has your best interests at heart. He only did what he felt was correct. Please sit, Mr. Evans. We have much more to discuss."

Mercer didn't move. Ned's constant badgering had finally pushed Mercer to want to take a swing at him.

Nigel begged, "Please, please, have a seat. Don't blame Mr. Lamb. I had my men follow you to ascertain whether you truly have the ability. Your meeting at the NYU Department of Physics intrigued us, but the visit to Brooklyn confirmed it."

Aniyah walked toward Mercer and stood before him with a stern look. Her presence diffused Mercer. He wasn't about to attempt going through her to get to Ned, so he sat back down. Everyone breathed a sigh of relief except for Nigel, who'd been breathing normally the entire time.

"Wait a minute," Mercer said slowly. Beginning to grasp his situation, Mercer started thinking like he did when he was on his game in front of a client. Everything that was said and all verbal and visual cues came into focus. He addressed Nigel, saying, "You said you 'represent' them. What does that mean?"

"Correct, Mr. Evans," said Nigel. "I represent the Leaf Runners by providing them with administrative services. I also ensure the proper level of discretion for business operations, preventing accidental exposure of Leaf Runner activities to those who may be less accepting of the group's abilities. I myself am too old to be a Leaf Runner."

"So the hired muscle is yours, then?" asked Mercer.

"The security personnel are in my employ, yes."

"Then can someone please tell me more about this 'transference ability' you keep talking about?" asked Mercer.

Aniyah piped up, "The specific abilities of each Leaf Runner may vary slightly, but the common thread is that we all have experienced life in the minds of at least one of our deceased ancestors. Many of us can…initiate this experience and travel back to a specific time in an individual's life. However, the link must be through a direct genetic connection to the Leaf Runner or someone in the immediate family of a direct connection, like a biological brother or sister. The experience can be quite different for each of us—the level of access to the ancestor's history and experiences, the senses and perceptions conveyed, and even the ability to…commandeer their ancestor's conscious mind. All of these are highly variable among Leaf Runners."

"Commandeer? What do you mean, 'commandeer'?" asked Mercer.

Ned said, "Some Leaf Runners can push aside the conscious mind of their ancestor for periods and control the ancestor's body as if they were in full control of their own body. They can even speak as their ancestor would, using their native language. It's a very dangerous thing to do because history is changed when this happens. An action you take on behalf of your ancestor may not be the same as your ancestor's action."

"Yeah, I think that happened to me," said Mercer. Aniyah and Ned shot a glance at Nigel.

With poorly concealed apprehension, Nigel said, "Mr. Evans, I cannot stress enough the importance of becoming a member of our community. You must seriously consider it. Without proper preparation, the actions which result from your ability could have serious consequences."

"All right, what's the catch?" Mercer quipped.

"Catch?" asked Nigel.

"There's always a catch. If you help me be a Leaf Runner, what's in it for you?"

Nigel said, "If any catch exists, it is this: I am in the employ of the collective group. They each contribute a portion of what they earn in their chosen professions to pay for my services. In return, I manage the day-to-day operations and provide other support. Although still a small organization, they have an elected council that performs governance duties according to a formal charter. It's all very legitimate and legal."

"You want me to pay you," said Mercer, incredulously.

"The fee is nominal and can be adjusted as necessary so as not to impede your admission. Mr. Evans, we can help you manage your ability. We can provide a safe space to interact with others like you. We can even give you opportunities to utilize your gifts to serve humankind."

"Serve humankind?" repeated Mercer.

In the most direct and sincere words that Mercer recalled Ned ever speaking to him, Ned interjected, "Think of it as purpose.

Imagine being given the gift of an entirely new and compelling sense of purpose for your life. Well, this is it. Why are we Leaf Runners? To protect history. Why protect history? Well, because it's *our* history. Failing to preserve this history threatens our very existence."

Ned's words struck a chord with Mercer. But still hesitant, Mercer said, "Do I have time to consider?"

"Of course," said Nigel. "But be wary. There are those with transference who are not part of our organization, those who espouse certain ideologies which do not align with ours, and those who are less hospitable than we are. They are probably already trying to seek you out. It is only a matter of time before they find you. Joining us will afford you a level of awareness and protection you would not otherwise have at your disposal. The sooner, the better."

Mercer knew that what Nigel said was true. He'd already experienced those who were less hospitable.

"I'll get back to you very soon. Can someone give me a ride home?" asked Mercer, eager to leave.

"Aniyah and a driver will transport you," said Nigel. "Until you commit to us, you cannot know our location. You must wear a head covering upon leaving the site and for some time thereafter."

With some hesitation, Mercer said, "All right." He stood, but before leaving, he addressed Ned while shaking his head and said, "I still can't believe you're a Leaf Runner."

* * * * *

Mercer wanted to talk to Aniyah on the ride back to his apartment, but without knowing who was in the vehicle, he waited until she pulled the bag off his head. Before speaking, he glanced at the burly man driving, the only other person in the car.

"How long have you been a Leaf Runner?" asked Mercer.

Aniyah replied, "For me, the nightmares started about a year ago. Nigel is very good at what he does. One of those things is the identification of Leaf Runners. He said my pattern of behavior and an experience I had with another Leaf Runner during one of my episodes tipped off his network that I might have transference. He was right. I'd planned to take my own life, but he found me before I had a chance."

Mercer's mind filled with questions, and he said, "You mentioned another Leaf Runner. How many are there? Who are they? How did they know you were one?"

Aniyah's eyebrows raised as she said, "My, aren't you inquisitive? Okay, there are less than one hundred Leaf Runners so far. If you join us, you'll meet some of them eventually. Nigel thinks it best to limit direct interactions with other Leaf Runners for our protection.

"As far as identifying me as one, some of the training Nigel provides to Leaf Runners helps them identify others who might have transference. Sometimes, Leaf Runners identify others during their transference events. That's what happened to me. I encountered a Leaf Runner when I first found myself in the past. Also, there are some character traits and demographics we can look for to help us narrow the pool of potential candidates. For example, Ned said you checked all the boxes: correct age range, born at Bellevue—we verified that—highly capable underachiever, et cetera."

"Highly capable underachiever?" glowered Mercer. Then he said, "Anyway, is this Nigel guy on the level?"

"Good question," said Aniyah. "I had doubts when I was first contacted. However, I wouldn't be here today if it hadn't been for Nigel and the Leaf Runners. I'm happy with my life now." She smiled at him. It wasn't just her mouth that smiled; her whole face lit up as she finished speaking. Mercer couldn't help but smile back.

Through the side window, Mercer recognized they were close to home. He considered coming up with an excuse to keep them going in circles for a while so he could continue talking with Aniyah. Then he remembered Lizzy had been in his apartment when he was taken.

Mercer said, "Well, here we are. Thanks for the ride. I'll bet my sister is panicking." Then sarcastically, he said, "If I had my phone, I could've called her."

After the car parked, Aniyah slid a phone out of her jacket pocket and offered it to Mercer.

"Sorry," she said sheepishly.

Mercer shook his head as the car sped away.

"Good job," he said to himself as he entered his building. "You had to open your big mouth, didn't you?"

An older lady leaving as Mercer entered overheard him, stopped, and scowled at him. Mercer gave her an embarrassed smile.

He opened his apartment door and walked in as Lizzy jumped out of the chair and ran to him. She pulled him toward her, and he put a hand against the wall to keep from losing his balance.

"What happened? Are you okay?" she asked.

"It's a long story," said Mercer. "The short version is that Ned Lamb ratted me out to an organization of Leaf Runners, who kidnapped me and knocked me on the head. But other than that, I'm fine."

Lizzy released Mercer and backed away, giving him the once-over. "Oh, thank God you're all right. I've been here all day and tried to do some of my classes online, but I just couldn't concentrate."

She picked up her phone and started typing on it.

"I'm sorry you had to go through this, Lizzy." After a momentary pause, he said, "Did you tell Dad what happened?"

"No. Given the distance between you two, I thought it best to wait a while. I'm messaging Connor," she said. "He's been really worried about you. He's been asking for updates all day, so I'm letting him know you're home safe."

"Oh, thanks," said Mercer blankly. It struck him as odd that Connor was worried about him. Most likely, it was Lizzy he was concerned about and was trying to comfort her.

When Lizzy finished, she gave Mercer a questioning look and said, "Who's Ned Lamb?"

Mercer told Lizzy about Ned, about the Leaf Runners and their organization, that the misguided reason they grabbed him was to protect him from himself, about the offer of membership they'd extended to him, and that they could teach him about his gift and give him protection.

After he finished, she asked, "Mercer, what're you going to do?"

Mercer pensively replied, "I'm not sure. But I know some not-so-friendly people out there will try to find me. Maybe they're already looking. Thcy will find me, whether I join the Leaf Runners or not. I've no idea what they intend to do with me, but I'm sure it isn't good."

Mercer stared into Lizzy's eyes, his glistening, before continuing.

"Also, if I'm in danger, so are the people I love. I need to do everything I can to protect you, Lizzy, to protect both of us."

"Then you already know what to do," said Lizzy. "Oh, by the way, the police are looking for you."

            ───────── 🍃11 ─────────

MERCER SETTLED INTO THE LONE recliner situated in the middle
of the room. Aniyah, sitting next to him on a stool near a rack of
instruments, placed some tiny sticky pads with metal snaps on his
scalp and some larger pads on his chest and torso. She connected
wires to each pad and flipped on the equipment to which the cables
were attached. Squiggly lines appeared on several screens as she
watched them for a few seconds. After adjusting several knobs
and a few electrodes, she looked satisfied.

"This allows us to monitor your vitals and brain waves,"
she said. "We do this as a precaution in case…in case your vitals
exceed normal ranges. Of course, that isn't expected. We can tell
if you're in control of your ancestor or under duress. We can even
tell when you've completed your transference. If Leaf Runners are
put in a situation where they take control of the body of an ancestor, hijack their consciousness, we like to make sure we can stop
the transference, if necessary."

"What the hell am I getting myself into?" asked Mercer
warily.

"It's simply a precaution. Remember, you'll feel your mind
wander like you're starting to go to sleep. It's during this time
that the ancestry pool can be accessed. You need to enter the pool
when you see it, or you'll just go to sleep. Also, and this is important, you are only to commandeer your ancestor's consciousness
while he is alone. You must not do anything that could harm him.
I don't want you in control for more than five minutes. Got it?"
she lectured.

"Yeah, I've got it," Mercer said.

"Now let's send you back in time." She smiled.

Aniyah dimmed the room lights and moved the noise-canceling speakers attached to the recliner into position on either side of Mercer's head. He closed his eyes and tried to relax, unsure what he was supposed to do to go back in time. The previous occasions had started on their own; he'd only learned how to control things once he was there, and he knew how to get back.

The chair was comfortable, and the room in the depths of the temporary Leaf Runner headquarters was dark and quiet. Mercer relaxed, and his mind retreated from the world around him. The familiar ancestry pool appeared. He observed it for a while, examining it from different perspectives to understand it better. As he loitered there, the pool began to withdraw. It moved slowly at first, and Mercer could move casually toward it to stay close. Movement became more challenging and impeded his ability to stay close to the pool. Not a moment too soon, he recalled what Aniyah said—enter the pool when you see it. Nearing a state of panic, Mercer fought to move toward the pool, pulling from every ounce of his resolve until he finally reached it, and he dove in. He kicked toward the bottom, and the trunk of Mercer's ancestral tree came into focus. Examining the branches, he moved along a path until he found the leaf he sought. Mercer touched the leaf and immediately entered its pool, rising quickly as he kicked toward its surface.

* * * * *

Striped hues of green flowed before me under a calm, clear blue sky. A stand of trees filled the space between two of the stripes. A quietly burbling stream interrupted the stripes, gently bisecting several verdant swaths. Other than the water, the only sound I heard was the chirping of birds. The air smelled of the earth but had a sweetness to it. My eyes focused more closely on the stripes, which resolved into rows of carefully tended vines.

I was in the most picturesque setting conceivable, a beautiful vineyard, a heaven on earth. I was in *my* beautiful vineyard. In the highly sought-after region of Bordeaux in France, Chateau Saint-Pierre was a winemaker's paradise. I, Corbin LaCroix, head winemaker at Chateau Saint-Pierre, always walked through the vineyard on days like this. Early morning was best. The sweet smell of the vines, the dew dripping from the ripening grapes, and the peaceful quiet that preceded the workers who tended the fields were inspirational to me. Each day living in the place was a joy to be alive, a glorious gift from God.

* * * * *

Mercer observed Corbin from the surface of his pool in the corner of Corbin's mind as he inspected the vines, strolling along the rows and stopping at some of the plants to peer at them. He chose the leaf with the birth date of 1784 on his ancestral tree, the same one he'd approached during his sleep a few nights earlier. Corbin was in the place of control, in command of his consciousness, and going about his daily ritual, unaware of Mercer's presence. With Corbin alone and in a safe situation, this was the perfect moment for Mercer to hone his ability to control his ancestor's body. He left the pool and started toward the consciousness. An invisible force pushed against him, trying to keep him from entering. It was like sprinting head-on into a gale-force wind. Aniyah mentioned he would experience this; it would be different for each ancestor. The stronger and healthier ones were the hardest. It was much easier with John Freeman, maybe because John was in such a weakened state. Corbin staggered slightly and dropped to a knee, placing one hand on the ground. As he was coached, Mercer explored the outer boundary of Corbin's consciousness until he thought he found an area of weakness. He asserted himself into this area and made steady progress filling it until he stood alone in the conscious mind.

The body's eyes looked where Mercer guided them. Its head turned as Mercer directed. He forced the body to its feet and stood in one place, trying to maintain balance. He'd been unable to stand when with John Freeman, lashed to that horrible waterboard. Having this much control was new to Mercer, and a bit scary, like the first time his dad put him behind the wheel of a car in the parking lot of a shopping mall in Newport. Mercer needed plenty of room to maneuver and was thankful the lot was nearly empty. Speaking of scary, he was glad his dad didn't make him drive back home through the Holland Tunnel.

Corbin looked like Frankenstein's monster as he picked up one foot at a time and jerked himself forward between the rows of vines. It was almost like having to learn to walk again, but Mercer discovered it took only a few dozen steps for him to acclimate to Corbin's weight and distribution. These legs had moved this body its whole life; they knew what they had to do. Continuing to move as Corbin did earlier, he walked down the rows, studying the vines. He noticed things about them.

This small bunch of grapes will need to be removed to favor the larger bunch near it, and some of the older canes will require more pruning during the offseason to favor the growth of newer ones.

He knew these things but had no idea how he knew them. He continued down the row until he reached the end of the field, so engrossed in examining the vines that he didn't hear footsteps coming toward him.

"Monsieur LaCroix, good morning," said a cheerful voice in French.

Mercer looked up to see a middle-aged man carrying pruning tools and a basket stop and look at him. He was wearing a broad-brimmed hat and work clothes.

"Um, uh, good morning to you… Henri," stammered Mercer, also in French. Henri was one of the peasant workers who tended the vineyards each day. There wasn't much else Mercer knew about Henri, which he found strange. Henri had been working in the vineyard for a couple of years. Still, Corbin never talked with Henri, other than giving him instructions each day and that cold winter's day when Henri had helped him after he twisted his ankle while walking the vineyard. Did he have a family? Was he happy with his job? Mercer hadn't a clue. Not knowing what he should do next, Mercer thought it best to recede into the ancestry pool and allow Corbin to retake control of his body.

Mercer continued to observe as Corbin's body shook when his consciousness was restored. Corbin staggered while easing his head around to look at his surroundings.

"Monsieur LaCroix, are you well?" asked Henri. His long strides brought him quickly to Corbin, and he grabbed Corbin's arm to keep him from falling.

"Oh, I… I don't know what happened. One minute I was walking the row, and the next minute I was standing here. I don't remember," said Corbin.

"Sir, I will take you to the château so you can sit. I am sure you will feel fine after a few minutes of rest."

"Yes, yes," grumbled Corbin.

They walked through several fields while Henri supported half of Corbin's weight. A beautiful white stone manor house stood among oak trees as they crested a hill. A gravel road crossed thirty paces in front of the house, and a stone path led through a manicured lawn from the road to a stone staircase leading up to large ornate wooden doors. The building had three levels aboveground, with a steep dark tiled roof, large dormers, and at least half a dozen chimneys, some spewing tendrils of woodsmoke. The two entered the building through the kitchen access door, and Henri led Corbin to a chair, helping him sit. A gaunt middle-aged woman wearing a petticoat and bustle and a linen cap covering her hair looked up from slicing carrots.

"There," said Henri, smiling. "I am sure you will be back in the vineyard in no time."

"Yes, thank you, Henri," said Corbin.

Henri addressed the woman, "Madame, Monsieur LaCroix is unwell this morning. I think he needs some rest, and maybe you can give him something to drink to help him?"

Camille LaCroix tentatively put down the knife and retrieved a mug from the pantry. She returned and filled it with liquid from a kettle warming by the crackling hearth.

"Thank you, Henri. That will be all," she said.

"Are you sure, Madame LaCroix?"

"Yes, yes, off with you then," she said. Henri bowed to her and left.

Mercer noticed the look of worry on Camille's face and got a sinking feeling. Something was wrong. Corbin's emotions overwhelmed Mercer as he lifted his head to look at her. The feelings were not the ones he'd expected. There was no love, no longing, and no desire. These were emotions of hate, resentment, and loathing. Corbin had no love for Camille, only hate, and Mercer could feel that hate welling up inside of him.

As Camille walked toward Corbin with the mug, time slowed for Mercer. Camille's eyes were diverted, trying not to make eye contact. Both of her arms were in front of her, ready to defend. She didn't face him directly but sidled toward him. He slapped the mug from her hand as she came within arm's length, smashing the full vessel to the floor, and grabbed her wrist.

"Do you think I cannot take care of myself, woman?" he howled. "Get your poison out of my face." He paused for a second, seeming to come to a realization. "You did this to me! You put something in my waterskin this morning before I left for the vineyard."

"No, *no*," she cried.

"Yes, you did. You want me gone. You need me, woman. Without me, you are nothing. Do not ever forget that. You…are… *nothing!*"

Camille cried as he pulled her toward him, holding her with one hand and slapping her on the side of her ribcage with the other. Each slap led to a scream of pain from Camille.

"Stop, please, stop, please," she sobbed.

He pulled up her dress to expose her leg to midthigh and pulled one of her stockings down. Time froze for Mercer. Her leg was black, blue, and green, almost every inch he could see through

Corbin's eyes. There were unhealed welts on top of healed ones, and this bastard was having another go at her. Mercer could see his hand hitting her leg repeatedly as time sped back up. He fought to regain control of Corbin, to force Corbin from consciousness. He was rebuffed, only now the shield seemed impenetrable. Corbin was in such a rabid state that his consciousness would be nearly impossible to control. Mercer could not take a pragmatic approach this time.

The beating and screaming of Camille continued as Mercer stood passively by. It was worse than torture, seeing this happen to another person, knowing there was a way to stop it, not being able to do so. Fresh welts and blood began to ooze from several spots on her leg, yet Corbin didn't seem close to finishing. Mercer could feel himself starting to boil, the rage bubbling inside and flowing over. He threw himself at Corbin's consciousness, ready to destroy whatever he needed to acquire it and stop this madness. He pressed on one side; he came at it from opposite sides; he came at it from every side, continuing to attack. He noticed the barrier starting to soften and that Corbin was slowing his barrage on Camille. Mercer fought even harder, gaining ground.

The beating halted, and Corbin stood still, breathing heavily, allowing Camille to drop to the floor, where she sobbed uncontrollably. This sudden termination of the offense caught Mercer off guard, and he gave up the precious ground he'd gained. Corbin was still mad with anger, but the beating had stopped. Mercer was unsure whether he should continue to press for control or wait.

After a few moments, Corbin yelled, "Where is Brigitte? Where is she?"

"No, please, you cannot," whimpered Camille.

"Where is she?"

"Oh god, please, no. Not Brigitte." Camille's plea was the most horrendous sound Mercer had ever heard. She would rather have Corbin continue to beat her than allow him to find Brigitte.

"It does not matter. I will find her. I will deal with you later," menaced Corbin.

Corbin grabbed an open wine bottle and immediately left the kitchen. Taking large gulps from the bottle, he went around the back of the building and opened the door to the cellar. He entered and closed the door behind him, leaving himself in near darkness because few of the wall sconces were lit. Rows and rows of oaken barrels filled the ample, chilly cellar space. He knew Brigitte, his fifteen-year-old daughter, usually came down here in the mornings to take the previous day's inventory and that she would be here somewhere. Mercer was unsure what Corbin intended; his emotions were a mix of anger, resentment, and frustration. Corbin's feeling of control was peaking, and the wine affected his judgment.

"Brigitte!" he called out several times as he walked.

Finally, near one end of the cellar, he heard Brigitte's timid voice, "Yes, Papa."

"Ah, there you are. What are you doing, Bigi?" he said. He had called her Bigi since she was a baby.

"I am taking inventory. Do you need something, Papa?"

"Yes, yes, I need something," he said. "You see, your mother has gone and upset me again."

She looked warily at his eyes and said, "Papa, you have been drinking. Please go and lay down. You are not well."

"But, Bigi. You can help me," he leered. He started toward her as she backed away.

"No, Papa, stop, *stop*!"

Mercer couldn't believe what was happening. This incestophile was going to take his daughter. He had to stop it, and he didn't have much time. He flailed his way into Corbin's consciousness, gaining a portion of it. Corbin prevented Mercer from gaining complete control, but Mercer was able to manipulate Corbin's left arm. Corbin forced Brigitte onto her stomach atop a wine cask, the girl's dress and shift were pulled up over her head, and Corbin started raping her. Corbin's eyes were closed, preventing Mercer from seeing anything. He flailed the left arm until he felt its hand bump into some tools on the wall. He rummaged blindly around the tools to determine what they might be and found the blade of a sickle. Grabbing the edge with their hand, he felt the sharpness of its cut and the warmth of trickling blood. Still holding the blade, he tried to detect Brigitte's hand by using the back of Corbin's hand and arm. She was weeping and seemed to have given up fighting. He located one of her hands and held the sickle so that she could reach its handle. She took the tool as he let go of it.

Mercer refocused on controlling Corbin, pushing harder and harder into the crevices. Corbin's ravenous state of mind suddenly abated, allowing Mercer to quickly move Corbin away from consciousness. Now he had control of the body and immediately pulled away from Brigitte.

He pulled her dress and undergarments back down and said, "I'm sorry, I'm so sorry. I tried to stop it, but I couldn't. He was just too strong, and I couldn't make him stop. Please forgive me."

He continued to back away as she regained her feet and turned toward him with her arms behind her, bawling and shaking her head, yelling, "Why, Papa? Why?"

She repeated it as she walked toward him unsteadily. Her right hand shot into the air, and Mercer saw the sharp metal blade of the sickle gleaming in the dim light. Mercer vacated the consciousness and dove for the ancestry pool as she wound up to swing the sickle. He went down to the ancestry tree and didn't immediately head toward the trunk and home. The leaves in this area of the tree were numerous, and he needed to study them for a time before he could understand all the relationships. His mind seemed like it was still being pumped full of adrenaline, which didn't help his concentration.

* * * * *

I came out of the fog as I had earlier, in a different place than where the fog rolled in. This time I was only a few feet from my original location. As before, my body was numb, and I was dizzy. However, I was able to see Bigi standing in front of me, disheveled, holding a sickle. Her face was sad, but a cold hard determination was also present.

I could barely stand in my stupor, let alone move, but I did notice a faint flash of light coming from the left side of my vision. Her arm holding the sickle moved quickly, and her face was no longer sad; it was angry. I had never seen that look on her face before. As her arm swept down, I felt the pain of a blade slicing through my left leg, causing it to buckle. I fell to my left and caught myself on my hands and knees.

"Bigi," I pleaded.

I heard her yell, "Never again!" as the hooked blade yanked at my neck, and I felt it slicing deep into my throat. I could no longer breathe; I was drowning in my blood.

My name was Corbin Hugo LaCroix. On February 18, 1748, I was born to Martin Liam LaCroix and Ninette Rochelle (De La Fontaine) LaCroix. I was head winemaker at Chateau Saint-Pierre, Bordeaux, in France. On July 2, 1784, I died at my daughter's hand.

* * * * *

Mercer found Corbin's leaf and saw three other leaves, representing children, connected by branches to Corbin's. They were Brigitte, born in 1769; Jean-Paul, born and died in 1770; and Claude, who was born in 1785. He also found Camille's name connected to Brigitte as her mother. Mercer was struck that Camille only had two children, Brigitte and Jean-Paul. Camille was not Claude's mother. Claude's mother was Brigitte. His father, and grandfather, were Corbin.

With a sparkling silver light, some of the information on two of the leaves changed before his eyes. Both Corbin's date of death and Claude's date of birth moved three months earlier. Mercer's actions had changed the future, but only slightly. He'd failed to prevent Corbin's heinous act upon Brigitte. If anyone or anything could have stopped this horrific incident, it was Mercer Evans. It was too late to go back and undo the horrible things done. Aniyah told him that once you fully enter the mind of an ancestor and then leave, you can never return. You have one chance to observe their life or take an action that would forever change their life and history. If you failed, you lost your only opportunity. Surrender was a lonely place.

Before returning to the tree trunk, he looked one more time at the leaves, at the lives of the people he'd just encountered. What started in a beautiful idyllic setting in a French vineyard turned into a vision of hell. Poor Brigitte and little Claude. He wondered what their lives were like. Mercer followed this branch of the tree and noted that Claude eventually married and had several children. Claude was one of Mercer's direct ancestors. Without Claude, Mercer might have never existed. He would certainly not be the same Mercer, genetically. Had he been successful at preventing Corbin's heinous crime, Mercer's role in history might never have been written. This was a sobering thought. Mercer drifted back toward the trunk and lazily floated to the top of the ancestry pool.

* * * * *

"Brigitte, oh Brigitte," Mercer mumbled with his eyes still closed.

He kept repeating the words, yet the instruments Aniyah monitored didn't show anything out of the ordinary. His vitals and brain waves were normal. She thought it odd since she had never heard a Leaf Runner vocalize during a transference event. Then Mercer's body started to twitch, but not violently. Twitching was not expected, and Aniyah was concerned. She texted, "need you now" to Ned, who'd been available on standby if something happened during Mercer's transference.

Seconds later, Ned bolted into the room and turned on the lights. Mercer blinked and shifted his gaze between Aniyah and Ned as his eyes slowly adjusted to the light. Aniyah was shaken by the panic that showed on Mercer's face, his eyes were wide, and his mouth was open.

Finally, Mercer said, "Oh my god."

$$12$$

"**WHAT HAPPENED, MERCER?**" ASKED A worried Aniyah as Ned stared intently at Mercer.

Mercer told them everything he could recall during his time in France, every repulsive detail. His ancestor was an evil, savage, and heartless man. Previously, those whom Mercer joined were good, honest, and respectable. Both offered Mercer positive character traits, which he readily accepted and intended to hone. What Corbin LaCroix offered was an intense hatred and a callous disregard for the lives of those closest to him, characteristics present only in the most sadistic and sociopathic. Corbin's actions ultimately led the one person he should have protected above everyone else, his daughter, to take his life. Mercer had no sense of loss for Corbin, only for his wife and daughter. Both had suffered heinous crimes at the hands of that beastly man. The trait Mercer discovered was not from Corbin; it was from Brigitte and himself. It was the trait of self-preservation. Mercer provided Brigitte with a way out of her tragic situation, and they both knew the cost. Neither would ever be the same.

Aniyah lectured, "Actually, you're pretty lucky, Mercer. You could've really messed up your personal history. Maybe now you can see just how dangerous transference is. There are times when we learn the history and, as you did, want to fight to change it for a different and better outcome. However, you must resist this… urge. It could be more destructive than you can imagine."

"Lucky?" murmured Mercer. "I don't feel very lucky."

Aniyah came close to Mercer, looked into his eyes, and said earnestly, "I know this probably won't seem very helpful, but I went through similar emotions after one of my experiences. It's tragic and…disheartening. But it's real life. It is your history. You have a chance to know your *actual* history, not just history based on the watered-down or…embellished stories passed down from generation to generation. Sometimes it's distasteful, ugly, or even brutal. But often, history is wonderful and inspiring. Use the knowledge you gained from this experience to enrich your life, not devalue it."

Mercer watched Aniyah and listened. The passion with which she spoke was enchanting. Her words and manner were soothing and comforting, and he knew they were true. Beyond what she said, he was also aware of how she would pause before saying certain words or phrases, searching to use just the right one to convey her message. He'd noticed her do this often. The tension in his shoulders and back waned, and Mercer relaxed.

"You're right," he said absently. "I've got a lot to process, but I'm so tired."

Mercer was silent for a couple of seconds, then turned to Ned with a serious expression and said, "Ned, I hope the Price proposal is ready. Your presentation is tomorrow morning, and I'm too tired to be of any more help today. I promise I'll be there for backup."

"I know what I'm doing, Mercer. I won't need your help," Ned said complacently.

"At least try to look enthused while doing it," gibed Mercer.

"Blow me," seethed Ned, while the other two laughed.

Mercer left them and numbly made the journey to his apartment. France had taken so much out of him, and he was eager to lay his head on his pillow.

* * * * *

Lizzy left her anatomy final walking on air. She knew she nailed the test and was already looking forward to next semester. However, at the moment, all she wanted was to celebrate. Some classmates were going to an acquaintance's apartment for some cocktails, so Lizzy gleefully tagged along.

As the group started the fifteen-minute walk, Lizzy called Connor to see if he wanted to join in the fun. When he answered, she said, "Hey, babe. I'm done!"

"Yay! How'd it go?" said Connor.

"Piece of cake," she said. "So a bunch of us are going out for some drinks. Can you join us?"

"Aren't you a little young?" chided Connor.

"It's only a few weeks until my birthday. Anyway, we're going to somebody's apartment. It'll be great, especially if you can come. Well?" Lizzy pleaded.

"All right," Connor said hesitantly. "I just need to finish a few things. I'll be there in an hour."

"I can't wait. I'll text you the address. See you," she chirped.

The cool night air was refreshing, and the friends chatted along the way as they enjoyed the feeling of relief that came with completing a semester. Not all were as optimistic as Lizzy about the test, but they were done, which counted for something.

The group arrived at a bustling penthouse apartment to the thumping sounds of house music. Drinks and snacks abounded, and Lizzy quickly lost herself in the joy and pleasure of being with friends and celebrating in a fun atmosphere. She'd lost track of the number of drinks she'd consumed by the time Connor appeared. A huge smile lit up her face, and she ran to him, hugged him, and kissed him. Then she leaned back and stared at him in a drunken daze.

He smiled and said, "It looks like you've been having fun."

"So much," she yelled over the music, louder than she needed to. Lizzy slurred slightly as she introduced him to her classmates, a few of which nodded approvingly. Connor didn't react, but Lizzy beamed. They spent another hour eating and enjoying them-selves, with Lizzy having another couple of drinks, after which, in a demure whisper, she asked him, "Can you take me home?"

"Uh…sure," he faltered.

He supported her as she staggered during the short walk to her apartment in Greenwich Village, and when they entered, she hugged him before he could close the door.

"Lizzy, you've had a lot to drink. Don't you think you should just go to bed?" he said nervously.

"Excellent idea," she purred. "Let's go."

"I'm not sure *that* is an excellent idea. What if your brother finds out you were drinking and that we slept together?"

"Mercer? How would he find out? I'm not gonna say anything. He's busy playing with his little Leaf People anyway," she said, waving her hands dismissively. She stammered, "I... I don't think he'd much care. Now quit talking about Mercer and help me get my shoes off."

"Leaf People, what Leaf People?" inquired Connor as he pulled off one of her shoes.

"Leaf People? No, silly, Leaf Runners," she annunciated. "Why didya call 'em Leaf People?"

"But you just... Anyway, who are these Leaf Runners?"

"They're just like Mercer. They can go back in time." She giggled.

"Really!?" Connor said absently. "Well, how did he find them?"

"He didn't find them. They found him... More like took him." She laughed as she fell backward onto the bed. "Come to bed," she said, staring at the ceiling.

"Took him?" asked Connor. Lizzy didn't respond. "Um, okay... Give me a minute. I need to go to the bathroom," said Connor haphazardly.

When Connor got back to the bed, Lizzy was fast asleep. He smiled, bent down, and gently kissed her forehead. She didn't react to his touch. He decided to stay awhile if she got sick, so he sat on the couch and turned on the television.

* * * * *

It was one of the clearest, bluest skies Mercer ever remembered seeing in the city as he stared out of the fifty-fourth-story windows of the Highbridge conference room where Ned was about halfway through his presentation to the Price delegation. Many others were also staring blankly out the window instead of the presentation screen. People rapidly lost interest, and some appeared close to losing consciousness as several heads bobbed sporadically. However, Winston's face was turning red like a boiled lobster. Ned knew his stuff, but his monotone delivery and slow pace were not engaging. He merely read the slides and presented data in gory detail while not providing much commentary. So far, Mercer had been quiet and let Ned run the show. Ned was ready to move to the main proposal, so it was time for Mercer to step in and attempt to rescue the meeting.

"To sum up, Ned. You're saying that although the hit rate is important, it's the slugging ratio that creates our successes. Is that correct?" Mercer could see some of the previously nodding heads in the room snap out of their stupor and become alert.

"Um, yes. I guess that would be a way to aggregate the information I presented on the previous slides," said Ned.

"Great, and the methods and algorithms we have in place have resulted in the slugging ratio here at Highbridge to be among the best in the industry, right?"

"That is technically correct," Ned said tentatively.

"Thanks for boiling that all down for us, Ned. Now that you've seen our standing in the industry and how we have a proven track record of success, Ned will get into the specifics of our proposal for Price. Are there any questions before we move to the proposal?"

Those around the table shook their heads, looking satisfied.

"Great, let's continue," said Mercer.

Ned continued with the presentation, and Mercer provided the color to keep the Price people engaged and attentive. The rest of the meeting seemed to go well, and the Price team was all smiles after they heard the full details of the proposal. As the meeting concluded, the Price representatives promised a timely response. There were handshakes all around, and even Winston looked pleased.

Ned escorted the visitors to the building entrance while Mercer went to his office. When Ned returned, Mercer asked him, "How do you think that went?"

"I thought it was going great until you broke in during the middle of my presentation. I had everything under control."

"No, Ned. You didn't. You'd almost lost them by that point. We were rapidly approaching the cliff, and you merrily kept on your way, heading straight toward it. I provided the necessary course correction. Did you not watch the audience to see their reactions? How about Winston? His face was so red I thought he was about to explode. Did you see any of that?"

"Well, no."

"You can't present to the slides, Ned. You have to present to the audience," said Mercer emphatically.

"Damn." Ned finally realized his presentation hadn't started very well.

"We have a long way to go, Ned. A long way," said Mercer, shaking his head.

Later that day, Mercer was eating lunch at his desk like he usually did when his phone buzzed. The call was from Connor.

"Hey, Connor," said Mercer.

"Hi, Mercer. Do you have a few minutes to talk?" said Connor.

"Yup."

"Great. I finally had a chance to read the papers by Dr. Warwick, as promised," said Connor.

"Oh, that's right. I almost forgot. What did you find out?"

"Well, not much more than what Professor Giannelli told us. There was a lot of work done on rats, with some promising results. However, there is very little human data, partly because they had difficulty convincing hospitals and patients to participate in the study."

"So Dr. Warwick took things into his own hands and performed a study without consent," said Mercer.

"Correct. The planned study was going to include over four thousand neonatal subjects from all over the world. They were to receive a series of injections before leaving the hospital and be followed for the next thirty years. A study like that would take a lot of time and money. So I looked closer at his funding sources and found very few of them. Most were shells, so nearly impossible to trace. But these very few donors planned to generate over fifty million dollars."

"Did you say fifteen or fifty?"

"Fifty. Five-zero. That's a lot of cash," said Connor.

"Well, he surely had *some* people convinced. Were you able to track down any of the donors?"

"The only one I could find has an address in Queens."

"Great work, Connor. Thanks," said Mercer. Connor gave him the contact information and hung up.

Mercer immediately called the number, and a quiet voice answered, "Leverton Ventures, how may I direct your call?"

"Yes, I would like to meet with Mr. Sigmund Leverton," Mercer said.

"Can I ask what it is regarding?" queried the voice on the other end of the line.

"Um...this is a private matter. I'd appreciate seeing him as soon as he's available," asserted Mercer.

"And your name is?"

"Mercer. Mercer Evans."

"Mr. Leverton is a busy man, Mr. Evans. I'm sure you understand. The earliest time he has available is two weeks from yesterday."

Tensely, Mercer said, "Two weeks...shit. Um...are you sure there's nothing sooner? I... I have information regarding a Dr. Amon Warwick." Mercer spelled the name.

"Dr. Amon Warwick, huh? All right, please hold," said the voice.

Blaring trumpets blasted Mercer's ear as the hold music clicked on, and he pulled the phone away so it wouldn't be so annoying, but he could still hear. Several minutes ticked by as

Mercer waited impatiently for the receptionist, or whoever he was talking to, to return.

Finally, the music was interrupted, and the quiet voice said, "Mr. Evans, are you still there?"

"Ah…yeah. Yeah, I'm here," said Mercer. "And can you turn down that hold music? It's too loud, just sayin'."

"Er…well, Mr. Leverton would like to inquire as to the specifics of the information you have related to Dr. Warwick."

Mercer was rattled. He wasn't sure how much he should reveal to Leverton. But since he started with a ploy about him having something on Warwick, he'd better play it out as far as possible.

"Well…um. I'd rather not discuss this over the phone. We need to talk face-to-face. Uh…that's the only way this'll work," said Mercer in a quivering voice.

The hold music blared on again and lasted another couple of minutes before the voice came back.

"All right. Mr. Leverton will see you if you can make it here by three."

Mercer thought for a second. If he left the office now, even with a quick stop at his apartment, he should be able to get to the meeting in time.

"I'll be there," he said and hung up.

Mercer hurriedly left the office and boarded the first train headed for 116th Street, messaging Ned that he would be out the rest of the day and to tell Winston he was unwell, if needed. Mercer was on edge as the train made its way toward East Harlem, unsure it was a good idea to use Warwick's name with Leverton, but he could think of no other way to convince the man to meet with him. Apparently, it worked. Leverton was curious.

Mercer opened his apartment door and was only there long enough to grab his jacket and helmet. He needed to be in Queens in an hour and would be cutting it close. The only way he could make it in time was on his crotch rocket, his pride and joy and the one thing he'd ever splurged on. The motorcycle was parked in a garage beneath his apartment building. It'd been a couple of weeks since he rode the machine, and he was eager to feel the thrill of speed the bike gave him. As luck would have it, he might have to dodge some traffic to make sure he didn't miss his appointment, which would give him a chance to stretch the motorcycle's legs a bit.

Mercer's luck continued with good traffic, and he pulled up to a simple brick three-story office building with two minutes to spare. The building had no signs indicating what lay within. He entered through a vestibule and came to a desk, behind which sat a receptionist.

"Hello, I'm Mercer Evans. I'm here to see Mr. Leverton," he said.

"Evans…yes. Mr. Leverton is expecting you," said the same voice he'd heard on the phone earlier. "Please follow me."

The receptionist went through a doorway, and Mercer followed him into a narrow hallway lined by a half dozen occupied cubicles with no natural lighting, toward a walled office along the front of the building. The receptionist knocked and waited for a response. A grunt came from within. The receptionist opened the door and extended his hand into the room for Mercer to follow.

"Mr. Leverton, this is Mercer Evens," said the receptionist.

"Thank you, Milo," said a man sitting behind a large walnut desk in a leather-backed chair in front of a window covered with partially open blinds, which provided an obscured view of the street. "That will be all. Please have a seat."

The receptionist closed the door. The bright sunlight beaming through the blinds and dim room lighting made it difficult for Mercer to make out the seated figure.

"I'm Sigmund Leverton. Now what do you have for me, Mr. Evans?" he said as he reached out a hand.

"It's Mercer," he said, shaking Leverton's smooth yet firm hand. "Well, Mr. Leverton, um… I was given your name as someone who might be familiar with um…a certain clinical research study that was planned to be conducted about twenty-five years ago. The principal investigator was a Dr. Amon Warwick from Bellevue hospital. Does any of this ring a bell?"

Sigmund cleared his throat, the reaction betraying his knowledge on the subject. "Well, that is privileged information. I am not at liberty to divulge—"

"Mr. Leverton," Mercer interrupted. "We both know Dr. Warwick is long dead, and the clinical trial never happened. However, I think we also know that Dr. Warwick raised a boatload of money for this planned study. You were one of the investors, and you probably haven't seen a dime of your investment returned. Am I correct, sir?"

Sigmund drummed his fingers on the desk in thought for a few seconds. After a big sigh, he said, "Yes, I invested. The man gave me a compelling pitch for his plan. I wasn't the only investor. Who would've thought it would all crumble when he died unexpectedly? He'd already spread the money around or spent it, so none of the investors were able to retrieve anything, as far as I know. That's pretty much the whole story… Mercer," said Sigmund, oozing with sarcasm as he said the name.

Mercer didn't react and continued, "Who else donated?"

"Wait, I thought you were coming here to give *me* information. Why are you the one asking the questions?" Leverton said sharply.

Mercer paused for a few seconds to carefully consider his next words. Then finally he said, "I think I was one of his subjects."

Leverton was shocked and sat back in his chair. "Wait, but I thought the trial never happened. How could you be…"

"Warwick obviously used your money for something."

Confused, Leverton said, "But how do you know—"

Mercer interrupted, "It doesn't matter how I know. I need to know who else donated."

"Even if I knew, I wouldn't tell you. But most donors were protected behind some shell or trust fund. Donors were not given specifics about other donors."

"So you don't know anyone else involved, and there was nothing more to it, as far as you know?"

"No. I'd almost forgotten about it until I heard the name when you called." Leverton's demeanor changed from off-balance to shrewd and calculated in the blink of an eye. "Tell me about this study you say you were a subject in."

Mercer stood abruptly and said, "I'm sorry, but I need to go."

"We still have much to discuss," Leverton said over his wire-frame glasses.

"It was a mistake to come here. I apologize if I've wasted your time. I'll see myself out, Mr. Leverton."

Mercer practically sprinted out of the office as he heard Leverton say, "But I'm not finished…"

Mercer rushed past Milo and quickly left the building. He'd hit another dead end. To make matters worse, he'd drawn attention to himself.

As he sat on his bike, ready to start it and head for home, his phone rang. It was Aniyah.

"Hi, Aniyah, what's up?"

"Mercer, we need you to come to the lab right now," she said in a rush.

"Come to the lab. Why?"

"We'll discuss it when you get here. It's a matter of some urgency."

Slightly annoyed, Mercer said, "I hear you, but I don't recall signing anything saying I had to drop everything and come whenever you call."

"No, of course, you didn't. But a…situation has come up that needs attention, and you are the person best suited for it."

"All right, but I'm about an hour away. I'll get there as soon as I can," he said.

As the sun sank toward the western horizon, he ended the call and started his bike. Cross Island Parkway was not very busy but had enough traffic to keep him alert as he headed toward the expressway. While he waited at a stoplight, headlights reflected off his side mirror. The mirror showed an SUV approaching him from behind. However, it wasn't the vehicle that caught his attention; it was the pistol sticking out of the passenger window and pointing at Mercer.

$$13$$

IT WAS A GOOD THING Lizzy didn't have any plans for the day. The throbbing headache she awoke to continued well into the afternoon. Fortunately, or maybe, unfortunately, the aches emanating from every muscle in her body sometimes diverted her attention from the headache. Her bed was her refuge: that, and as much water as she could drink.

When Lizzy initially woke up, Connor was gone. She wondered if he was there the night before or if it was just a dream. He stopped around noon to check on her, temporarily stepping away from his lab duties, and brought some bananas and an omelet. The food was welcome, but the bouts of nausea continued. The best medicine was sleep, so sleeping was how she spent most of her day.

When midafternoon rolled around, Lizzy felt much better. She needed to get out and move, so she showered, put on comfortable clothes, and left her apartment to get something to eat. The order taker at her favorite corner deli greeted her warmly; Lizzy knew everyone who worked here. After placing an order for her usual chicken panini sandwich, she sat at a small table in front of the window and waited for her food.

The traffic whizzed by on the street outside, and her mind wandered. The events of the previous night were a blur. She remembered celebrating with her friends and eventually leaving the bar with Connor, but everything after that was blank. As with most who've experienced a severe hangover, Lizzy vowed to herself never to do *that* again.

The sandwich was delicious, and Lizzy was comforted that her stomach was finally receptive to food. Connor should be finishing up at the lab in an hour, which would give her plenty of time to enjoy a walk before she met him at the physics building. Lizzy left the deli and started for Washington Square Park, the perfect place for a quiet late afternoon stroll on a fabulous, clear day.

As she stepped into the Sixth Avenue crosswalk, a white van with no windows squealed its tires and lurched to a stop beside her, causing her to jump back reflexively. Two men wearing dark clothes and Guy Fawkes masks jumped out when the van's sliding door opened and seized her before she could run. One of the men smothered her face with a gloved hand so she couldn't scream. People in the area stopped and stared as she kicked and tried to escape, but no one did anything while the men forced her into the van. Then it sped away, and Lizzy was gone.

* * * * *

Everything happened in slow motion. Reflexively, Mercer leaned to his left, gunned the throttle, and popped the clutch, causing the rear tire of his bike to spin and squeal as he shot past the car in front of him and through the red light. Two loud popping sounds came from behind. The intersection was empty, and he shifted and opened the throttle as he regained his balance, quickly exceeding the speed limit and flying by cars on the two-lane boulevard. The next light was green, so he kept rolling, checking the mirrors for his pursuers when he got a chance. Some distance back, car headlights weaved toward him through the traffic.

Vehicles waiting at the next intersection blocked his path, and he slammed on the brakes, letting the rear wheel slide so the bike could get sideways. He let off the brakes and accelerated onto the cross street, going as fast as he dared to maintain control of the motorcycle and react to traffic. Mercer hadn't noticed anyone tailing him for several blocks, so he slowed to the posted speed. He was crossing an intersection when, out of the corner of his right eye, two motorcycles bounced over the curb and sidewalk and gave chase. He gunned the throttle, and the bike's front wheel lifted off the ground. Fighting for control, his mirror flashed with reflections from the headlights of the cycles in pursuit. They were right behind him, and he swerved through the slow-moving traffic to shake them. Congestion blocked his way, so he veered into the opposing lanes of traffic. Oncoming cars skidded and swerved to avoid him as he cut through the lanes to evade the vehicles hurtling toward him and stay ahead of his pursuers. From behind came a loud crunching sound, and in his mirror, Mercer saw one bike flipping through the air without a rider as the other closed on him. The careening bike impaled the windshield of a parked car and burst into flame. Farther back were the wobbly lights of a vehicle zigzagging through the traffic, still chasing him. Even farther back, he could see the red-and-blue flashing lights of the police.

The street ended abruptly as it reached an embankment, forcing Mercer to turn onto a one-way street. Traffic was light, so he opened the throttle and gained speed while a motorcycle hung with him about ten car lengths behind. He pulled away slightly after the road narrowed but hit the brakes hard to avoid crashing as he came to a sharp bend. Over his shoulder, he could see one bike and a car in the distance still in pursuit. The surge of adrenaline that had started when Mercer saw the gun hadn't let up, and his heart was racing as he pressed on. Although he thought himself a skilled rider, he wasn't a match for the one chasing him. The gap was closing.

The road forked, and Mercer veered onto another one-way. As he rapidly approached some vehicles stopped at a traffic light, he braked hard and slid sideways. When he'd slowed enough to regain control, he drove onto the sidewalk and narrowly missed a woman and two dogs. He continued driving on the crosswalk into crossing traffic when a screeching car lightly clipped his rear wheel, and he lost control. The motorcycle hurtled down the sidewalk, with Mercer barely holding on while pedestrians screamed and scattered. The uncontrolled bike charged recklessly toward a chain-link fence until Mercer was finally able to squeeze the hand brake and bring the motorcycle to a halt as the front wheel bumped lightly against the fence. He glanced over his shoulder to back the bike away from the fence and saw his pursuers closing in. The motorcycle tailing him on the sidewalk had an easier time maneuvering because everyone had already moved out of the way. In seconds it would be upon him.

Mercer realigned the bike toward the road, twisted the throttle, and accelerated, jumping the curb and launching out into the street. The expressway loomed in the distance, and Mercer focused on getting to the on-ramp heading toward the Bronx. Sirens came from somewhere as he sped up the ramp and joined the traffic flow on the expressway. The other bike was close behind, and Mercer could not shake it.

Mercer moved to the shoulder of the road to gain some ground and sprinted past traffic. The other rider quickly used the same tactic and matched Mercer's speed. As he approached the bridge, the shoulder disappeared, forcing him to weave back into the lanes of traffic. He aligned himself with the lane markings on the road and darted through the narrow spaces between vehicles. Twice during the half-mile ride on the bridge, he quickly reacted to cars crossing lanes directly in front of him. He'd lost track of his pursuer. Up ahead, with the end of the bridge in site, there was a break in the traffic. He accelerated and found himself between the rotating wheels of a semitrailer on his left and a garbage truck on his right, both only inches away. Miraculously, Mercer navigated his way through the gauntlet unscathed and into the clear, where he increased speed and created separation between himself and the vehicles behind him.

As he reached the end of the bridge, Mercer looked in his mirror for any sign of the other motorcycle. In that instant, a semitrailer careened off the bridge wall, crossed the traffic lanes, and crushed two cars against the inside retaining wall, forcing one car to cartwheel over the wall and into oncoming traffic. The semi came to rest crosswise on the bridge, blocking all northbound traffic. More vehicles plowed into it from behind as the chaos unfolded, and the air was filled with the sounds of tires squealing and metal crunching. Mercer slowed and pulled over to the side of the road, then watched as the tangled wreckage burst into flame and lurched each time another vehicle rammed into the pile. The crashing sounds gave way to popping and sputtering as the heat of brilliant orange flames quickly spread over the wreckage, its black smoke blotting out the sky. A wobbling, crushed motorcycle helmet launched out of the carnage like a grape dislodged by the Heimlich maneuver. It tumbled along the empty pavement before coming to rest in the middle of the road.

Mercer sat on his motorcycle for several seconds, dazed and trying to catch his breath as his heart pounded. The sounds of sirens in the distance tugged him out of the trance. Trembling hands guided the bike as he continued into the Bronx, then headed for Manhattan.

Forty minutes later, he pulled into the underground garage of the partially constructed office tower which housed the Leaf Runner's temporary headquarters. Even though the chase shook him, Mercer had remembered and used the procedures Nigel's trainers taught him to avoid being tailed. Once Mercer stood on solid ground and took a few steps, waves of anxiety and fear washed over him as the shock of nearly being killed overwhelmed him. Mercer was a target; of this, there could be no doubt.

He entered the laboratory, and concern spread over Aniyah's face. Uncharacteristically, she exclaimed, "Jesus, Mercer. You look like hell."

"Someone just tried to kill me. I feel like I'm being hunted."

Aniyah lightly grasped his shoulder as her face softened. She reassured him by saying, "You're safe now, Mercer... You're safe here. I think we should go talk to Nigel."

Her soothing tone helped steady him, and his anxiety ebbed during the walk to Nigel's corner office, where Nigel sat staring at his computer screen. As they each took chairs facing his desk, Nigel looked up.

Aniyah spoke first, "There's been an attempt on Mercer's life."

Mercer told them about the chase and being shot at after visiting Sigmund Leverton.

Nigel pleaded, "Mercer, you can't be taking things into your own hands like this. As long as you are with us, you will be safe. Someone will always be nearby in case you need help. Just don't go running off without giving me a heads up first. All right?"

"I think I can do that," Mercer muttered.

"So why did you meet with this, Mr. Leverton?" queried Nigel.

"He was an angel investor in Amon Warwick's research. I was trying to get more information about it. It was another dead end."

"Maybe you should let that little piece of history be. I don't believe there is much to be gained by pursuing it further," said Nigel stiffly.

Mercer gave a noncommittal shrug.

Nigel spoke earnestly, "Now time is of the essence, and we have something important to discuss. Other groups of people have transference, like the Leaf Runners, but some choose a different path. They desire to affect history in such a way as to permanently modify outcomes to attain a certain benefit for their cause."

"Nigel, what in the hell are you talking about? Enough with the usual flowery eloquence. Get to the point," Mercer interrupted.

"I am getting to the point, but some background information is necessary, so kindly bear with me. As I was saying, they affect history by using transference to change the actions of key ancestors of members of their group, thus affecting a permanent historical modification. Specifically, they want to change or eliminate events that, they surmise, have had a significantly negative effect on the history and impact of their religion, which is based on what they believe to be the one true God. Their goal is to remove what they see as a tarnish created over the past two thousand years on the Catholic Church. They feel it is their mission to adjust history, and thus the perceptions of all of humankind, to make their God the center of our lives. Effectively, they are religious extremists who will stop at nothing to achieve their goal."

"That's unbelievable. Is it possible for them to do that?"

"Oh yes, it is possible. Have you ever heard of Jacob Samuel Drummond?" Nigel said.

"Who?" asked Mercer.

"Exactly. He was a nobody. Yet in a different history, the history that prevailed before this group disrupted it, he was a captivating speaker and writer. Drummond preached humanist ideals and was the first person to bring such ideas into the mainstream. In this version of history, the church withered as it was eclipsed by a tide of humanism, a tide catalyzed by Jacob Drummond. His message that religion was not a prerequisite for morality, that understanding the world requires reasoning and science, not divine intervention, resonated with the people. Yet you will not find his name in any history book, and he doesn't exist on the internet."

"Then how am I supposed to believe in this…alternative history?" queried Mercer.

Aniyah went from being softly reassuring to the consummate professional as she said, "As Leaf Runners, we observe many things which others can't. For example, remember how some information on your ancestral tree changed after you visited France?" Mercer nodded. "We can see how history changes by seeing how our tree changes. As long as the change doesn't remove us from history or significantly impact who we are or where we came from, we can know that the change has occurred. For example, you would not be a Leaf Runner if you were born somewhere other than Bellevue Hospital. Understand?"

"Yes, I think so," said Mercer hesitantly.

Aniyah continued, "I and other Leaf Runners observed a… significant change in our trees a few weeks ago. We noted that the prevailing humanism movement had almost vanished. We traced this to an alteration in the historical record. In the original history, graduation was a pivotal moment in Jacob Samuel Drummond's life, launching him on a path toward popularizing humanism. In the altered version of history, the version in which we now live, he was killed in 1989. The so-called accident happened on the day he was to graduate from college."

Mercer sat back in his chair with a look of astonishment.

Nigel said, "We believe it was an uncle of a member of this terrorist group who brought about Jacob's demise. It was no accident—it was murder."

Mercer had already met someone who was trying to change history. "Lutomir," he said. "The man who tortured John Freeman. He thought I was a Leaf Runner. And I thought he was one, but now I don't think so. He must be part of this group. Who are they?"

Acerbically, Nigel said, "They call themselves God's Left Hand."

The room was quiet for a few moments. Then Mercer said, "Aniyah, since I'm a Leaf Runner, why didn't I notice this significant historical change you mentioned?"

"You had your first experience after the event occurred. You would've never known since you hadn't seen your ancestral tree before that experience," said Aniyah.

"Maybe they're the ones…," stammered Mercer, trailing off.

"Pardon?" said Nigel.

"I think God's Left Hand is trying to kill me," said Mercer. "But why?"

"Well, it may be for the same reason we brought you here tonight," said Nigel. "We have been made aware of a plan being executed by these radicals to affect the historical record, as they did with Jacob Drummond. This plan has one of their operatives targeting a figure of major historical significance. You happen to have an ancestor who might be in a position to thwart their plan."

Sarcastically, Mercer said, "So I'm an operative now. Is that what I signed up to do when I became a Leaf Runner?"

"In a way, yes. Leaf Runners was established five years ago to provide a community for those with transference and to create and enforce a set of governing principles intended to prevent others with the ability from significantly altering history. We failed recently. We cannot fail again," said Nigel.

Mercer had initially joined the Leaf Runners to protect himself, but after today's harrowing experience, it was evident that he still took unnecessary risks and put himself in jeopardy. His first controlled transference as a Leaf Runner, an ill-fated attempt to affect history when he wasn't supposed to, didn't go so well. Mercer realized it came down to a simple question: could he trust the Leaf Runners with his life? He'd found it difficult to trust anyone. But relying solely on himself hadn't been working too well of late. He needed to trust someone.

Then he thought back to the day he met the Leaf Runners on what Ned had said to him about purpose. Mercer had a gift. They were asking him to use that gift to prevent history from drastically changing course. If they were right, the present world might become a vastly different place if he declined and the radicals were to succeed. The very future of humankind was at stake. To Mercer, the choice was not obvious. Why shouldn't he just accept whatever happens? If he weren't a Leaf Runner, the future would be preordained. Then out of the blue, he recalled something his father always told him, "Not having the ability to take action and having the ability to take action but choosing not to are two very different things." His father carried a profound sense of duty, and this adherence to duty led Mercer to rebel against his father. Rebellion against his father was the second-worst mistake of his life. The worst was having too much pride to make amends with the man. He needed to take action because he could.

"Okay, tell me what I need to do," Mercer said.

Nigel displayed a world map on the large monitor in his office. The map contained annotations at specific locations and a hand-drawn line that had arrow marks along it. The line started in England and passed through the Atlantic Ocean to the coast of South America, around South America, and across the Pacific Ocean to Australia, around the southern portion of Australia across the Indian Ocean to Africa, around Africa across the Atlantic Ocean to South America, and ended back in England.

He said, "This is a map of the circumnavigation of an English ship from 1831 to 1836. The importance of this voyage would not become widely known until twenty-five years later when a gentleman who undertook this journey published an analysis and findings of his exploration of many of the ship's destinations. The ship was called the HMS *Beagle,* and its captain was Robert FitzRoy. One of the ship's hands was Alexander John Williams, a brother to Charlotte Fidelia Williams. Charlotte is a direct ancestor of yours, Mercer."

"So you want me to be on this ship in the mind of Alexander Williams. Then what?" said Mercer.

"Then you will foil a murder by covertly identifying the per-petrator and stopping him from succeeding at his task," said Nigel.

"A murder? Who's murder?"

"By any means necessary, you will prevent the murder of the father of evolution, Dr. Charles Robert Darwin."

MERCER WAS TAKEN ABACK BY Nigel's words. Astonished, he said, "*The* Charles Darwin?"

"Correct," said Nigel. "We expect the attempt on Darwin's life to take place while the ship is at sea during one of the longest legs of the voyage, somewhere between the Galapagos Islands and New Zealand. Therefore, we need you to transfer to Alexander on October 20, 1835."

Aniyah said, "But before you go, I'm giving you a crash course on being a Leaf Runner. You're not ready to do everything you need to yet."

Mercer was in shock as Aniyah led him to the lab, and he dropped down in the recliner he'd used earlier. Another recliner was positioned next to it, which Aniyah settled into after she'd dimmed the lights.

"Wait, aren't you going to put the sticky wires on my head again?" asked Mercer.

"Not this time. This time, we go together," Aniyah said with a smile. "Since I chose a fairly controlled setting, and I'll be there with you, we don't need the equipment. I'll put that stuff on you before you transfer to Alexander. For now, we're going…somewhere else. Do you like snow?"

"Huh?" Mercer muttered.

"Okay, so you already know how to move along the branches of your ancestral tree and find each leaf. I want you to follow your father's branch to Charles Proctor. He was a brother to your great-grandmother, Eunice. Now instead of diving into the pool that appears on the leaf, I want you to touch the leaf first. You'll see a timeline. The timeline represents every second of the life of that person. You can slide to any date and time, then enter the pool there. This places you into that person's life at a precise moment. Does this make sense?"

"Yes, I think so," said Mercer as he squirmed in his seat.

"All right, let's give it a try. I want you to find Charles and go to February 18, 1928, at 13:58 hours—it's a twenty-four-hour clock. Remember, do not enter his conscious mind. You are only there to observe until I give you further instructions. Got it?"

"Crap, I don't know. What if I enter at the wrong time? What if I accidentally take control? How will I find you?" Mercer said anxiously.

"Mercer, you'll go to the right time. Taking control could be deadly, so don't do it. Finally, I'll find you. Now close your eyes and relax. If you're too nervous, you won't be able to transfer."

Mercer's head was spinning with numbers and instructions. Aniyah made everything sound so easy, but he was having trouble sorting through it all. He watched her as she rested her head and closed her eyes, and within seconds appeared like she was asleep. She looked…peaceful.

All right, he could do this. *Just lie back, get comfortable, and relax*, he thought. *Piece of cake—Charles Proctor*. Mercer wondered who Charles Proctor was. He was going back almost one hundred years. Would he be a farmer, or a salesman, or…

There was the pool. Mercer didn't wait around this time; he dove into the pool and started up the trunk of his ancestral tree, moving along the branches until he came upon the leaf of Charles Nancrede Proctor. He touched the leaf, as he was instructed to, but it wasn't his real finger that touched it. It was more like the ghost of his finger. His body didn't exist in this place, just his… essence. He imagined this is what people meant by an out-of-body experience.

Like a shot, what appeared to be an arrow whizzed past his face from the right, but it was the longest arrow he'd ever seen. It kept moving past him until he finally saw its tail, where the arrow halted abruptly. The date on the timeline was visible; it read February 1, 1996. Mercer reached up and touched the timeline. It didn't feel like anything, but when he moved his ghostly finger side to side, the line moved with it. Like on his phone, he swiped to the right, and the line moved. Years flew by and counted down, moving back in time. He swiped until he reached the front of the arrow, where it came to a stop. The date here was January 4, 1906. And there was the life of Charles Proctor, from death to birth. Charles died about a year before Mercer was born.

Mercer swiped the timeline back to the left. As the timeline approached 1928, he slowed. The timeline began sliding in units of months, then days, then hours. The slower he went, the finer was the time resolution. He stopped at precisely 13:58 on February 18, 1928.

"Well, here goes nothing," Mercer said to himself. He entered the pool on the leaf and rose to the surface…

A dazzling white snow-covered landscape spread before him. In the distance, towering peaks filled the horizon, with rocky cliffs visible where snow could not cling. Majestic pine trees with deep green branches supporting tufts of white snow filled most of the land on either side of him. The air was crisp yet comfortable. Charles lowered his gaze, and Mercer wished he could close his eyes. Charles was precariously perched atop a mountain, peering down a steep snow ramp with skis strapped to his feet. Hundreds of people lined the slopes on either side of the ramp and even more surrounded a circular area at the bottom of the hill.

Charles reached up and adjusted his goggles, then raised his arms straight in front of him, allowing Mercer to see his multi-colored coat. Then Charles leaned forward and started dropping like a stone. Mercer felt the same bombardment of sensations as when he'd ridden his first roller coaster at Coney Island. The skis Charles wore barely touched the ground as his speed quickened. The trees and people flashed by, faster and faster. The sound of the wind rushed past them, and Mercer felt like he was flying down the hill. Then he noticed the slope didn't continue smoothly downward. They were headed for a jump traveling faster than a commuter on an empty expressway. As Charles reached the end of the jump, he sprung into the air and leaned over the tips of his skis. Now Mercer *was* flying; only he never felt so out of control. They were falling down the hill a dozen feet above the snow for what seemed like forever. Charles kept his eyes on his landing point, forcing Mercer to watch and feel every sensation. He wasn't about to take control of Charles now. It was too late for that.

Then the ground seemed to come up to them quickly, and Mercer braced himself for a horrific crash. But at the last possible moment, Charles straightened himself and lowered his skis, touching down in a perfect Telemark landing. Now they were hurtling down the hill on skis and heading directly for the circle of spectators at the bottom. Again, Mercer envisioned a terrible bone-crushing crash into a horde of people and prepared to brace himself. Charles smoothly turned his skis to the side and cut the edges into the snow, rapidly slowing, so they reached the edge of the crowd at a standstill.

Charles screamed and yelled in excitement and exhilaration as he raised his hands enthusiastically in the air celebrating an excellent jump. Mercer knew he would have filled his pants by this point if he could. Yet the excitement of what Charles had just accomplished was not only felt by Charles. Mercer felt it, too. He experienced the same emotions Charles did. Feelings that allowed Mercer to know that Charles was filled with pride in himself and that he was here, in St. Moritz, Switzerland, representing the United States of America at the 1928 Winter Olympic games. Charles had nothing to hide, which gave Mercer an unobstructed view into who Charles was. In seconds, Mercer knew that Charles Proctor was an infinitely better person than Corbin LaCroix had ever been.

Mercer observed as Charles walked through the crowd and was congratulated by people from his team and people who didn't know him and just wanted to acknowledge his performance. Charles eventually ended up in the chalet and sat by himself for a pint of beer to celebrate. The jump was his last event of the

Olympic Games, and even though he didn't medal, he'd given his best alongside the best in the world, doing what he loved most.

The barmaid brought his beer and asked in broken English, "Will there be anyone else joining you, or are you socially distancing?"

"What? No, I'm not expecting anyone. I just wanted to enjoy a nice local beer before leaving Switzerland," said Charles.

"Are you sure there is no one else coming? I thought a man named Mercer was supposed to meet you here," she said.

"Who? Mercer? I'm sorry, but I don't know…," Charles trailed off as Mercer scrambled to fill his consciousness.

Charles's body swayed in the chair and nearly fell out of it after Mercer took control.

"Jesus, Aniyah," Mercer said in a harsh whisper, reeling as he tried to balance Charles. "You could be a bit more discreet, couldn't you?"

"I am sorry, sir," said the barmaid. "But are you all right? Who is Aniyah?"

"Um…oh, ah, sorry," said Mercer. "I thought you were someone I knew."

She sat down across from him with a smile and wink, leaned back in the chair, and said, "Hi Mercer. Long time no see."

"Damn it, Aniyah," Mercer said incredulously. "This is no time to be goofing around."

"I know. And I'm sorry, Mercer," she said, still smiling. "I just couldn't help myself. So what do you think of Charles Proctor?"

Mercer sighed and said, "You're getting a kick out of all this, aren't you? You placed me with Charles at the exact moment he made that jump. You could've warned me what was about to happen. It was terrifying."

"I know. Although I have to admit, I got lucky with the timing. I could have been off a couple of minutes in either direction. I did it for a reason."

"Reason, what reason?"

Aniyah became more serious as she said, "Mercer, you never know exactly what situation you might be facing at the moment of transference. It's disorienting and unsettling when you're thrust into a situation without the proper…context. One tends to want to take control immediately, which could've been fatal in your case. Luckily, I didn't leave you enough time to think about it, and you let Charles do his thing. The lesson is to observe and assess before taking action."

"You could've just told me that," Mercer said, slightly miffed.

"Would it have had the same effect?"

"Well, probably not." Mercer softened. "I guess you're right. I won't soon forget *that* experience."

"Next, did you notice anything odd about me before I said your name?"

"Odd, what do you mean, odd?" inquired Mercer.

"Was there anything I did or said that might've captured your attention or seemed out of place?"

"Uhhh…hmmm. Damn, I don't remember."

Aniyah said, "Charles reacted when I said 'socially distancing.' It's a phrase that doesn't fit in this time and place but is familiar in ours. You need to be aware when someone is doing or saying something which seems out of place. You've already seen this happen when a Leaf Runner takes control of an ancestor. They act and say as *they* would in a situation, not as their ancestor would."

"Makes sense," said Mercer with a slight nod.

Aniyah leaned forward and spoke quietly but earnestly, "One of the most important lessons is that those first few seconds after you transfer are critical. It's when you learn the most about your ancestor, their history, hopes, joys, and fears. You'll get to know more about them in ten seconds than anyone else will in their entire lifetime. Even more amazing is that you can project your own thoughts toward your ancestor when they are in control of their conscious mind. This allows you to convey information, such as filling in the gaps of what happened while you were in control. Isn't that incredible?"

Mercer stared into her eyes and felt the passion as she spoke. With her light brown hair, most of which was hidden under a scarf, and her pale white skin, she looked nothing like Aniyah. Yet it *was* her. Aniyah was there, with him, in Switzerland, in 1928. Yes, it was incredible.

He must have been staring at her because she eventually produced a slight smile and then leaned back in her chair and sheepishly turned her head to look anywhere else but at him.

Then she said, "Let Charles enjoy his beer. He deserves it. I'll see you later for a few more lessons."

There was that little grin, and she was gone. The face gave a blank stare, and then the eyes blinked a couple of times. The barmaid quickly regained her senses and then looked at Mercer. Somewhat embarrassed, she jumped up from the chair, turned on her heel, and hurried away.

"Wait, what's your name?" Mercer yelled.

The barmaid briefly looked over her shoulder but kept walking. Again, Mercer would have to wait for Aniyah to reach out to him because he didn't know anything about the barmaid. Mercer dove for the pool, and Charles quickly regained consciousness. After a couple of shakes of his head, Charles gave the mug a puzzled look, then held it up and swirled it while he inspected its contents.

* * * * *

Tomorrow would be the beginning of a long journey home, and Charles was exhausted from days of stress and grueling athletic competition. He looked forward to a night of restful sleep. But before turning in, he took one last walk along the shores of the quaint St. Moritzersee. Dusk came early this time of year, and the streetlights spread their dim lights throughout the bustling town of St. Moritz.

Mercer had been on the lookout for the barmaid since talking to Aniyah. He wasn't sure what she still planned to teach him, and he was becoming impatient. He had uncomfortably little control over his present situation. *Maybe this is all part of the lesson*, he thought.

Three days later, Charles boarded a train in Paris that would take him to the port in Cherbourg, where he was to board a steamship bound for New York. As Charles settled into his seat in one of the cabins, Mercer had had enough. He'd expected Aniyah to reveal herself before they left St. Moritz, but there had been no contact since that day in the chalet. It was as if he was on a stakeout waiting for something to happen, and he was getting bored. This so-called training was one big waste of time; he had more important things to do.

Mercer had occupied his mind with thoughts of murder and espionage to fill the time. It was like he was forced to play a scene in a suspense movie without a script. Would he be able to stop a murder? Would he do something that could change history for the worse? There were so many things to consider, so much that could go wrong, and he had precious little training to deal with situations that might arise. He was a stock analyst, for Christ's sake. What did he know about espionage?

Mercer doubted whether he could do what the Leaf Runners had asked him to. He thought about what might happen if he failed, how his life would be different, how humanity's understanding of the world would change, and if the world would become a better place or a worse one. Mercer knew the actions of the terrorists were an attempt to change history, to reshape the future to one they desired. Did they have any idea what kinds of unintended consequences could result? Was it ethically correct to impose such a change on human history? No. It wasn't. He might be the only person who could stop it, the only one standing in their way. He needed to act.

He'd reached the same conclusion several times since arriving in St. Moritz with Charles. It was time to move along and leave Charles to his dull, slow travels. Mercer wasn't about to spend two weeks on a ship crossing the Atlantic. He was preparing to dive into the ancestral pool when a woman sat in the seat across from Charles. Wait, wasn't that…

"Are you still with me," said the barmaid from the chalet, smiling coyly.

"I beg your pardon," Charles said.

Mercer dived into Charles's consciousness instead of the pool.

"Damn it, Aniyah," exclaimed Mercer. "What took you so long?"

"Good," she said with a satisfied expression as she glanced around to make sure no one else could hear. "I would've been disappointed if you were gone already. You've barely begun."

"What? I've been waiting here for three days, doing absolutely nothing. I thought this business with Darwin was so urgent. What are we waiting for?"

"The first lesson is this: time is not linear when you've transferred. I'm sure you already know this from your prior experiences, but it's one of the greatest things about being a Leaf Runner. You could be Charles for months and come back to Mercer only seconds after sitting in that recliner back in the lab."

"Again, couldn't you have just told me that?"

Ignoring him, Aniyah said, "The second lesson is that you need to be on your guard the whole time. You were too slow to react when I sat down just now. Charles should barely have an image of me before you take over. You gave him time to process and respond. Every precious second counts, so stay alert and ready. Would this have made sense if I'd merely told you rather than had you experience it?"

"Well, no. I guess you're right," Mercer said. She *was* right. He'd become involved in his thoughts and had let the world Charles was living him start to pass him by. He'd become inattentive and indifferent to the present.

"You are here, so act like it. *Be* here," she said.

There was that passion again. He looked into her eyes and saw Aniyah. It wasn't her face, but it was her.

"Tell me," he said as he leaned closer to her. "Do you enjoy this?"

"Enjoy what, Leaf Running? Yes, I do. It's an amazing and rare gift."

"No, do you enjoy tormenting me?" He smiled, keeping her gaze. "Or is this how you treat all Leaf Runners?"

Aniyah's eyes opened wide, and she stumbled, "I…um… well. You're different." She sat back slightly as if she was trying to get away from him.

The train's whistle blew several times, and Mercer said, "Different, hmm? Different how?"

The train lurched, catching Mercer off-balance and causing him to fall forward into Aniyah's lap.

With a genuine look of surprise, she said sheepishly, "Lesson's over."

Mercer froze.

In the next instant, she went through a range of emotions. After a blank stare, her face went back to surprise, then recognition, and finally turned to anger as the barmaid exclaimed in an accent, "I beg your pardon!"

She glanced down at her chest. Mercer looked down absently and noted that his hand rested on her breast.

"Shit! It's time to go," he said and dived for the pool.

Mercer hated to leave Charles in such a precarious position, but he knew enough about Charles that he felt confident he would be able to handle the situation. He spent a moment observing Charles's leaf and the leaves around it to make sure history hadn't been modified. There were no flashes of change on the leaves, and Mercer was relieved. He continued down the trunk to his own name and floated to the surface of his pool.

* * * * *

Immediately after Mercer opened his eyes, the lights in the room came on full bright, blinding him temporarily. Aniyah walked nervously from the wall switch to the equipment without acknowledging Mercer or looking at him. She aggressively flipped switches and turned knobs on the equipment, then tore into a tangled mass of wires trying to separate them.

"That was interesting," said Mercer.

"Hmm… Oh, yeah," was all Aniyah said, still not looking at him.

After an uncomfortable pause, Mercer said, "I left Charles in an awful predicament."

Aniyah said, without taking her eyes from her work, "Charles will be fine."

"How do you know?"

Aniyah stopped working and turned to Mercer with a hand on her hip, then said, "Did you notice any changes on your tree when you left him?"

"No, I made sure to check."

"And did you see who he married?"

Mercer thought, then said, "I didn't pay close enough attention to remember any other names."

"That's all right," she said. "He married Elena Graf in 1929, and they lived happily ever after." She returned to her work.

"Okay," Mercer enunciated. Then his brow crinkled as he said, "Who's Elena Graf?"

Her shoulders slouched as she tossed the wires onto the bench. She stared into his eyes as she said, "Elena Graf was the barmaid and my great-grandfather's sister."

His brow uncrinkled and then went straight up as he stammered, "Wait, you mean we're related? You…and me…we're related? Damn!"

"It was one place in history where I knew our paths would cross," she said apologetically. "It was a simple training exercise. I was just having some fun, but then you touched me and I didn't expect to feel…" She turned away from him, embarrassed.

Mercer watched her, and in the most honest admission of his life, he said, "Neither did I."

She turned her head slowly and looked into his eyes. They stared at each other, unblinking, for an eternity.

"Are you sure there isn't more that I need to prepare for this?" Mercer finally asked.

After she collected herself, Aniyah said, "You've been through training, and we've told you everything we know about the situation. You can't take anything but your mind, so you have all you need. We'll know you've succeeded if this is still here when you get back."

She held up a leather-bound book for Mercer to see. It was titled *Origin of Species*, and the author was Charles Darwin.

"It's time," she said intently.

Aniyah finished placing the electrode pads on his scalp as Mercer closed his eyes and tried to relax. He noticed the pool and was surprised at how quickly it had appeared for him. He was getting the hang of transference, so he dove and soon found the leaf containing Charlotte Fidelia Williams. Another leaf on the same branch displayed the name, Alexander John Williams. He touched the leaf and slid along Alexander's timeline to October 20, 1835.

Mercer rose back through the pool, kicking toward its surface until he reached it. Alexander's consciousness was before him as he floated in the void above the pool, but he did not seek control. He was in the mind of Alexander Williams and could sense the world as he did. At the moment, Alexander—Alec, as he liked to be called—was currently looking out across the sea at the horizon. Mercer could feel motion. He experienced a gradual rise and lateral movement, which took several seconds, followed by a gradual fall and opposite lateral movement. The motion repeated while Alec continued to stare at the horizon. Mercer noted the ghostly outlines of mountains covering portions of the horizon. Momentarily, Alec looked down, which would have made Mercer's stomach empty if he had it with him. Alec stood on a small platform near the top of the tallest mast on a ship, holding the wooden mast with one hand and leaning so that most of his body was hanging out over thin air. The deck of the vessel was eighty feet below.

15

Muffled voices, speaking in a language Lizzy didn't understand, were drowned out by the roaring of the van's engine and the squealing of its tires each time it took a corner. She could tell they were speeding and weaving through traffic but stopped at lights. She could hear more of what the men were saying during those stops, in Italian, she thought. The dark bag over her head and the gag in her mouth drowned out any sounds she attempted to make. Her bound hands and feet prevented her from doing much at all. She was petrified and had given up fighting against them. They were too strong and struck her when she fought back. A rib on her left side might have been cracked as stabs of pain racked her when she tried to turn her body a certain way. Her helplessness, aloneness, and lack of control filled her with terror and made her body tremble.

It could have been minutes or hours. She had no concept of time as the van continued, each tight corner causing her to wince in pain before the vehicle finally came to an abrupt stop. Doors opened, and hands grabbed her exhausted body, pulling her out. Someone tossed her over their shoulder and carried her like a sack of potatoes, ignoring her muffled cries of pain. More voices could be heard; some of them were speaking English.

"Are you sure you have the right one?" asked an impatient female voice.

"It is the woman in the picture," said another man with an accent.

"What took you so long?" the woman said.

"She did not leave her apartment until later in the day. We had to wait."

"We must get her to the bunker as soon as possible."

Lizzy could smell ocean water and hear it slapping against the hull of a boat. She was lifted from the man's shoulder and laid on a hard floor. The swaying of the floor led her to conclude she was on a boat. Her journey had not ended. The boat engine started and revved, and she felt the boat accelerate. Soon the jarring of the boat's bow hitting waves at high speed made the torturing rib pain unbearable. With each buffet, her body slid along the wet floor until it came to rest against a wall. The violent jolts, the shooting pain, and sheer panic made every inch of her body tingle. She was numb, and the sensations and sounds of this horrifying experience became ever more distant. Her body experienced sensations as if she was atop a long flexible rod. The rod would bend to and fro, causing her whole body to sway. The rod kept getting longer and the swaying more severe, picking up speed and growing in intensity until she thought she would be thrown high into the air, as if from a catapult. Extreme fatigue finally overtook her, and she passed out.

* * * * *

Liquid splashing the side of my face wrenched me from a deep sleep, and I opened my eyes wide. Darkness was all around, yet I could see a rectangle of very dim light in front of me. I realized I was staring through a window into a dark, eerie night filled with pouring rain. The pitch-black was interrupted when a flash in the distance pulsed light through the window. I turned my head to see what was around me. Other flashes from outside created more pulses of light, allowing me to form a picture of a room. I was in a bedroom in a house. The walls were flat wooden timbers with chinking filling the cracks between them.

I tried to sit in the bed where I was lying, but my girth prevented me. After tossing both of my legs over the side, I was able to sit upright, although I still needed to lean back slightly due to my enormous belly being in the way. I saw through the window from the illumination produced by the ever more frequent lightning that there were gardens close to the house and farm fields beyond, filling the distance to the slight rolling hills along the horizon. Thunder rumbled across the land as I stood at the side of the bed. I stretched an arm out to the wall to brace myself because most of my extra weight was in front of me, pulling me forward. I felt the area around my stomach with my other hand and found that my belly was protruding immensely as if I had eaten a watermelon whole. With my bare feet, I felt a puddle of cool water that had collected on the floor as raindrops streamed through the open window.

A bout of dizziness overcame me, and I stood still for a few moments trying to gather myself. The cool puddle suddenly felt much warmer, and I wondered why that same warmth seemed to be creeping down my inner thighs. I warily reached my hand down to determine the source of this warmth and felt warm drops of liquid splashing against my palm. The liquid was coming out of *me*. I screamed.

A grunting sound came from the other side of the room, and I turned from the window to see what hideous beast was lurking there.

"Bea? Bea! Bea, are you well?" said a man's voice.

"Bea?" I said.

Beatrice Walters. That was me. Richard was calling me. My wonderful, loving, handsome husband was calling my name.

"Yes, Richard. I am well. But I think the baby is coming."

Richard jumped out of bed and lit the lantern sitting on the bedside table. "I shall awaken Nellie immediately."

"Thank you, dear," I said.

"Please, Bea. Lie down on the bed. I'll fetch you some water and start some more on the boil. Please lie down," he said.

I laid back down on the bed and continued to feel the warmth seeping beneath me. My belly grew hard, and the cramping was very uncomfortable. After about a minute, the contraction passed, and the discomfort eased. Nellie, the midwife, arrived to assess the situation.

"Your bag of waters has broken," she said. She felt around my belly with both of her hands, the furrow in her brow deepening with each press. "Oh, dear. The baby is breech. We must try to turn it."

Painful contractions continued as Richard and Nellie attempted to turn the baby by pushing hard on my stomach. The pain of their efforts made me scream, and I felt Richard release his pressure.

"Keep going, Richard!" yelled Nellie.

Richard exerted, and the pain flooded back. I tried not to scream, but it was the only way to get through it. The contractions temporarily subsided, and I could relax and breathe for a couple of minutes. Richard gave me water, and as I sipped, I could see the redness of crying and worry in his eyes. I knew he didn't like seeing me going through this. Once the baby was turned, he would be able to leave the room.

After an hour of trying to turn the baby between contractions, they gave up. They were both exhausted, and I became faint from holding my breath during the pain of each contraction and their manipulation attempts.

"She must save her energy," Nellie said to Richard. Then she half-heartedly told me, "You will deliver the baby as it is."

Before Richard left the room, he looked into my eyes and said, "I love you, Bea. I am sorry you suffer so. I wish I could take the pain from you and bear it myself. If I could, I would." As he leaned over me to kiss my forehead, tears dropped from his eyes and splashed onto my face.

"I know. I love you," I said hoarsely, trying to clear my throat. My screaming over the past two hours had strained my voice. Richard left the room, ruefully looking over his shoulder as he did so, and closed the door behind him.

Contractions continued, coming more frequently and lasting longer. Minutes turned into hours. My fatigue was so severe that I slept between contractions, but these short naps kept me going even though the rest was fitful. Nellie was incredibly kind. She remained with me and made sure I had water and was as comfortable as possible.

* * * * *

When I awoke, Richard was present, his eyes hollowed and darkened from lack of sleep, and a deep look of worry was etched upon his face. The cramped room spinning before me prevented me from opening my eyes for very long; the light in the room inflamed my throbbing headache whenever I did. The contractions were still there, but my body had so little energy left that they were nothing more than a tug. I was barely able to take water. The dryness of my lips made it difficult for the water I could get into my mouth to remain there before it dribbled down my cheeks. Nellie often held my hand but otherwise paced the floor nervously. She started doing this after the rain had stopped the previous afternoon. The black of this night came hours ago. I had been in labor for almost two full days.

They called upon Dr. Naismith earlier to see if there was any help he could provide. He told them something that I could not hear and then left. Richard was visibly shaken and would not look at me for a short time, and I fell asleep again. When I awoke, Nellie was there, and she called Richard into the room.

In a distant voice, I heard her say, "Push, Bea, push! The baby is coming now. *Push!*"

Her final yell brought me out of my dazed state, and I understood. With all the strength left in my body, I pushed and pushed. I fell into the darkness for a time, utterly exhausted. I could barely breathe. I was shaken awake with Richard standing over me and yelling at me to continue pushing. I just couldn't… I just couldn't do it anymore.

"I see the baby," Nellie shouted. "It's coming. It's coming!"

I gave one more push, and the darkness returned. The pain was gone; I felt nothing. My exhausted body shuddered and would not stop. Richard's voice in my ear brought me back. His wonderfully beautiful voice gave me something I could run to, away from the darkness. As I opened my eyes, I heard a yowl, like the cats would sometimes make in the middle of the night.

With a smile on his face and tears in his eyes, Richard handed me our newborn child. "It's a boy," he whispered excitedly. "What shall we name him, Bea?"

Barely able to speak, I whispered, "His name is Nathaniel. Nathaniel David Walters."

He was beautiful. The most beautiful little creature I had ever seen. It was more than I could have imagined, the joy I felt at that moment. I had finally brought this little light of mine into the world. I couldn't wait to watch him grow into a strapping young man. I knew he would make his father and me proud.

As I became lost in these thoughts and hopes for the future, the panicked voices of Richard and Nellie pulled me back to the present.

"Oh my god, there is blood everywhere. I cannot get it to stop. She is bleeding, and I cannot stop it!" Nellie was anything but calm.

The situation was dire. As the hopes for our future together faded from my mind, the present, the here and now, was most important. Nothing else mattered. I stared into my beautiful son's tiny face, a cherub, one of God's beautiful creations. Richard would raise him well. I knew he would. Richard would see his first steps, help him with his studies, give blessings to him and his new wife at their marriage, and be one of the first to hold our new grandson. I envied Richard, but I knew he would always have my memory in mind when these fantastic events of life unfolded, taking me everywhere with him. As long as Richard was there, so would I be. But now I must go.

My name was Beatrice Sylvia (Haynes) Walters. I was born on February 23, 1848. My parents were Victoria Anne Haynes and Everett Milton Haynes. On March 16, 1870, I died after giving birth to my only child.

* * * * *

Rough hands pinched the outside of Lizzy's thigh as she felt herself being tossed over some brute's shoulder again. She was shaking from the dream. Maybe it was the boat's movement or the pain still emanating from her ribcage, but the dream seemed real. In the dream, a woman had given birth and died shortly after, but Lizzy saw, heard, and felt everything the woman did, yet she could do nothing. She was only a spectator. It was a horrible experience. Like her, the baby would never know its mother. The dream might have had some deep Freudian meaning relating to Lizzy's mother, someone she was too young to remember, someone she'd only seen and heard in long-forgotten family videos and pictures.

The weirdest part was that she was no longer paralyzed by fear. Yes, she was in mortal danger, but the experience of the dream had changed her somehow. There was a new resilience. She was no longer a victim. To Lizzy, only two options remained, fight or flight. As long as she had nowhere to run, she would fight in a way that allowed *her* to choose the battle.

Nathaniel David Walters. The name was familiar, but she couldn't place where she'd seen or heard it. Someone opened a car door, and the stupid pack mule carrying her dumped her into the backseat. The car lurched forward, and after only a couple of minutes, it stopped, and she was manhandled out of it. Rather than being hoisted onto another shoulder, the bindings around her ankles were removed. She was prodded by a hand on her back and forced to walk, a welcome relief from the humiliation of being carried and less painful. She knew she was moving from daylight into darkness from the brightness she could detect through the cloth bag covering her head. Someone guided her with a firm grip on her upper arm through several twists and turns until she was finally forced to sit in a chair, her hands still bound. Then the bag came off and the gag was removed.

The dingy room appeared to be an old workshop, with only a couple of bulbs to light the space and no windows. A muscular man stood like a statue near the only visible doorway. Looking around revealed little, just some workbenches piled with useless rubbish. Everything was gray and drab and probably would have remained so even in bright sunlight. Lizzy sat quietly, waiting for battle, expecting it at any moment. This battle wouldn't be physical. She'd already tried that and knew she didn't have a chance in a fight against the neckless guy near the door.

After several minutes, a woman wearing dark tactical clothing walked into the room, followed by a man in an ill-fitting suit. Other than the suit, there was nothing remarkable about him. He could have been any average Joe. The woman stood in front of the door as the man approached Lizzy.

"So you call this a bunker," Lizzy scoffed. She didn't know if this was the right tactic against these pricks, but she had to start somewhere. She was still filled with fear, but it was walled off in a place where she had control over it, for now.

"Ah yes," said the man. "This has to be Elizabeth Evans. The salty demeanor must run in the family." Sneering, Lizzy said nothing. "Well, don't you have any questions? Aren't you wondering why you're here, precious?" he said, leering at her.

"What do you think?" she seethed.

"I know that I'd have many questions. Many, many questions." The man walked around her chair as he talked, drawing his hand along her shoulders as he rounded her. "But you're right. We don't plan to answer your questions, so why bother asking. Things should go smoother that way, my dear."

"People will be wondering where I am," she said defiantly.

"Let them wonder," he said. "They won't find you here." He paced in front of her with a look of contemplation. It seemed like he was trying to goad her into asking a question. She didn't speak. "You're here as a hostage. Until we get what we want, you'll remain here. Well, most of you will. Parts of you might disappear from time to time. The longer you're here, the fewer parts you'll have. That's how it works." He paused, stroking her hair. "It's a shame, really, to disfigure such a pretty one."

"Go to hell," she sniped, shaking her head and pulling away from him as tears filled her eyes. Her rocky facade was starting to crumble.

"That's what will happen to you should we fail in our mission. What is our mission, you might ask? Well, I'll tell you. We are God's Left Hand. We're here to change history by removing people who've diminished the glory of God and the church by their words and actions. You already know who sits at God's right hand. Well, with our abilities and our mission, we're sitting at his left. We fight a war against God's enemies throughout time.

"Now if you behave, you'll be treated well. Should you attempt to escape or cause any disruption, you will not. Understand?"

Lizzy didn't respond. The woman in tactical clothes must have moved toward her like a cat while Lizzy wasn't paying attention because her gloved hand slapped the side of Lizzy's face, causing her ear to ring while she nearly fell out of the chair.

"Understand?" he said again. Lizzy nodded as tears fell. "That's better, my dear. Now that you understand, *you* can answer some of *our* questions. Where is your vile brother, Mercer?" the man said with distaste. Lizzy betrayed her surprise as her eyes widened. "Yes, that's right. We're looking for him. Can you tell us where he is?"

"No," she said. Another whack to the side of her head made her see stars.

"No? Hmm. No, you can't tell us, or no, you won't tell us?"

Lizzy said, with panic in her voice, "I don't know. I don't know where he is."

"That's okay, doll. We don't really need you to tell us anything. News of your capture has been delivered. I expect we'll hear something fairly soon, given the time pressures we've applied. You see, if our demands aren't met within the hour, one of your parts will be specially delivered to the interested party as a demonstration of just how urgently things must be resolved." He smiled at her, the corner of his mouth twitching slightly. As he walked to the door, he said, "For now, we'll leave you to your thoughts. I'll bring either good news or bad news when I get back. It shouldn't take you long to figure out which it is."

After he exited, the woman and guard followed, closing the door behind them and leaving her alone. She turned to look at the bindings around her wrists and realized they were handcuffs. These weren't coming off easily. She stood and walked around the room, looking for anything she could use to try and cut them off. Lizzy quickly determined that there was nothing here she could use to remove them. She walked to the door and put her ear to it, hearing muffled voices outside. Then she paced around the room, trying to think about what she could do to escape, looking in every nook and cranny to see if there was another way out. There was none. She was trapped and had never experienced anything like this. The emotions were too much to hold in, and she sobbed uncontrollably. Lizzy sat back down in the chair and let the tears flow as quietly as possible.

Amid her sorrow, her mind suddenly jumped back to Nathaniel Walters's name, remembering. Mercer told her about their ancestors from Madagascar, and she recalled that Nathaniel Walters had a son with a Malagasy woman who died during childbirth. The boy was named Jonah. Was it merely a dream that she'd experienced, or was there more to it as if she'd been there?

"Is it possible?" she thought. "Could I be like Mercer? Could I be a Leaf Runner?"

As she was pondering the possibility, the door flew open, and the man in the suit walked in, followed by his entourage.

"It's nearly time," he said, glancing at his watch as he strolled toward her. "We haven't received any response. While Sam goes to get the tools she needs, I'll tell you a bit more about your situation, my beauty."

The woman left the room, and the guard closed the door, leaving Lizzy alone with the suited man. She trembled as he approached her. The gleam in his eyes rattled her.

He glanced at the door and then spoke in a commanding tone, "As I mentioned earlier, we're made up of people with transference, like Mercer, like the Leaf Runners."

Lizzy's look of astonishment didn't go unnoticed.

"Yes…yes, that's right. I figured Mercer would've told you about the Leaf Runners. But, well, let's just say our goals are different. Mercer has chosen evil, and he could get in our way. We're hoping that having you will prevent him from doing so."

Lizzy spoke in a rush. "You're the evil one. Mercer is a good man and wouldn't do anything to hurt anybody. You don't know him. You don't know who he is."

"My dear, that is where you're wrong," the man said. "I know exactly who he is. I've worked with him for a couple of years now. Mercer Evans deserves everything he's going to get. Maybe he's mentioned me. My name is Ned Lamb."

16

ALEC MOVED ALONG THE RIGGING and around the mainmast like a spider tending its web. In addition to keeping watch for any vessels in the distance, he checked and rechecked the uppermost sails, the tangle of ropes and pulley systems, and the horizontal beams that framed the bottoms of the sails. As Mercer observed Alec doing this work, terms and phrases describing the different parts of the ship came to him out of nowhere. He noticed that one of the clews on the upper main topsail was loose. Alec slid along the yard of the lower main topsail and tightened the sheet to allow the sail to grab more of the wind. Alec moved along the mast and sails like he was moving on solid ground. The wind gusted, and the smell of the sea was pungent. The assault on the senses gave Mercer reason to panic, yet the constant barrage was a minor annoyance to Alec. The ship currently had favorable winds and was under full sail toward the setting sun.

The sound of a boatswain's pipe made Alec freeze. As the piping continued, Mercer recognized it was the call to mess. It was time to eat, and Alec wasted no time climbing down to the deck. The rest of the crew did the same, and before long, everyone was gathered for dinner in the ship's mess hall.

A man sat on the bench next to Alec after they'd received their meals from the ship's cook.

"Blimey, the food is so much better when it's still fresh, don't ya think so, Alec?" said the man.

Having weighed anchor that morning, there was plenty of fresh food. The crew would have up to a week of fresh fruits and vegetables before the long slog of salt pork, lobscouse, dandy funk, and ship's biscuits began.

"Ya got that right, Tunney," said Alec as he heartily chewed one of the unusual fruits brought on board from the Galapagos archipelago.

"Won't be too long, and it'll be bags o' mystery for every meal, right Alec?" said Tunney.

"Yup."

"I'm already lookin' forward to Tahiti. Aren't you, Alec?" asked Tunney.

"I am," said Alec.

The men ate their rations briskly. Somehow, Tunney could talk and eat at the same time. Alec mostly ate. They left the mess within fifteen minutes.

Although Tunney was going on duty, Alec's watch was over, and he walked posthaste to where the hammock netting was stored along the bulwark. He selected a hammock and went down the stairs of the main hatchway to the midshipmen's berth to find a ceiling space to tie it up. Alec's next watch was only a few hours away, and he wanted to get as much sleep as he could before then. There was nothing comfortable about the hammock. Others hung from the ceiling such that there was barely enough width between for the men to occupy them. Whenever a sailor shifted in his bunk, the men on either side were jostled. The quarters weren't quiet, but the lighting was dim, the muscles were tired, and the gentle rocking of the vessel made for a short time before Alec dozed off.

While Alec slept, Mercer could not sense much of the outside world. He heard frequent footsteps above and below him, the muffled ring of the ship's bell every half hour, and the thrum of snoring. The ship's rocking would have made him nauseous had he been in control. It gave him time to think about how to accomplish his mission. The challenge was significant given his inexperience and lack of information about who, when, and how the murder of Charles Darwin was to take place. He determined that his best option was to allow Alec to go about his business and interact with other members of the crew as he usually would, not attempting to usurp Alec's body until he either encountered someone he thought was a suspect or got impatient enough to try and make something happen. Mercer didn't know what Charles Darwin looked like, but he expected that Alec would recognize him when he saw him.

The sounds of the pipes rousted everyone out of their bunks; it was time for the next watch. Alec was awake, alert, and standing in seconds, rubbing the sleep from his eyes and stretching his arms and legs to get the blood moving through them. He untied the hammock and climbed through the main hatch onto the upper deck and into the twilight. Walking over to the bulwark, he stowed the hammock and reached for the mainmast rigging, scaling the outside of the rigging to end up on the platform above the yard of the mainsail. He climbed more rigging to the next platform, examining the sails, yards, rigging, and halyards during his ascent, ensuring everything was secure. The ship was still under full sail. As Alec looked toward the horizon, Mercer wondered in awe at the vast expanse of open ocean. There wasn't the light of land or another vessel in sight.

As Alec went about his duties, Mercer grew to appreciate how difficult the work of a sailor was. There were many repetitive tasks, but the attention to detail that Alec and the other sailors paid to their work was admirable. The strength and endurance exhibited by these men were inspiring.

The routine continued for a few days with slight variation. Watch after watch, each four hours long except for the two-hour-long evening dogwatches. He worked for fourteen hours on one day, then ten the next, repeat. Outside of working with the maintop men, the only time he interacted with other sailors was at mealtime and in the evenings when the men not on watch would gather in the mess and do any number of things. Some sketched or painted, and some drank grog. One fiddled while another played the flute. A few wrote letters. Sometimes the group would include others on board who were not sailors: several Royal Marines, a few passengers, Darwin's servant, Syms Covington, and a missionary.

Tunney stuck by Alec's side whenever he could. It wasn't Alec who sought Tunney out; it was the other way around. Alec tolerated Tunney and seemed to enjoy his company, while Mercer was annoyed by Tunney and would often allow his thoughts to wander when Tunney got talking. Other sailors were cordial to Alec, but most of them avoided Tunney.

On Sunday, all joined in a Bible reading, as was customary for sailors on such a voyage. This was Mercer's first opportunity to see all those on board, including Mr. Darwin and the murderer, although Mercer didn't know who that could be. This was also his first chance to observe the ship's officers other than those who directly commanded Alec, including Captain FitzRoy. The officers never ate with the sailors and had their own quarters. Interactions were confined to duty. Mercer thought it would be easy to spot a person who might perpetrate the murder. However, there was nothing remarkable about anyone that he could discern.

As Alec slept on a chest one afternoon between watches, Mercer contemplated taking action to see if he could move the mission along by gathering information to identify the potential perpetrator. He knew the risks and weighed them against the possible consequences of acting too late. He concluded that he needed to do something, so he decided to take control of Alec's body during the next watch.

The boatswain's pipe finally sounded, signaling the change of the watch. Alec ascended to the upper deck, and before he could reach the rigging to climb, Mercer forced himself into Alec's consciousness. Alec's body staggered for a few moments as Mercer took over and tried to manage the movements of Alec's body for the first time. He reached the portside bulwark and steadied himself, gaining his bearings and looking around the ship. He changed direction and headed across the deck toward the starboard bulwark, attempting to familiarize himself with Alec's gait, balance, and muscle strength. Crossing back to the port bulwark, he repeated this a couple more times until he confidently controlled Alec's body. He was ready to undertake his plan. Other sailors filed past him, ignoring him as they intently crewed their stations and went about their work.

Mercer nonchalantly walked toward the stern of the ship. He descended the steps to the gun room and shuffled around, pretending to inspect some of the equipment. There were few men here at this time of day, and those would be gone soon as they finished returning their equipment from the watch. Mercer retreated to the shadows and waited for the remaining men to leave. Then he sneaked to the closed captain's door and put his ear to it to listen. Hearing nothing, he gently knocked, having prepared a story about accidentally bumping the door in case Captain FitzRoy happened to be there. There was no answer, so he struck more forcefully. Again, there wasn't an answer. He unlatched the door and walked into the captain's cabin, closing the door behind him.

He didn't know what he should be looking for, but he thought this would be an excellent place to find useful information. He carefully looked through the papers and maps on the captain's desk and any cubbyhole or drawer, reading what he saw and trying to spot anything out of the ordinary. Of course, he wasn't sure what was ordinary, but he expected he would know something out of place when he saw it. Uncertain of when the captain would return, he wasted no time. He found a doorway at the back of the cabin, opened it, and walked into another room that appeared to be used for storage. This room was full of stuff, everything from plates to pitchforks. It would take him a month to go through it all. He didn't have much time, so he took a cursory inventory, and as he was about to leave, something made a scraping sound on the ceiling above him. He listened quietly and could hear muffled voices above. The only words he understood were "Mr. Darwin." He waited a bit longer, craning his neck toward the ceiling, but the voices were too quiet to understand.

He turned and left the storage room, closing the door behind him. As he crossed the captain's cabin, the door opened. There stood a surprised Captain FitzRoy.

"My good man," he said. "What business have you in my cabin?"

"Um… I… I came to retrieve a…a sextant, sir," stumbled Mercer.

"Damn it, man. Under whose direction are you being asked to enter my cabin to retrieve something that should not be here?"

"I thought… I mean…"

"Mr. Fuller!" yelled Captain FitzRoy over his shoulder. "Fetch Lieutenant Wickham for me, will you please?"

A voice in the gun room said, "I shall proceed without delay, sir." The sound of boots on the stairsteps receded from the gun room.

"What is your name, sailor?" said FitzRoy as he withdrew his knife and pointed it toward Mercer.

Mercer considered diving back into the pool and letting Alec deal with the situation. It would be an easy way out for Mercer but would leave Alec in a confusing situation without understanding how he got there. In any case, physical and reputational harm would come to Alec because of Mercer's actions. Receiving the immediate pain of any punishment doled out was the least Mercer could do. This had been a foolish and risky endeavor, and to what end? He had no plan other than to go bumbling around to see what he could find, selfishly putting his hardworking and loyal ancestor's life and career in jeopardy. He would have to find some way to make amends.

"Alexander Williams, sir," said Mercer.

Footsteps came through the gun room toward the captain's cabin. Standing in the doorway was Lieutenant John Wickham.

"Yes, Captain," said Wickham. "What situation arises that you should wish my aid?"

"Lieutenant Wickham," said FitzRoy. "This man, a Mr. Alexander Williams, was found trespassing in this cabin. Please check to see if he has taken anything."

Wickham walked to Mercer and patted his jacket and pants pockets. The only item discovered was Alec's sailor's knife.

Mercer said, "I've taken nothing, sir. I entered this room by mistake. I… I apologize for any harm m…my actions might have caused. I should be at my watch. May I please go?"

"No, you absolutely may not," said FitzRoy. "There is a penalty for trespassing in the captain's quarters. You must be punished for this crime." To Wickham, he said, "Take him up on deck and give him two dozen, then send him back to work. And Mr. Williams," he said as he approached Mercer, lowering the knife and glaring into his eyes. "I will not see you in this cabin again. The next time could be fatal. That will be all."

Wickham grabbed Mercer's arm and pulled him out of the cabin, up the gun room stairs, and onto the upper deck.

"Bosun, signal All Hands," said Wickham.

Mercer heard the pipes sound and watched as all sailors aboard the ship descended to the upper deck or came up from below decks. Once all were gathered, Wickham spoke.

"This man was caught trespassing in the captain's cabin. Such an act will not be tolerated. Therefore, as an example to the rest of the ship's company, observe the punishment now enforced. Strip to the waist!" he shouted at Mercer.

Mercer pulled off his coat and shirt to bare his back.

"Seize him!" called Wickham.

Several men seized Mercer's arms and braced him against the starboard bulwark. His back was exposed. Mercer glanced nervously over his shoulder as Wickham raked the fingers of his left hand through a cat-o'-nine-tails while holding its handle with his right. Mercer faced forward and closed his eyes. The whooshing sound was all he heard before searing pain exploded on his back.

17

AS EACH FURROW WAS CREATED, it felt like sharpened fingernails were digging into the skin of his back, then slicing down its length, pulling flesh away. He had barely enough time to take a breath before the next strike. At first, he tried to count the lashes, but the pain made him lose all concentration. He could sense the presence of Alec near him, trying to regain consciousness. Mercer's struggle to deal with the pain and fend off Alec at the same time was almost too much to bear. Then the lashes stopped.

Expecting the men to let him go, Mercer relaxed. The men did not let him go. The sound of boots scuffling on the deck prompted Mercer to look over his shoulder and see another man, one of the marines on board, remove his coat, roll up his sleeves, and take the cat from Wickham. The look of disgust and determination on this man's face, and the strength of his build, made Mercer tremble with fear. Wickham's lashes felt like puffs of air compared to those he received from this soldier, the pain being so great that Mercer couldn't prevent Alec from regaining consciousness. Mercer's relief was immediate. He thought about diving to the bottom of the pool, back toward his ancestral tree, to escape the torment. Then he remembered that he would be unable to come back to Alec's body if he returned to his own. Charles Darwin would die if he left now.

Alec lost consciousness within a few seconds, giving Mercer a chance to regain control and experience the fiery pain again. He'd committed himself to spare Alec from as much torment as possible, so Mercer filled Alec's consciousness. The torturous pain flooded back, and he could hear the soldier grunting with effort before each lash struck. The lashes finally ended, and Mercer leaned against the bulwark after the hands released him.

The soldier who struck him approached and murmured, "I've always wanted to do that. I hope you screw up again. Then I'll get another crack at you."

He chuckled and walked away. Mercer immediately knew that something about the man's accent was wrong. He looked like an English soldier but didn't sound like one. The problem was that Mercer's mind and body were in shock after the brutal assault. He could not think coherently.

Most of the crew returned to their duties, but Tunney came to him. He helped Mercer gingerly don his shirt and guided him belowdecks. Mercer caught a few men staring at him as they entered the mess hall, then diverting their eyes when he looked in their direction. No one, save for Tunney, spoke to him.

The watered-down grog Tunney brought was precisely what he needed, and as he relaxed, his mind gradually distilled the recent events. The words said by the marine who lashed him were strange. The soldier seemed eager for the task; he'd probably volunteered. That anyone would enjoy such a thing was disturbing. But Mercer was sure about one thing: an English soldier with an East Coast accent didn't belong here. Mercer had a suspect.

"Tunney, do you know anything about the soldier who lashed me?" asked Mercer.

"That be one of the marines assigned to Mr. Darwin's detail," said Tunney.

"Mr. Darwin's detail?"

"Yeah. Wherever you see Mr. Darwin, you'll see that one. His name is Middleton, I think."

How convenient, thought Mercer. "Thanks for sticking with me, Tunney. You're a good friend. Now I need to get back to my watch."

Mercer finished his grog and rose from the bench. The pain of the shirt touching his back and sliding on the sensitive skin and open wounds made him wince and jerk. This would be the most challenging watch to get through, but he had to show the other sailors that Alec was resilient. After observing Alec perform his duties each day since he'd arrived, Mercer knew what to do and when to do it. He resolved to do everything possible for Alec to regain his fellow shipmates' respect and trust. Mercer would be the one dealing with the pain on this day.

He completed the watch, thoroughly exhausted physically and mentally, and after tying up a hammock, he carefully entered it to get some rest. It was the first normal sleep Mercer had since arriving, and it was welcome. When he awoke, it was time to allow Alec to regain consciousness until Mercer had reason to take over. As he vacated, allowing Alec to return, the pain and weariness disappeared. Alec awakened and crawled out of his bunk, moaning. He touched his back and yelped. Mercer could feel Alec's anxiety and the panic building inside him. Desiring to help, Mercer recalled what Aniyah told him about conveying information to his ancestor. He had little practice doing this with Charles, but Alec needed to know what happened to him. Mercer pushed along the edges of the void but did not attempt to enter. He relayed his thoughts to Alec as if speaking to him by projecting with his mind the words, "You will be fine. The pain will subside. You are one of the best sailors on this ship, and you are valued. You made a mistake, going into the captain's cabin uninvited, but you are important for the survival of Mr. Darwin. Life will go on." Mercer wasn't sure what to say, but these words seemed to calm Alec, causing his panic to subside.

The next day, Alec was back into his routine. The pain was significant but manageable.

Mercer needed to act soon. If he didn't, the murder of Darwin might happen before he could stop it. Although he was pretty sure he knew who would carry out the attack, the when and how were still a mystery.

After the meal and while Alec was between watches in the evening, he joined other men in the mess to relax. Syms Covington played a light tune on his fiddle as the sailors listened. As Alec listened to the music, Mercer decided to tell Covington that Darwin was in danger. He hoped this might make Darwin more alert and help prevent an attack. He took control of Alec's body and approached Covington after the young man finished playing.

"Mr. Covington, you have a talent for the fiddle. These men and I enjoy hearing you play," said Mercer.

"Why, thank you, sir," beamed Covington.

"I wonder, Mr. Covington, could you spare a moment or two? I have some vital information for your master."

Covington looked at him dubiously. "Vital information," he repcatcd. "What vital information?"

In hushed tones, Mercer said, "I have reason to believe that someone aboard this ship intends to murder Mr. Darwin."

Covington drew a deep breath in surprise. Then his look became dubious. "Were you not the man who was flogged for trespassing in the captain's cabin?"

Mercer struggled, "Yes, I was, but that doesn't make—does not mean I am a liar. I snuck—trespassed because I heard a man talking about killing Mr. Darwin and was trying to find out more. It was a mistake to enter the cabin, but that d—does not change what I heard." Mercer gave up trying to sound like Alec and pleaded, "You need to warn Darwin. He has to be ready for something to happen at any moment. I mean it. Please tell him. Tell him for his own safety."

Covington stared in disbelief. He finally said, "Are you mad, man? You sound like a raving lunatic."

Shaking his head, Covington turned on his heel and left the room. Dejected, Mercer moved to a seat on the other side of the room, blending in with the other sailors. That had not gone well. He closed his eyes and receded consciousness, allowing Alec to return. Alec opened his eyes and looked around. Upon seeing other sailors near him, some of whom were napping, he grunted and closed his eyes, quickly falling asleep.

The following day, as Alec crossed the deck to check the portside rigging lines, Mr. Covington approached him.

"Mr. Williams," said Covington with his brow furrowed. "Mr. Darwin would like you to accompany me to his berth in the poop cabin."

Alec said, "Huh, why?"

"Why? Of course, it is regarding the information you provided me with yesternight," said Covington.

Mercer commandeered Alec's consciousness, causing his body to stagger slightly.

Covington noticed Alec's unsteadiness and said, "Are you well, Mr. Williams?"

"Yes, I'm fine. Wait, I thought you said I was crazy. But you still told him what I said?" puzzled Mercer.

"I did. I felt it was my duty to inform him. However, I was clear that I do not believe you are to be trusted. No matter, he would like to see you."

"Okay, let's go," said Mercer.

"Very well," said Covington, who turned and walked aft.

Mercer followed, wondering why Darwin wanted to see him against the advice of his servant. The poop cabin was aft, at the stern of the ship. It sat atop the captain's storeroom, where Mercer had overheard the voices before being caught by Captain FitzRoy. As they passed the stairway that led down to the gun room and captain's cabin and approached the helm, Mercer saw Middleton standing against a wall. Covington knocked on the door of the poop cabin while the soldier glared at Mercer, who tried to ignore the man's gaze. An authoritative voice came from within, and Covington opened the door, beckoning Mercer to follow.

Mercer entered the room. Behind a large desk littered with sheets of paper and artifacts that appeared to be taken from nature sat a serious-looking man with a high forehead, sizeable bushy brown eyebrows, and lamb chop sideburns. The gold chain of a pocket watch stood out against his dark green vest. Mercer stood with his mouth agape and stared at the one and only Charles Darwin. The pictures of Darwin that Mercer recalled seeing were of a much older balding man with a long white beard. The only similarity between the image in Mercer's mind and this man was the dour expression. He did not look up, nor did he acknowledge their presence. After closing the door, Covington and Mercer stood quietly. The men waited for several minutes until Darwin closed his journal and capped the ink bottle, raising his head and giving Mercer a stern look through his dark, piercing, deep-set eyes.

"Mr. Covington has relayed to me some disturbing news you have no doubt fabricated, but news which I shall hear straight from its source," Darwin said in a commanding tone.

Realizing it was his turn to speak, Mercer said, "Ah, sir, I heard a man say that he planned to murder you at some point during our journey. I don't know exactly when or how this will happen."

"Mr. Williams, do you know this man, the one who intends to murder me?"

"I… I do not," Mercer said with a slump in his shoulders. He couldn't claim he knew who the murderer would be because he had no proof.

Darwin's hard stare at Mercer continued as he said, "Am I to believe that I shall be murdered by an unknown man, at an unknown time, by an unknown method?"

"Y… Yes, sir," Mercer mumbled.

Darwin shook his head, then said, "Mr. Covington also told me of your punishment, one recently enforced for a crime committed aboard this ship. Is that correct, Mr. Williams?"

"It is, but…"

"Enough," boomed Darwin. "Please take your leave now. It would be best for you to focus on your assigned duties as a midshipman and allow storytelling to remain in the domain of novelists and bards. We will not speak of this again."

Darwin returned to his work as Covington opened the door to the room, motioning quickly for Mercer to leave. Middleton watched as Mercer passed the helm and went forward toward the mainmast. Darwin had no interest in taking precautions, making him an easy target. His survival depended on Alec and Mercer now.

Mercer walked to the portside mainmast rigging and left Alec's consciousness, leaning against the bulwark as he did so. Alec took over and shook his head, mumbling something about losing his mind. After he regained his bearings, Alec continued going about his duties.

Early the following day, in the inky blackness of night, Alec was on watch and performing a portion of his shift that had him moving around the deck, ensuring that various halyards and blocks were secure. From above, he heard yells.

"Lower the main staysail!"

The main staysail, a triangular sail between the main and foremasts, had become torn and needed to be taken to the sailroom. Sailors above lowered the canvas sail to Alec, who gathered it up and headed belowdecks. The sailroom was empty, as was usual for this time of night. After stowing the damaged sail so it could be repaired later in the day, he started up the ladder toward the fore hatch. There was a scraping sound from above, and a boot crashed into the side of his head, knocking him from the ladder. Lying on the floor of the sailroom, he saw stars. Then a face appeared before him, illuminated by a lantern held by a man. It was the soldier who had flogged him.

Alec said, "Hey, what is this about? Who are you?"

"My name is C… Marine Clay Middleton of the Royal Marines. I'm here because someone's on to me, and I think that someone is you," said the soldier.

"On to you? What do you mean?"

"I saw you enter Darwin's cabin with his servant earlier," said Middleton. "Why?"

"I am not sure I understand what you are talking about."

"All right," said Middleton as he unsheathed his dagger and held it toward Alec, who immediately backed into a wall. "Maybe this will draw you out."

"Draw me out? You are…crazed," said Alec indignantly.

As the knife came closer to Alec's throat, his eyes glanced at the shiny blade, and he yelled toward the hatch, "Help! Help!"

The knife pressed against Alec's neck, drawing a trickle of blood, and he trembled and became silent.

Middleton smiled and sneered. "That's better. We're deep inside the ship. No one can hear you. Show yourself. Now. I won't hesitate to slit this man's throat. I could care less if he lives or dies."

His icy blue eyes glared into Alec's, who tried to look away.

Middleton continued, "You're not from this time, are you? You've been sent to try to stop me. You warned Darwin."

Suddenly, his face lit up with excitement, "You know, you may have just given me a way out of this, a way to cast suspicion onto someone other than *my* ancestor. Oh, that's perfect!"

Middleton was giddy. He was planning to make Alec a scapegoat. The crew would likely hang Alec by the neck from a yardarm until he was dead. It was also clear Middleton would be true to his word and kill Alec if he needed to. Mercer had to figure out how to keep Alec alive and salvage any chance of preventing Darwin's murder. He quickly filled Alec's consciousness.

"There are others on board who know of your plot," Mercer said defiantly. "I won't give you their names, but they know who you are."

Middleton laughed. "I knew it! Nice try."

The knife tip pressed harder into his throat, and Mercer croaked, "I know who you are."

"I'm sure you think you do, but you don't. You don't have a clue who I am."

"You're one of those God's Left Hand zealots, trying to change history because of some warped notion that it would help God. God doesn't need your help."

Middleton paused, then said, "'The best way to predict your future is to create it.' Do you know who said that, Mercer?"

Mercer was shaken. Somehow Middleton knew it was Mercer in Alec's body. Mercer said nothing.

"Abraham Lincoln did. Fitting, isn't it?"

Mercer recalled something from one of his prior transferences.

"No fucking way!" exclaimed Mercer disdainfully.

"Oh, yes. You do remember. Lutomir is one of my favorite ancestors. He and I are a lot alike. I almost exposed you. But then you ran away, coward. Yet you gave me enough to be able to track down who you were after I returned. It took me two years to find you."

Mercer was incensed and tried to pull away, but the knife only pressed deeper, and blood started running down his neck.

"Ah, ah, ah," taunted Middleton. "We're not done yet. There's one more thing I need you to know. After I kill Mr. Darwin and, of course, your ancestor here, you'll find things are a mess *if* you get back home. Who knows what things will be like after Mr. Darwin's history ends today? Also, someone's taken your sister, Lizzy. She's probably in grave danger."

A wry chuckle came from Middleton.

$$18$$

MERCER WAS DUMBSTRUCK. IF HE believed this sociopath, someone, probably the terrorists, had kidnapped his sister. No doubt her life was in jeopardy, and he needed to get back to help her. On the verge of returning to his own body, he stopped himself. Once before, he'd nearly broken his link to Alec and was almost goaded into doing so again by Lutomir, Middleton, or whoever this guy was. Leaving now would accomplish nothing, and the consequences could be dire. Lizzy's abduction would need to be dealt with after he left Alec. He needed to stop Middleton.

One chance, a single opportunity, was all Mercer had. If anything went wrong, and Alec was severely injured or killed, the mission would be a failure, and Charles Darwin would be dead. Mercer needed to do whatever he could to play this out to its successful conclusion, that being both Alec and Darwin alive and safe.

"Back to the business at hand," Middleton hissed. "Find a length of rope so I can bind your hands."

Mercer didn't move.

"Now!"

Mercer stood and searched the room in the dim light. Since this was the sailroom, pieces of rope were plentiful, so he found one of an appropriate length and offered it to Middleton.

"Back against the wall, and don't try anything," said Middleton.

As Mercer stood with his back to the wall, Middleton pushed him against it, reigniting pain from the scourging he'd endured, and pulled his arms forward. Middleton brought Mercer's hands together and wrapped the rope around them. The binding was tied tightly, so wriggling out of it would be near impossible. Middleton patted Mercer's clothes until he felt Alec's sailors' knife in a pocket, then took the knife. He then sheathed his dagger.

"You'll go first. Follow my directions, and don't say anything. I'll have a knife ready to slice you if you try anything," said Middleton.

Mercer climbed the ladder, made more difficult with his hands tied.

"Through the fore hatch," Middleton pointed.

Mercer walked up the steps through the fore hatch and onto the upper deck. The sailors on deck were busy working, and few noticed him and Middleton emerge from the hatch. Those who did, Middleton ignored, urging Mercer toward the stern. They walked the length of the ship, finally reaching Darwin's cabin, where Middleton nodded his head toward the only guard on duty. Then he knocked several times.

"Mr. Darwin," he said. "This is Marine Middleton. I am very sorry for the interruption at this time of night, but I have a matter of some urgency. Could you please open the door?"

Mercer heard sounds coming from within Darwin's cabin, then the door opened.

"Marine," said an exasperated and weary Darwin. "I was in the depths of slumber. Can this not wait until the morn?"

"Again, I am sorry, sir. But there is an issue that I need to discuss with you urgently."

Darwin noticed Mercer standing with his hands tied in front of him.

"Mr. Williams? What is going on here, Marine?"

"I am assigned to your detail, sir. Please allow us to enter so we can talk in the privacy of your cabin," said Middleton.

"Very well," an annoyed Darwin said.

They entered the room, and Darwin sat at his desk. His bunk was no longer stowed, and it hung in the middle of the ceiling. On the desk was a stack of papers, atop which sat his closed journal, and various other items, most unidentifiable by Mercer, were strewn about the desk. There were many pieces of what looked like bone, most of which were small, but the biggest bone, about a foot long, looked like half of a jawbone of a crocodile. Everything appeared to be very old, and Mercer suspected these were fossils discovered by Darwin.

Middleton unsheathed his knife with his right hand, pointed it toward a chair, then said to Mercer, "Have a seat, Mr. Williams."

Mercer sat in the chair in front of Darwin's desk with bound hands in his lap while Middleton stood at one end, keeping his knife trained on Mercer.

Middleton addressed Darwin, "I beg your pardon, sir. I must keep my blade at the ready. This one is dangerous."

"Well, Marine, what is the matter?" said Darwin.

"Mr. Darwin, I must first verify something with you. Is this the same man who entered your cabin earlier today and produced a fantastic tale about a plot to murder you?"

"Yes, it is the very same. I do not know what his game is, but I directed him to interfere neither with me nor my servant for the rest of our voyage. Yet here he is, interfering with my sleep. Why is this?"

"Sir, I have ascertained that it is, in fact, this man who intends to perpetrate the heinous crime of murder upon you. I have uncovered his devious plot and intend to see justice prevail. I am here to confirm his identity and, as a courtesy to you, inform you of my discovery before taking this information to Captain FitzRoy," said Middleton smugly.

Darwin paused for a moment. "Marine Middleton, I am sincerely grateful to you for bringing this grievous plot to my attention. I expect you to ensure this scoundrel will be punished to the extent the law allows."

Middleton smiled broadly, then said, "It is my pleasure, Mr. Darwin. Now there is one more item we need to discuss before I take my leave. Can you tell me your purpose for being on this ship?"

"Hmm, I do not understand. What has this to do with an attempt on my life?" queried Darwin.

"Indulge me for a few more seconds, sir," pleaded Middleton as he removed his jacket and draped it over his forearm. His knife remained in his hand, still directed at Mercer.

"Well, I suppose, but this had better be quick. I am here as a scientist to explore the natural world. These artifacts I have discovered could lead us to a better understanding of how things came to be as they are today."

"Have you considered how your studies might impact man's belief in God?" said Middleton.

"What? Man's belief in God? What has this to do with God? Marine Middleton, what is your point?"

Middleton watched Mercer as he sheathed his knife and pulled Alec's knife from his pocket. Then Middleton took a half step toward Darwin and pointed the blade at him. Mercer stood quickly, and Middleton thrust the knife toward him, his eyes boring into Mercer until he sat back down.

Middleton's voice and language reverted to an apparent East Coast upbringing as he and his knife turned back to Darwin, and he scornfully said, "This is my point, Mr. Charles Darwin. You're an ignorant fool. You have no idea what you're messing with here, no idea how much you'll set humanity back with this…this so-called work, and with your life." Then he exploded, "This has everything to do with God!"

For the first time, Darwin showed fear as Middleton came unhinged. Darwin gestured toward Mercer and said with quiet disdain, "And you accuse this man of the very crime you intend to commit. You are stark raving mad."

"Mr. Darwin, if you believe in God, you'd better start praying to him," said Middleton. He turned toward Mercer and said, "Here's what happens next. After your knife kills Darwin, I'll kill you with my dagger, having been unable to stop you from getting to Darwin because you stabbed me. A minor self-inflicted flesh wound is a small price to pay, don't you think?"

Middleton plunged Alec's knife into his own leg and quickly pulled it out, wincing in pain. Then he stuffed the jacket into Darwin's face with his left hand to muffle his screams and raised

Alec's knife. Darwin swung his arms wildly, trying to fight back. He had seconds to live.

Mercer moved without thinking. He reached for the large jawbone with his bound hands, standing as he did so. Gripping it tightly, he raised the fossil over his head, bumping it against the ceiling. The distraction startled Middleton, making him pause before he thrust downward with the knife. Mercer rammed the bone as hard as possible against Middleton's head as he turned toward the noise. There was a crunching sound, and instead of stopping abruptly, the jawbone continued into Middleton's skull for a couple of inches. Middleton fell with a thud, the side of his skull dented and bloodied. Darwin cast the jacket aside as Mercer dropped the bloody bone on the desk, and they watched as the body lay twitching on the floor. Mercer expected the evil had already left it, leaving behind the corpse of its ancestor. What remained was probably a good man, a man who needn't have died, a man who Mercer killed.

Mercer dropped into the chair with a shocked look on his blood-spattered face. He was numb, couldn't speak, and was shaking visibly. The two men sat in silence, staring at each other.

Darwin spoke first. In a trembling voice, he said, "I owe you my life, Mr. Williams."

Darwin slowly stood and approached the cabin door, opening it and yelling for assistance. Within minutes Lieutenant Wickham and the ship's surgeon, William Kent, were present in the cabin. Kent verified that Middleton was deceased. Then he checked the two men and instructed they be brought water and given a few minutes to recover from their ordeal before answering questions.

Wickham questioned Darwin and Mercer about the events leading up to Middleton's death. Darwin praised Alexander Williams for saving his life and told Wickham that Middleton attempted to frame Mr. Williams for the murder.

Alec was relieved of his watch duties for the remainder of the day and allowed to rest. Mercer badly wanted to leave Alec and return home but was unsure how to do so without causing Alec great confusion. As he slept in his hammock, Mercer receded from

Alec's consciousness, but not entirely. Alec filled the remaining space, and Mercer relayed the day's events to him. It was like Alec was hypnotized; Mercer spoke into his mind to convince him that the events had happened to Alec.

When Alec awoke, he found Tunney sitting on the floor, sleeping with his back against the wall.

"Tunney, what you doin' down there?" said Alec from his hammock.

Tunney awoke with a start and stood groggily. As he recognized Alec, he spouted, "Alec, you're a hero! It seems everyone on the ship wants to be your friend. Even the captain wants you to mess with the officers tonight. How 'bout that, Alec?"

"Huh. How 'bout that," said Alec with a slight grin.

It was time for Mercer to go, so he dove for the bottom of the pool and reached his ancestral tree, looking at the leaves before moving down toward the trunk. The leaves remained as they were; there were no changes. The impact of this episode of transference on his family history left no trace. He moved back toward the trunk and his carved name, then rose through the pool to its surface.

His eyes opened to the same dimly lit laboratory he remembered being in almost a month ago. The room was unoccupied. He sat up, stretching like he'd just woken from a nap. The door to the room opened, and Aniyah stepped in. Her ever-present smile warmed him, but her expression was foreboding.

"Lizzy, where's Lizzy? We have to find her!" he pleaded as he attempted to rise from the recliner.

"Just a minute," scolded Aniyah. She quickly detached the wires from Mercer's skull as she said, "The monitors show that you completed the transference, so I was coming to wake you. And you're right. We received a message from God's Left Hand only moments ago. They kidnapped Lizzy and want you in exchange for her." She pointed to the copy of Darwin's book lying on a bench. "At least it looks like your mission was a success. I wish there were enough time to hear how things went."

Mercer stood, then said earnestly, "Yes, I killed the man who tried to kill Charles Darwin. He told me Lizzy was taken and that she may be in danger. I need to get her back. How do we make the exchange?"

* * * * *

"Ned Lamb? You're Ned Lamb. Mercer trusted you," Lizzy scowled at Ned. "He tried to help you."

"It was an excellent bit of deception. I don't think anyone could have gotten closer to Mercer Evans than I did," said Ned. His words and mannerisms seemed theatrical, as if all of this was some reality show and he was playing for a crowd. Every so often, he glanced, very briefly, up toward the corners of the room as he spoke. Lizzy had the sneaking suspicion that someone unseen knew everything that happened in this room.

Ned continued, "'Poor Ned Lamb. He's got potential, but he's so drab and boring. He's the perfect partner for someone like that too-big-for-his-britches Mercer Evans. If a little of Mercer could rub off on Ned, we'd have one helluva team. Do you see? Do you see how easy it was to get to him? I had Mercer in my sights for quite some time before I was sure he was a Leaf Runner. But I stuck with it and didn't give up. That's what makes me so good at my job."

As Ned was talking, the door opened, and Sam, still in her tactical outfit, walked in carrying a briefcase. She set it on one of the workbenches and opened it, revealing an array of what appeared to be medical instruments. She selected two particularly gruesome-looking items from the case and sauntered toward Lizzy.

Ned said, "Now Sam looks ready to do what she's good at. But first, I need to check to see if we have a response. I'd hate for one of your pretty little ears to be lopped off if it doesn't need to be."

He smiled.

* * * * *

Gazing into his eyes, Aniyah said, "Mercer, it's not that easy. They'll want you to do things. Things that you won't want to do. If you don't, they will kill you. That's the only outcome I can see happening unless you decide to help them." Her words trailed off, and she looked away from him.

"What choice do I have? I won't let them harm Lizzy." Pausing for a few seconds, he finished saying, "If I die…so be it." The last few words were a whisper.

"Then they win. They'll be successful in changing history," she said with a faraway look. Then she turned back toward Mercer. "Your family tree is unique, you know. Most of the Leaf Runners are immigrants with ancestry primarily from countries in Africa, South America, Indonesia, and Asia. Surprisingly, we have few Europeans where God's Left Hand…targets most of its efforts. You play a key role in helping to stop them. That's probably why they want you."

"But I can't sacrifice my sister for this. This whole thing is surreal, and I wish I'd never been a part of it!" Mercer cried out.

He was angry, angry at his sister's captivity and his feelings of helplessness, angry at the realization that killing Clay Middleton would likely not be the last time he would need to take a life, angry that he could see no easy way to end this. However, getting angry never solved anybody's problems. Taking action could.

"We need to make the exchange," he said determinedly as Nigel walked into the room.

Nigel said, "Mr. Evans, I do not advise this course of action. God's Left Hand will have an insurmountable advantage with you entering their fold, even if you choose not to help them. In which case, they will kill you."

"I'm aware of the consequences, Nigel. But I need to save Lizzy. I'll figure some way out of this after she's safe."

"Very well. It so happens that they have threatened to remove one of her ears if we don't respond to their demands within the hour," said Nigel.

"Then respond now!" shouted Mercer.

The instructions they were given after accepting the demands required Mercer to take a train to Coney Island and await further instructions. If he wasn't there in seventy-five minutes, Lizzy would lose an ear. This gave them very little time to plan an exit strategy. As Mercer walked out the door, Nigel's people were already boxing up the offices and getting ready to clear out. Once in the grasp of God's Left Hand, they could not expect Mercer to be able to withhold the secret location of the Leaf Runners.

                                 19

As Mercer crossed Surf Avenue on his way to the boardwalk, the dimming sun approached the western horizon, pale orange due to smoke carried by the wind from wildfires hundreds of miles away. He found the red, white, and blue garbage can and sat on the nearby bench, fighting the urge to swivel his head around to check his surroundings. The instructions said he was to sit and face forward until contacted.

A noise came from behind him, but he had no time to react as a bag was pulled over his head and his arms held in front of him. The only sounds were the ratcheting of cold handcuffs around his wrists and seagulls squawking. Hands patted him down roughly and dug into his pockets. He was pulled up to a standing position, then led quickly by the arm for several steps before being shoved into a car. The trip was a short one. Mercer was dragged from the car and had to jog to keep pace with his captors. Their clomping footfalls eventually lead to the gurgling thrum of a boat motor. He stumbled as hands pulled him down some steps and then tossed him into a seat. The boat's engine revved, and he felt the vessel gain speed and plane itself above the water. The ride became rough, and a man's voice growled, "This won't take long."

* * * * *

"Well, my lovely little tulip, it appears you'll get to keep those pretty little ears. I'm sure you'll find this news agreeable," said Ned. "We keep our promises, and, as promised, you will be taken back to Greenwich Village once we receive our gift."

"Gift? What gift?" demanded Lizzy.

"Ahh, you're curious. Yes, everyone likes getting gifts, don't they? This gift is special to us. It will help us win our war against those who demean God."

Lizzy rolled her eyes, saying, "It sounds like you're more of a mindless disciple than a warrior."

"Oooh. You're sassy. I'm sad you're leaving us. I'd like to keep you around to play for a bit longer," said Ned.

The guard entered the room and proclaimed, "He's on the boat."

"It's time to go," barked Sam.

"Okay, I need to talk with this one for a minute," said Ned.

Sam closed the door, leaving Lizzy alone in the room with Ned, who unbuttoned the top button on his shirt, loosened his tie, and then walked behind her chair.

"It's getting warm in here, don't you think?" he said. She heard a click followed by the whirring of a fan as it sped up and blew air around the room. The clattering sounds of his footsteps on the hard floor made her heart skip a beat as Ned came around to face her.

He shouted, "This won't hurt very much." Then in a whisper she could barely hear, he said, "Tell Nigel I'll take care of Mercer, and it's Luther at Wittenberg. Remember, Luther at Wittenberg." He waited for her to nod her head slightly, then said, "Sorry about all this."

He slapped her face hard enough to cause pain and leave a mark, but not so hard as to break anything. Lizzy hardly noticed the slap. Instead, she tried to process the words Ned had just said. Then, covering her head with the cloth bag, he lifted her arm, made her stand, and ushered her out of the room.

* * * * *

After an hour-long ride, Mercer was lifted from the boat onto a dock and pulled by a strong hand that pinched his arm as he walked. After a couple of minutes, he was pushed down into a chair and the bag was yanked from his head. The room was bright and luxurious, with many windows looking out over a beautifully sculpted lawn, beyond which was a rocky beach and, finally, the open ocean. It was difficult to see much more in the dimming twilight, but he figured he was somewhere on Long Island or the Jersey shore.

A young man dressed in a suit and tie held a tray toward him, which contained a glass filled with a clear liquid, a lemon wedge, and ice. "Water?" said the servant.

Mercer took the glass, his hands still cuffed, but did not drink from it.

The room was spacious and decorated in a nautical theme. Windows adorned with blue-gray draperies held back by brass finials shaped like dolphins spanned two adjacent walls. Beneath the drapes were sheer white curtains, many of which were moved aside to allow clear ocean views. A large flat-screen television was mounted to another wall, while the final wall was covered in mirrors behind a well-stocked bar. Several matching couches and chairs furnished the room, and books were strewn over the coffee table sitting at its center.

The man who brought Mercer into the room left through a sliding glass door, leaving him alone with the servant and a muscular guard who stood by the doorway that led into the rest of the house. Mercer sat for several minutes, wondering what he was waiting for when a person entered the room.

"Professor Lazarro Giannelli," exclaimed Mercer. His initial shock turned to recognition as he realized Giannelli was aware of Amon Warwick's work and in a perfect position to exploit it. "Of course. Who else would have as much insight into what Leaf Runners can do?"

"Leaf Runners," spat Giannelli as he sat on a chair opposite the couch occupied by Mercer. "What a detestably stupid name. I imagine it is something you call yourself when you have no clearly defined purpose. Now the name God's Left Hand immediately suggests the most pious and noble of purposes, don't you agree, Evans?"

"I don't understand how killing Charles Darwin can be considered noble. That man had some of the most insightful ideas ever formulated in the human mind. Why would anyone want to kill him?" said Mercer.

"Do you not realize how many souls his blasphemous ideas have caused to drift away from God? The story of creation has been systematically dismantled over generations, all due to the seeds of doubt planted over a century ago by one man. However, what is done is done. We lost our only real chance of getting to Darwin. Since you were, unfortunately, successful in thwarting his removal, we need to move on to our next plan of action. One in which you will play an important role," said Giannelli.

"I have no interest in playing any role for you," snarled Mercer.

"Do you value your life? You will die should you choose not to ally with God's Left Hand. Your part in this will help ensure success, but you're not our only possible move. My best operative will also be involved in this mission. Although a bit messier, we can still accomplish our goals without you, making you expendable if necessary. Either choose to join us and change history for the glory of God or be his enemy and deal with his reckoning."

"And if I help you, what do I get in return?"

"Eternal glory in heaven," said Giannelli. "It is not the trappings of earth which will be your reward—it's the crown of glory in heaven."

"Your trappings of earth are pretty nice," Mercer said as he looked around the room. "It seems like you're getting some of your rewards early."

Giannelli ignored him as Mercer remembered something Giannelli had said.

"Wait, your best operative? Do you mean the one who failed to kill Charles Darwin?" taunted Mercer.

"I mean the one who is good at changing the past and is also good at what he does to affect the present. He has positioned himself close to you. Soon he will be spending some quality time with your sister, Elizabeth, as another way to ensure your compliance."

"Wha…what are you talking about? You said you would let Lizzy go if I gave myself up!" Mercer was agitated.

"Oh, Lizzy has been freed, for now. To further assure your compliance, she will be monitored closely and restrained again if need be. As to the who, it is someone Elizabeth trusts, maybe one of the first people she would call if she needed help. He's also one of the first I call when I need something to be done, something that I can't do myself, something that only a Leaf Runner like you could do, or someone like Connor Walsh."

"Connor Wa—Wait." Puzzle pieces clicked into place in Mercer's mind. "Connor Walsh was Lutomir in Korea?"

"He was, and he was also Clay Middleton on the HMS *Beagle*." Giannelli was so smug.

Mercer's mind reeled. His thoughts were all jumbled. Connor was the one who had discovered Mercer in John Freeman, the one who tried to kill Charles Darwin. He also had Lizzy's confidence, and she didn't know what he was capable of. Mercer struggled to bring himself back to the present.

"You're a bastard, Giannelli. Both you and Connor will rot in hell!"

"Oh, Evans, you can plainly see you have no option but to help us," Giannelli said. "Help us, or you and your sister die." He looked at the guard and nodded.

The large man near the door started toward Mercer.

As he reached down to cover Mercer's mouth with his gloved hands, Mercer said, "Wait! Stop!" Mercer saw no other option than to do as Giannelli wished. It might give him time to find a way out of this predicament. "Just promise me something, Giannelli. Promise that you'll let Lizzy be. She's not part of this. You don't need her to get to me anymore. You already have me. *Leave her alone.*"

Giannelli motioned for Mason to back away and said, "I don't make promises that I don't intend to keep. Since you seem so excited to begin working with us, first, I think we'll perform a little test to make sure that you can follow simple instructions."

* * * * **

Lizzy discovered the car was entering Lower Manhattan when the hood was removed from her head. The handcuffs were removed two blocks into Greenwich Village. Finally, the car door opened, and Lizzy was given her purse and allowed to exit the vehicle. As she stepped onto the sidewalk, the car sped away. People were still walking the sidewalks at this time of night, but not many. She was a block from her apartment and was eager to get home, as a phrase repeated in her head. "Tell Nigel I'll take care of Mercer," was what Ned had said. What did he mean by saying that he'd take care of Mercer? She had to call him.

As she walked up the stairs to her apartment, she tried calling Mercer but was immediately rolled over to voice mail. Two more attempts had the same result. After she unlocked her door, entered, and slumped down on the couch, she called the next person on her list, Connor.

"Lizzy, what's going on? I've been trying to call you all day and stopped by your place to check on you. Where've you been?" Connor sounded concerned.

Lizzy started to cry. "Oh, it was terrible. Some horrible people kidnapped me. One of them was a guy that Mercer works with."

"Kidnapped! Are you hurt? Did he do anything to you?"

"I think I'm okay. They didn't hurt me. They threatened me but apparently got what they wanted and let me go. I'm not even sure what it was they wanted. I feel like I should call the police and report what happened to me, but I'm so tired. I just want to sleep." She continued sobbing.

"Um, no. Just wait. Don't call anyone. I'm coming over. I'll stay with you," said Connor hurriedly.

"Are you sure?" she said.

"I'm sure. I'll be there in ten minutes."

After the call ended, Lizzy thought she should clean herself up before Connor arrived. She was at the sink dampening a washcloth when her phone rang. An unknown number showed on its screen as she set down the towel and picked up the phone.

"Hello," she said.

"Hello, Ms. Evans?" said a voice.

"Who is this?" Lizzy asked in a shaky voice.

"First, I apologize, but I must insist. Are you Elizabeth Evans?"

"Y… Yes."

"My name is Nigel Trowbridge. I must tell you that your brother, Mercer, has been taken by a group of terrorists in exchange for you."

* * * * *

Mercer was still handcuffed and sitting on the couch as Giannelli stood and walked over to him, holding a large book with his finger stuck between the pages. Opening the book to the page he had marked, he held it so Mercer could read it. It was a copy of a handwritten list of names and dates, a manifest.

Giannelli said, "This is a listing of immigrants that passed through Ellis Island during March of 1911. It was a time when a major influx of immigrants entered this country, all seeking a better life, a life shielded from oppression, war, and hunger. All were eager to experience the American Dream, as they called it. Anyway, there is a name on this page that you will ensure does not appear. You will somehow prevent the person with this name from entering through Ellis Island. It doesn't matter how you do it, just that it is done."

"So you're basically telling me I need to kill somebody. Like throw them off the ship or something."

"As I said, I'll leave the means up to you."

"What name?" asked Mercer.

"First, let me show you another name on the page."

Giannelli moved his finger down the page until it reached a line. On the line was the name Rudolf Janik.

"Janik," said Mercer. "Who's that?"

"He would be a great-great-granduncle to you, Evans. His brother, Tomasz, was your great-great-grandfather and had immigrated from Poland a year earlier. Of course, we don't want to change his history because that could change your history, but we're not worried about poor Rudolf. He is someone history has forgotten, making him the perfect vessel for your mission. Now I'll pick another name from this page." Giannelli scanned the names on the page. "Here, Julianna May. To prove that you can do what is asked of you, you must keep the name Julianna May from appearing in the book. After you've completed your mission, all we need to do is review this book and have another who has transference check that history was changed to verify your task was carried out."

Mercer, inside, was incensed. He needed to find a way to get out of this place, but until then, he had to stay alive. His only option was to find a way to erase the name Julianna May from that book.

"Damn it!" Mercer said under his breath. "I guess I can give it a try."

"You'll need to do more than 'give it a try,' Mr. Evans. You must succeed," said Giannelli, looking at the imposing guard. "Mason is all too willing to finish his task."

* * * * *

"Mercer's been taken?" Lizzy said.

"Well, he actually voluntarily gave himself to them so they would free you," said Nigel.

"Oh my god. These are awful people. They'll do horrible things to him. What was he thinking?" she gasped.

"He was more worried about the horrible things they would do to you. We are working on a plan to retrieve him, but we may arrive too late to impede history from being changed by Mr. Evans or others from the group. They have transference, like Mr. Evans. And now they have Mr. Evans, as well."

"I know they have transference," she said. "One of them told me who they were. He was a beastly man who threatened to cut parts off of me! He said he works with Mercer, and his name is Ned Lamb."

"We know. Mr. Lamb is actually one of *our* operatives. Did Mr. Lamb say anything else to you, anything at all that might assist us?"

Lizzy paused for a few moments, confused and in shock. Recalling Ned's last words, she finally said, "Well, yes, he did. But I couldn't believe what he whispered to me. Not after the repulsive way he talked to me. He told me to tell you that he'll take care of Mercer. I thought he might have meant that he would kill Mercer. Ned is a Leaf Runner?"

"Yes. He will do what he can to protect Mr. Evans without jeopardizing his own cover. I am certain you were being watched the entire time while you were held captive. I expect Mr. Lamb said to you what he did so that his cover could remain intact," said Nigel.

Struggling to process everything, Lizzy said tentatively, "I can't believe Ned is one of the good guys. But we need to get Mercer back as soon as possible. Should I call the police?"

"I do not think it is wise to involve the police just yet. For now, the best thing you can do is go about your normal business. I will have some of my people in your vicinity watching out for you should you need assistance. Is that acceptable?"

"I guess so," she said hesitantly. "Maybe the best thing for me right now is to get some rest. It's been a long day."

"I am sure it has, my dear. I will contact you at this number if I have any updates for you," said Nigel.

"Thank you, and good ni—" Suddenly, she remembered something else Ned had told her. "Wait! Mr. Trowbridge, are you still there?"

"Yes, I am here."

"I almost forgot. Ned also told me something else, something that made no sense to me."

"He did? What did he say?" asked Nigel.

"He said something like, 'It's Luther in Witt… Witt something or other.' I don't remember exactly."

"Luther? Gracious!" Nigel exclaimed. "Luther. Could you please hold on a second?"

"Sure," she said. The buzzer from the front entrance sounded, so she went to the intercom and covered the phone. "Hello?"

"Hi, Lizzy, it's Connor. Can you buzz me in?" She went to the intercom and pushed the button to open the door for him. Connor would be up to her apartment in a minute. She went back to her phone. "Mr. Trowbridge, are you there?"

"Um, Yes. Yes, I am here. I think I found what I needed. Could it be Wittenberg?"

"Yes! That's it. Wittenberg. 'It's Luther in Wittenberg.' That's what he said."

"Thank you. This information is vital. You must not tell anyone of this. Do not trust anyone. Do you understand, Elizabeth?"

"Yes, I understand. What's so important about it?"

As a knock came on her door, Nigel said, "While you were held captive, Mr. Evans transferred to an ancestor who was a sailor on a ship called the HMS *Beagle*. Through this ancestor, he prevented the murder of Charles Darwin while on the voyage."

"What," she stammered. "I can't believe…" She paused for a couple of seconds. "But what does that have to do with what I just told you?"

The knock occurred again, so she walked toward the door to open it as Nigel said, "This information means that God's Left Hand intends to kill Martin Luther before he can submit his famous disputation."

She opened the door to see Connor standing there. "What? What's that?"

Nigel said, "They intend to kill Martin Luther before he can post his Ninety-Five Theses, to prevent the Protestant Reformation from ever taking place."

————————————— 20 —————————————

THE BRANCH SEEMED TO GO on forever, filled with other smaller branches and thousands of leaves, too many to count. As Mercer searched for the leaf that contained the name of Rudolf Janik, he paused for a moment to take in the tree's enormity. Although he'd already experienced its grandeur, he was still amazed by it.

Mercer continued along the branch that held Rudolf's leaf, eventually finding and studying it. Rudolf was born in 1890 and lived until 1930. His parents were the only leaves connected to him, so he'd never married and had no children. It must have been a lonely life, thought Mercer. Touching the leaf revealed Rudolf's timeline, and since Rudolf entered Ellis Island on June 8, 1911, he must have disembarked from somewhere in Europe at least two weeks earlier. This would be a nearly impossible task if Rudolf and Julianna did not come over on the same ship. Given that they appeared on the same page of the Ellis Island manifest, Mercer pinned his hopes on them arriving on the same boat.

It was time to go. He added a few extra days and transferred to Rudolf on May 21, 1911. Reaching the pool's surface, Mercer stopped to observe. He wanted to understand more about Rudolf, his interests, acquaintances, and how he came to emigrate to America.

* * * * *

Blurring flashes of people and wagons moved in every direction, surrounding me. The whinnying of horses, the cracking of whips, the squeaking of wagon wheels, the screams of children, and the deluge of a thousand voices swamped my senses. Where was I? How did I get here? I froze in place, afraid that movement in any direction was unsafe. I was trapped, so I lifted my hands to my face to afford even the tiniest sense of protection from the multitudes. However, the warm skin of my hands was not what greeted my face. A slightly wrinkled sheet of paper, with holes in the corners where it had been folded and unfolded many times, was pressed against my nose and mouth. Due to my surprise, I jerked the page away and found it contained writing in a familiar hand. It was a letter addressed to "My dearest brother Rudolf."

The anxiety of the moment must have played tricks with my mind. After seeing the greeting on the letter, I was instantly aware that I was Rudolf Janik from Lodz, Poland. The warmth of relief replaced the tingle of apprehension that had overcome me.

Then came the realization of where I was. I had finally made it to Hamburg! The letter from Tomasz brought with it such bittersweet feelings. To have the opportunity to travel to America, as so many other Poles have done, and to see the excitement in their stories had such a pull on my heart that I needed to catch my breath as I thought about it. All my life was spent on the family farm outside of Lodz, where life was never easy, but it was home. For many years my homeland was in the midst of a constant tug-of-war between Russia and Germany, and many of us native Poles were the victims of this battle. The lack of food and money became a part of each day, one from which I could not wait to flee. I had lived with fatigue and the pangs of hunger for far too long.

So when I received the letter from Tomasz months ago saying that he would pay for my passage to America, I was overjoyed. The letter stated that I must have a passport and arrive in Hamburg to board the ship, SS *Finland*, on May 24. Besides what I was wearing, I had very little for the journey; just a bag with some clothes, a journal, my traveling papers, and a ring from my mother. She told me I was to look at it to remember her when things became difficult. She said I would always be in her thoughts.

I had never been this far from home, so everything I had experienced since arriving in Hamburg was unfamiliar. Lodz was a large city, but this place made it look like a small berg. Food was plentiful. I could eat some fresh fish, which I hadn't tasted in more than ten years. It was glorious!

After the long journey from Lodz, I found a boardinghouse where I could rest for a few nights before being at the docks to board the ship. It was nothing special, but it had a roof to keep out the rain and allowed me some privacy, and it was a place I could afford.

Since I had nothing to do, I decided to explore the town. The people who I passed came from everywhere, it seemed. Some wore clothing like mine and walked along as I did. Others wore fine clothes and were pulled along the cobblestone streets in horse-drawn carriages. Some rode by sitting in those noisy horseless carriages. The sounds of steam trains could be heard frequently, but I found it best to avoid areas with rails. Rarely did I have occasion to get near a railroad. The only time I'd ever ridden one was on the journey from Lodz to Hamburg, but being near the rails as a train went by was frightening.

The layout of the city streets made it very easy to get lost, so I had to draw myself a map to be sure I could find my way back to the boardinghouse. I frequently paused to update the map as I walked. On one of these stops, as I was squatting down to draw an intersection with street names, a group of Poles, about half of which were young women, walked past me. As I looked up at them, they immediately turned away. This is something to which I had grown accustomed. I was born with a cleft lip that was surgically repaired when I was an infant. The surgery allowed me to eat and speak almost as well as my brothers and sisters and live a nearly normal life. However, the visible scarring and malformation of my upper lip were evident, and the mere glimpse of it by an unsuspecting person would elicit a grimace or incent them to divert their gaze. Throughout my life, I thought that smiling at someone was one of the worst things I could do to them, so I never smiled. The result was that most people preferred to avoid me, even many whom I had known my whole life. Concerning girls, this was a significant problem. I had never been close to any other than my sisters.

I came to accept that I would never find a woman who could overlook my deformity and want to have a relationship with me, even a cordial one. Although I had hoped the people in Hamburg would be more worldly and accepting of me, the reaction of this group continued to reinforce my thoughts on the subject. Desiring to protect my emotions, I determined to continue to push thoughts of a relationship with any woman from my mind.

My exploration of the city continued into the evening when I decided to look for something to eat. A simple meal of knackwurst and beer, the comfortable down bed in my room at the boarding-house, and the fatigue from traveling were enough to cause me to sleep soundly.

The next day I explored the dock area where my ship would be boarding in two days. My anxiety to ensure I knew what I had to do and where I had to go drove me to understand every detail of the place, including where the emigration office was and what papers I needed to bring. I checked to ensure I had everything I needed and was too excited to sit for another day with noth-ing to do. A uniformed man sitting inside a small building near the entrance to the gangway told me I would need to answer a couple of dozen questions and that I needed to have money. The letter from Tomasz warned me about the money, so every penny I owned was on my person. Thinking about the questions made me nervous, but when I mentioned this to the woman at my board-inghouse, she told me there would be no problem if I answered truthfully.

On the day before my departure, I decided to take a more extended tour around the city, still using the map I created on my first day in Hamburg but adding to it as I went. Some of the build-ings I saw were very tall with beautiful architecture, such as Saint Michael's Church and the great Church of Saint Nicholas, with its tower climbing hundreds of feet into the air. Sitting down to rest in a beer garden within full view of the church, I drank a beer and relaxed as the warm sun bathed me. Groups of people nearby were also enjoying the fine day and fine local beers. Sitting near me was a group of Poles, many planning to emigrate to America, I supposed, laughing and enjoying themselves. Periodically, words could be overheard, but I paid no attention as I did not know anyone and preferred my own company.

* * * * *

"...Julianna," Mercer heard out of the chaotic sounds of human voices talking, laughing, and singing. Hearing the name jolted Mercer, like when his phone rang while watching a movie in front of the TV. It was time to commandeer Rudolf's consciousness to determine if the name he picked up was that of Julianna May. After doing so, he scanned the area and paid close attention to the group where the word came from, not appearing too eager to pry into their gathering. He listened for a while but did not hear the name. Mercer became more assertive when it looked like the group was getting ready to leave their tables.

"Excuse me," he said. No one answered. "Excuse me!" This time it was loud enough for members of the group, and others around them, to hear. "I am sorry to interrupt, but I wonder if any of you know anything about the SS *Finland,* a ship leaving for the port of New York tomorrow." Several heads nodded in recognition. "Wonderful. It seems I have forgotten the time of departure. Would one of you be so kind as to tell me?"

A few faces turned slightly to not look directly at him. One petite young woman who seemed unfazed by his appearance answered without hesitation, "The ship departs at eleven in the morning, but all must be on board by ten."

"Excellent, my lady," Mercer said as he approached her. "I am Rudolf Janik of Lodz, and I sincerely thank you for your kindness."

Bowing slightly as she brought her right arm forward, he kissed her hand, then smiled at her as he let it go. She smiled back, a broad smile that fit well with the high cheekbones on her round face. Her fluffy dark blonde hair was pulled up under a bluish-gray wide-brimmed hat that complimented her piercing deep blue eyes.

"I am glad I could be of assistance," she said.

She turned to follow the others and started walking away.

"I'm sorry," Mercer said a little too loudly. "But I did not get your name."

She paused, looked sideways at him over her shoulder, and then said, "I did not give it, Rudolf Janik of Lodz."

Sheepishly, Mercer said, "I beg your pardon, ma'am. It was rude of me to yell after you. My sincerest apologies." He bowed toward her ever so slightly.

After a short pause, she said, "I am Julianna May of Warsaw."

"Pleased to make your acquaintance, Julianna May of Warsaw," beamed Mercer.

She turned and left with her group. Now Mercer had a face for the name. He dove for the pool.

* * * * *

I found myself staring after a group of people walking away from me, the same group seated near me a short time ago. I don't remember standing, but what was most disconcerting was that I was smiling. What came over me? Was the journey affecting me in some way? Then I saw the faces of some in the group as they looked back at me with scorn, so I turned away and left quickly.

Despite this strange incident, I enjoyed my last day in Hamburg with no further unexplained episodes, but I knew tomorrow would be a big day and wanted to be sure I would be prepared and at the docks on time. Therefore, I returned to my room in the early evening and rechecked all my belongings and papers to ensure I had everything. Then I packed my bag and placed my passport and ticket in a place I was sure would be safe. I did not have much with me, but it was all I owned in this world and was important to me. Sleep that night was fitful.

The line was long when I got to the dock by eight the following morning, so I waited patiently until it was my turn to talk to the boarding attendant. A scowl was etched into his face, and I was unsure if it was due to a problem with my papers. Of course, it could be that he was born that way. He asked me many questions: where did I come from, how old was I, what was my occupation, could I read or write, had I been to prison, was I married, and many others. After every answer, he wrote on the manifest list.

My next stop was in a room with a doctor for a medical exam. He listened to my chest with some tubes and checked my reflexes. The exam went quickly. However, the vaccination created some discomfort as he produced a long needle and proceeded to pierce my left buttock with it.

Before climbing the gangway to the ship, I and my bags required disinfection. The fluid used had a strong smell of medicine, and because every immigrant was subjected to this process, I was not alone in having to endure this bit of embarrassment.

Finally, I was aboard the SS *Finland* and needed to find my place on the ship. The ticket from Tomasz indicated that I was in steerage, the least costly accommodation, so I was ushered past some machinery toward the rear of the ship, downstairs to below deck, and into a room with narrow bunks and close conditions. I had never been on a ship and was unsure what to expect, but this would be a two-week journey with little personal space and people everywhere. Apprehension for what was to come welled up inside me. My expression must have been evident because a young man lying on the bunk below the one I took said to me, "It is not going to be so bad. My brother wrote to me that the destination is well worth the journey."

I introduced myself, and he told me he was Hugo Brunner from near Krakow, another Pole, and that some of his family was on board. I told him I was alone but looking forward to seeing my family living in America, as many on board were. Hugo was a rail of a man, really more like a boy, and was very friendly. We talked about many things, but mostly we talked about growing up on a farm since we both had done so. One of Hugo's older brothers had emigrated to America two years before, and Hugo was planning to meet his family in Chicago. The letter from Hugo's brother was similar to the one I had from Tomasz, filled with exciting possibilities, and food was plentiful! After our talk, I forgot about my worries about the journey ahead because the future was brighter than I ever felt it could be. Any angst I felt was a small sacrifice I willingly made to experience my exciting new life to come.

As the ship got underway, its railings were crammed with passengers. Everyone wanted to watch as we left the harbor, and the city buildings shrank into the distance. The Elbe was a wide and busy river. I overheard someone near me say it would be near nightfall before we left it and entered the North Sea. The mesmerizing shoreline slowly slipped by as I stood at the railing and watched after most others had left. Steadily chugging, the two steam engines which drove the ship's propellers caused the vessel to vibrate in a hypnotic rhythm. After another hour, I looked along the railing. The ship's structure made only a portion of the railing visible, so I could see only one other person, a young woman, holding the railing tightly. She was beautiful, and as I looked at her, she looked back. I thought I saw her smiling but didn't dare linger for fear my face would repulse her.

* * * * *

Mercer saw her image for a mere couple of seconds. With no one else on the deck in this portion of the ship, now might be his best chance to get rid of Julianna May. If she went over the side here, near the ship's stern, it would be a while before someone found out she was missing. She was a sweet, innocent young woman with her whole life ahead of her, and here he was trying to figure out the quickest way to kill her. Well, wasn't that what Giannelli wanted him to do? Could there be another way? There had to be, but an opportunity to complete this useless assignment was at hand. He didn't have much time before this chance would disappear, so he leaped into Rudolf's consciousness and immediately turned to face Julianna. She was still looking in his direction, but with a fading smile until he walked toward her. He covered the ten paces between them as she leaned against the railing, watching him approach.

Mercer scanned the deck once more before reaching her. Covering her mouth and tossing her over the railing would be easy. Then he would need to leave the area quickly and stealthily so he couldn't be identified as the last person who might have seen Julianna May alive. Thinking that he'd figured out a plan, he reached her, ready to act. But instead, he froze. She looked at him as though he were a friend, someone she could trust. How could he do this? It was senseless.

As he stood wrestling with his conscience, she stared into his eyes, waiting for him to speak. Suddenly he detected movement out of the corner of his eye. Hugo stepped from behind the bulkhead and walked toward them along the starboard railing. Mercer retreated to the pool.

21

It happened again.

Somehow, I stood at the railing in the ship's stern, close to the woman, staring into her face. She was staring back in expectation as if waiting for me to speak. Time stood still, and it felt like I would never be able to move my gaze away from her. She was the most striking woman I had ever seen, blonde, blue-eyed, and beautiful. The wind gently tugged at wisps of her hair, causing them to brush her creamy porcelain cheeks. The large birthmark at the corner of her mouth made her fetching smile all the more joyous, yet at the same time, there was serenity. I had never met this person before, but I felt that I knew her. I knew that her soul was pure, and her demeanor was delightful. But I didn't know how I knew it. I just did.

Hugo approached us along the railing and said, "Hey, Rudolf, who is your friend?"

I stood there, not knowing what to say and not knowing the beautiful woman's name.

"Well, Mr. Janik," she said. "Have you forgotten my name already?"

Wait, she knew my name? How? "Julianna May of Warsaw," I blurted out. Where did *that* come from?

"Yes, you do remember." She smiled at me again, a broad beaming smile that melted my heart.

"It is a pleasure to meet you, Miss May," said Hugo. "I am Hugo Brunner, a friend of Rudolf's."

"Pleased to meet you," she said, smiling so sweetly.

I was unable to speak and did not know what to say. The first words that finally left my lips were, "Why are you standing here alone?" What a stupid thing to say. Anything would have been better than this feeble attempt at conversation.

Slowly she started, "Well, things were feeling cramped belowdecks, and I needed to get some air. So here I am."

"How wonderful," I said jubilantly.

She giggled at me. Was this the best I could do? My lack of experience in such matters was apparent, even to Hugo, who tried to hide a snicker.

"I think I will continue stretching my legs and leave you two to yourselves," said Hugo. He elbowed me slightly in the ribs as he brushed past me, and I looked at him. He was wearing a wry smile, and his eye gave me a wink; I think it was his way of encouraging me.

As Hugo walked away, I turned back toward Julianna, who was watching the roiling water churned up by the ship's propellers. Entranced by the effervescent wake, she eventually said, "Do you ever wonder what it would be like to be born somewhere else? To grow up and live in an entirely different country?"

Finally, I could speak. Her questions opened the door for me to feel more at ease, and so I said, "I had not thought much about the rest of the world until I received the letter from my older brother, Tomasz. All I knew was the farm and the city of Lodz. I had not traveled more than a day's horse ride from my home in my entire life. When Tomasz left home, I worried about him, worried that he would not be able to survive the dangers of the unknown. Life outside of this…this little bubble of the world that I knew was never something I had considered for myself. It was something I feared. The letter from Tomasz brought me a gift, a way to look at the world from a whole new perspective. What he says about America makes it seem like heaven on Earth. I cannot wait to get there and experience a brand new life."

"I am so excited, but I am also scared. I have no idea what it will actually be like," she said. "My greatest fear is not knowing anyone and being alone amongst a sea of people."

"Are you alone on this journey?" I asked.

"I have a few friends on the ship, but we will go our separate ways once I arrive in America. I am to travel to Philadelphia to see my aunt, but beyond that, I do not know what my future holds…" She let the words trail off and continued staring at the churning water below.

* * * * *

Mercer considered his options now that the two were alone. He could still attempt to carry out his plan to throw Julianna overboard, but it was an awful plan that would destroy both of these lives. Besides that, he knew he couldn't kill Julianna, anyway. Rudolf's emotions were a mix of excitement, desire, and fear. He seemed interested in Julianna—very interested.

Mercer needed to find a more ingenious way to complete this mission.

* * * * *

Until the diminishing daylight made it difficult to see, Julianna and I talked about our families, our homes, our dreams, and our fears. I did not want to leave her side, but we both were hungry and needed some rest. We promised each other we would meet again in the morning in this exact location. There was something in my heart I needed to ask her before we parted, so I said, "Julianna, may I ask you a question before we retire for the night?"

"Of course, you may, Rudolf."

I said sheepishly, "Why do you not seem afraid of me, of my face, I mean?"

Looking relieved, she said, "Oh, Rudolf. Is that why you shied away from me at first? Do all girls avoid looking at you?"

I did not reply immediately because this was something I locked in a secret place inside of me. "People react to me when they see me for the first time. Many look away or divert their eyes, so they do not look directly at me. I have grown accustomed to it, especially with women. That is why I am asking you. What makes you different from them?"

"I do not know, exactly, what makes me different, Rudolf. But my brother, Antoni, you remember, the one who used to push me in the tree swing and saved me from drowning in the lake when I was twelve?" I nodded. "Antoni has a face much like yours. I always saw warmth and happiness in that face, constant kindness, and a steady presence that unwaveringly supported me. Yet I noticed the way others avoided looking at him. I believe it hurt me more than it did him to see people so repulsed by his appearance. Once, he found me crying after we traveled to the city, and he asked me what was wrong. I told him I had seen the people turning away from him, and all I could think about was if I was in his shoes, how would I feel?" A tear rolled down her cheek as she spoke, but her eyes never left mine.

My heart leaped into my throat. I swallowed and had to catch my breath. My mouth was dry, and my legs were shaking. I do not know what possessed me, but I reached for her hand and clasped it between my hands. "I do not know what to say, Julianna. Your kindness is unmatched. I… I look forward to tomorrow and wish you good night."

She said good night to me, and we parted. My body and mind were numb, and I do not recall much about that night, other than sleep was elusive.

* * * * *

Stepping into the apartment and closing the door behind him, Connor said, "What's the matter, Lizzy? You look like you've seen a ghost."

Lizzy lowered the phone from her ear and stood frozen, staring at Connor. She was trying to process everything she'd just heard and all she had endured during the past day.

"Mercer gave himself to the kidnappers so they would let me go," she sobbed.

"Oh no. That's terrible. I'm so sorry, honey," he said as he embraced her. She could sense the strength of his arms around her, and it made her feel safe.

* * * * *

Connor knew someone had already gotten to her. It was probably the Leaf Runners on the phone telling her Mercer was gone. Tonight, it would be best to play the concerned boyfriend. The Leaf Runners were off-balance, and Mercer was under Gianelli's supervision. All was well for God's Left Hand.

Even better, he had Lizzy right where he wanted her. As they hugged, he allowed a smirk to appear on his face, a smirk that she could not see.

* * * * *

"Have you eaten anything?" Connor asked concernedly as they released their embrace.

"No. Now that you mention it, I haven't had anything since this morning," said Lizzy blankly.

"I'll take care of it. Just have a seat on the couch and relax, honey," he said with more care in his voice than she was accustomed to.

Lizzy sat and turned on the TV. As she searched through the streaming movie options, something was eating at her. Her mind went back to thoughts of being a Leaf Runner. Could she actually be one? She had no other explanation that would fit her experience. Should she tell someone, maybe Connor? Then something else crept into her thoughts, confusing her even more. Honey? Connor had called her that twice since he arrived. She'd never heard him say it before. That was new.

Doubt slithered its way into her consciousness. Lizzy started to wonder if the trauma of her kidnapping had somehow changed her and increased her paranoia. She didn't know who to believe nor who to trust. Fear and panic rose inside her. Her lips quivered, and her muscles trembled.

Connor was in the foyer with his back to her and talking on his phone, presumably ordering food. On an impulse, she quickly texted Nigel, "I think I might be a Leaf Runner."

* * * * *

I awoke early, not having slept much at all. Julianna's face was so deeply ingrained in my mind I could not shake it. Apprehension about whether she would continue to express herself to me the way she had yesterday eroded my confidence. However, I could not let a lack of confidence deter me. I needed to know if my feelings for her were just a passing fancy or the seeds of love. Love, there was a word I had not thought about for a very long time. Yet there it was. I could not escape what I felt toward Julianna, nor did I want to.

I finished breakfast, thoroughly enjoying the bakery food, and went up on deck to the stern to stand at the railing, where we talked the night before. The SS *Finland* was now in the open sea, and the ocean's swells rocked the ship much more than when we were running on the Elbe. It was still quite early, so I expected to wait for a while before Julianna arrived. The minutes stretched into hours, and the excitement of seeing her waned. Maybe she did not feel the same as I, and my feelings and yearnings of last evening were a mirage, faint and fleeting, never to be reached.

The sun's heat was making me uncomfortable, and my hope was diminishing, so I turned to leave the railing and find some cooler air. And there Julianna was, walking along the railing toward me, pale and somewhat gaunt. She looked sick and unsteady, so I ran to her and put my arm around her to give her support.

"I am so sorry, Rudolf," she cried. "The seasickness has me retching horribly. I am dizzy and flushed."

"Have you eaten or had anything to drink?" I asked.

"I do not feel up to it," she said.

I took her below and sat her in a comfortable place while I brought her food and water. I told her to sip the water slowly and only take small bites of the food until her stomach felt better and her nausea lessened. Her color was much better within half an hour, and her smile had returned.

"Again, I apologize, Rudolf. I meant to be up at the railing earlier than you," she said. "I wanted to be there for you."

"I will admit, I was worried that you would not come. And I was becoming disappointed. Your smiling face occupied my mind, and I urgently wanted to see you again."

She grinned, then said, "I think it would be best if I went back and laid down for a bit until I am feeling better."

"Of course," I said.

She stood to leave but did not go immediately. Instead, she stared into my eyes. She said, "I, too, could think of little else than the sparkle in your eyes, Rudolf." She gave me her hand, and I bowed to kiss it. Her smile widened, then she turned and walked away. I had never felt such longing.

Julianna's seasickness improved over the next few days, and we spent a great deal of time in each other's company. We laughed and cried as we moved about the ship, and I quickly realized what I was experiencing was more than a passing fancy. I believe she felt the same.

* * * * *

He was in love, thought Mercer. Rudolf was head over heels in love with Julianna. And only a fool could miss that Julianna felt the same for Rudolf. These two should just get married.

Wait, that's it!

* * * * *

A thought suddenly struck me, an idea which I would never have usually considered after such a short relationship. I could not believe I was thinking it now, but something deep inside compelled me to move the conversation into an uncomfortable area.

"Julianna," I said as we stood near the railing at the ship's bow, bathed in the glow of the setting sun. "There is something that I have been thinking about more and more. I guess I am too young to have thought much about it before, but I am compelled to do so now. Have you ever considered what it would be like to have a family of your own someday?"

She searched my eyes and said, "I thought I wanted to spend my days seeing the world and traveling. Well, it seems that life aboard a ship may not be my future." We both had a good laugh. "But I have been thinking about what it would be like to have a family and be a wife and a mother. These are things I have not spent much time thinking about until recently, very recently." Her eyes twinkled.

"And are you excited or scared about these thoughts?"

"I am not scared," she said softly, then inhaled deeply.

"Neither am I," I said. Pulling my mother's ring from a pocket and holding it toward her, I knelt on one knee on the deck and saw her hands fly up to her mouth as I said, "Julianna May of Warsaw, will you marry me?"

The wait for her reply was the most prolonged moment of my life. It felt like forever. Would she say yes, or would she laugh at me and tell me I had entirely misunderstood? I had never felt so vulnerable before, pulling my heart from my chest and placing it in her hands, hoping she would not crush it.

"Oh, Rudolf," she said slowly, tears filling her eyes. "I… I… yes. Yes! Yes, I will marry you!" She dropped down to me and kissed me with her full lips for the first time. Dreams could not compare with such a kiss. Love filled us as we embraced and let time and the ocean pass. Nothing else mattered.

* * * * *

Mercer couldn't believe it. So far, he'd only coaxed Rudolf at a few key moments, enough to get him to take the initiative. The rest all just happened naturally. Mercer wasn't out of the woods yet, though. He needed them to be married before they reached Ellis Island, or Julianna's maiden name would still appear in the manifest. Getting Rudolf to hurry things up so the marriage would take place on board the ship might take a little more than coaxing, but he had little choice. If he was unsuccessful, he had to consider what else he could do. They were still seven days from arrival, in the middle of the Atlantic Ocean, so his options were severely limited. He had not expected Julianna and Rudolf to fall in love. Still, even if they hadn't, he now knew that dying at the hand of Giannelli and his radicals would be better than living with the guilt he would always carry by destroying the lives of innocent people.

* * * * *

News traveled around the ship quickly. The morning after our engagement, almost everyone I met, whether Julianna was with me or not, had words of congratulations for us. After breakfast, I was at our usual spot when she arrived, radiant as ever. Julianna said, "Good morning, my love." My mouth became dry, and my throat constricted. I still could not believe this beautiful woman wanted to be my wife. Yet here she was.

"You are the most beautiful woman I have ever seen," I said, speaking my true feelings. She smiled, and then we kissed. I imagined every day would be like this for the rest of our lives, and happiness welled inside me as I said, "My dear, have you thought yet about when and where we should be united in marriage? Where shall we have our wedding ceremony?"

"I find it interesting that you should ask," she said. "This has been on my mind since the moment I said yes. For what reason would we wait?"

I was taken aback, for I was planning to suggest we get married as soon as possible, not knowing exactly why. I usually did not make such hasty decisions, but something drove me to push forward. Here she was suggesting the same! Was this some fairy tale? I could not believe what was happening.

"My thoughts exactly," I said. "I would like to talk with the ship's captain to see what arrangements could be made for a ceremony before we reach America. Then we can enter the country as husband and wife!"

She jumped into my waiting arms, and I spun her around. Her happiness was exceeded only by my own.

Later that day, we received unwelcome news. The captain stated that he could not act as an officiant for a wedding. We would need to find a priest on board. The captain also said that a marriage could not be performed until we were out of international waters and in the coastal waters of the United States of America, which meant that even if we could find a priest, we would need to wait until the morning of our arrival to be wed. However, these setbacks did not deter us. The need for a priest to perform the ceremony quickly spread throughout the ship.

By evening a man came to us and identified himself as Father Finlay Duncan, traveling to America from his homeland of Scotland. He was called to a church in California and would be traveling by train across America after landing in New York.

"I dinna think I can do as you request," he said. "Even though you are both Catholic, performing the sacrament of marriage aboard a ship is highly unusual and requires special permission from a bishop. The marriage is usually performed in the church of either the bride or the groom."

"But we are immigrants," said Julianna. "We do not yet have a church in America. Is there no way we can be married here, on this vessel, in front of you and any necessary witnesses such that we are wedded lawfully and truly?"

I so loved this woman.

"Well, 'tis not unheard of in the Scottish tradition for a wedding to take place outside of a church. I ken I've done it before. How different is a ship than a home in this regard?" He thought for a few seconds, then said, "Aye, lass, it can be done. But I'll need to speak with the bishop before leaving New York."

* * * * *

Mercer observed as Rudolf and Julianna stood facing each other on the deck of the SS *Finland*, with the wind blowing their hair and the Statue of Liberty in the distance. Since there were no flowers aboard for a bouquet, Julianna substituted her mother's Bible wrapped in her grandmother's kerchief, which she clutched as she smiled, never taking her eyes from Rudolf. Rudolf repeated the vows after Father Duncan, then slid his mother's ring onto Julianna's finger. Hugo stood beside him as a witness, beaming. After Julianna repeated her vows, Father Duncan announced that they were husband and wife, and they kissed. A cheer came from the crowd, and with the ceremony completed, Father Duncan had them and their witnesses sign the appropriate papers. It was now official. They would be known as Mr. and Mrs. Rudolf Janik from this day forward.

22

"HOT FOOD SHOULD BE HERE soon," said Connor as he sat beside Lizzy on the couch.

"Thanks," she said wearily. "I appreciate you being here for me. I kind of feel on edge. Like I'm going to have a panic attack at any second."

"Things will be okay," consoled Connor. "I'm sure we'll get Mercer back safe and sound. Do you still think we should call the police?"

Lizzy gave a start, then said hastily, "No, not yet."

If the Leaf Runners had contacted her, that was the answer he expected. There was no question about that now. She trusted them for some reason.

"Okay," he said. "I'm sorry for asking, honey. But do you think you're going to be all right? I mean, you've been through a very traumatic experience. Should we find someone who could help you…process everything?"

"I don't know. Yes, it was terrifying. I just think I need some time to think before deciding if I need outside help."

"I get it," said Connor. "I don't want you to feel like you're being pushed into anything. But I do know someone who might be able to help. We haven't talked about this yet, but I want you to know that I'm part of a church. And there's a guy there who's very good at helping people who've gone through difficult times."

"Church, huh?" said Lizzy. "That's not something I ever did while growing up. My parents were focused on their careers and children. It was never a part of my life."

"I understand. That's the case for many people these days. I guess I consider myself lucky, in a way. Church has always been important to me. It was a central part of everyone's life for many centuries. But that's changed over the years."

Connor needed to be careful. This was an opportunity to explore Lizzy's feelings to see if she might be open to the ideology of God's Left Hand. He purposely hadn't delved into this topic since they'd met. He wanted to develop a closer relationship first for fear of pushing her away. Her traumatic experience made her vulnerable, and since their relationship had matured, maybe it was time to work on recruiting her.

"I'm a bit surprised," said Lizzy. "You've never mentioned this before."

"I know, and I'm sorry. It's not something I usually bring up unless the time is right. I'm not ashamed of that part of me, but I also know that discussing religion can make people uncomfortable. It's not a good topic to bring up in the Physics Department." He chuckled. "Many wonder how I can be both a physicist and a believer. I tell them that physics tells me *how* things are the way they are, but not *why*. I need both in my life."

He paused for a few seconds to let his words sink in, then said, "It just hasn't come up with you and me until now, I suppose."

"Yeah, I guess not," she said as she yawned.

"Anyway, help will be there if you need it," reiterated Connor.

* * * * *

Lizzy knew Connor was only trying to help, but she didn't want to have this talk, at least not yet.

"Thanks for the thought, babe," she said. "And I'm sorry, but I'm too tired to continue this discussion right now."

As she spoke, the intercom buzzed.

"No worries," said Connor, somewhat distracted. "That'll be dinner. I'll go grab it."

He was back in a few minutes with wonderful-smelling bags, and Lizzy realized she was famished. As they ate, she could feel some of her strength returning. Connor was focused on his phone, and his leg was bouncing nervously, but Lizzy was grateful for quiet, so she didn't speak until she was finished eating. He appeared to be anxious.

Lizzy said, "Is everything okay?"

Connor looked up and said, "Oh, it's just that I have an early lab tomorrow, and I can't seem to find someone to fill in for me. I want to be here for you, but I think I need to go."

"It's fine, Connor," she said. "I'll be okay. You go do what you need to do."

She saw the consternation on his face, so she held his hands, looked into his eyes, and said, "Really, I mean it. I will be fine. And thank you for dinner. I'm feeling much better."

With relief, he said, "Thank you, I'm sorry. I'll see you tomorrow."

He smiled at her and kissed her goodbye.

Soon after Connor left, there was a slight knock at her door. Lizzy saw a beautiful woman standing in the hallway through the peephole. She'd never seen the woman before and tried to remain silent so she would leave. A whooshing sound came from under the door as a sheet of paper slid across the tile. Picking it up quietly, she read it.

> Lizzy,
>
> My name is Aniyah Wright, and I'm a Leaf Runner. I waited for Connor to leave the building before approaching your room. Nigel sent me. I'm here to help.

Lizzy grabbed a pen and wrote below the other words.

> Why should I trust you?

She slipped the paper under the door and waited. In less than a minute, the sheet shot back into the room.

I can teach you how to be a Leaf Runner.

* * * * *

Mercer waited as Giannelli talked with someone on the phone. He was not pleased as the call ended but walked toward Mercer with a complacent look.

"You think you're pretty clever, don't you, Evans?" he said with a wry smile. "I told you that you were supposed to prevent her from appearing in the manifest. Yet there she is, Julianna Janik, as verified by Connor when he looked at the historical changes."

"You told me Julianna May wasn't supposed to appear in that book, and the name doesn't appear, so I accomplished my mission, as requested," Mercer said indignantly.

Giannelli stared unwaveringly at Mercer. "You will require some hand-holding, someone to remind you about the true intent of orders. They are not open to your interpretation. I expect the next assignment to be completed exactly as I intend. Connor will be here in the morning so the mission can commence. For now, Mason will show you to your room. You'll need rest, so don't waste the hours trying to figure out how to escape."

Mason grabbed Mercer's arm and forced him to stand, pulling him toward the inner hallway. Before they reached it, Mercer said, "What is this mission you're talking about?"

Giannelli replied, "You will find out only when necessary. I don't trust you, Evans. I'm not about to have you mess this one up."

As Mercer was being practically dragged through the house by Mason, he noted that it was huge and filled with expensive furniture and religious art. Most of the art looked like stuff that he'd seen at weddings he had attended in traditional churches. Here lived a man obsessed with the church. This, Mercer believed, would befit someone who proclaimed that he and those who follow him sit at God's left hand.

Mason pushed Mercer into his assigned room and closed the door. The space had a decor that matched the rest of the house.

Although not very well concealed, it had hidden cameras in every ceiling corner. He continued nonchalantly exploring and checked the attached bathroom for more of the devices. Finding some there, as well, Mercer mused that Giannelli was not concerned about the privacy of his guests.

The growl that emanated from his stomach while sitting at the desk chair reminded him of how long it had been since he'd eaten.

"I wonder where I can get some food around here," he muttered as he stood to leave the room and look for something. The locked door wasn't surprising, but he jumped when it opened as he stepped away from it. The butler who had served him earlier entered the room holding a silver tray carrying a covered plate and some beverage glasses. The man didn't say a word as he placed the tray on the desk, removed the cover, and served the food. As quietly as he had come, he left Mercer to his meal. Mercer examined the food and imagined it was probably laced with something that would knock him out. But it looked good, and its aromas were incredibly enticing. He sat down and dug in. Not surprisingly, the meal rivaled those he'd eaten while taking clients out to some of the best restaurants in New York City. He felt no ill effects after finishing it.

Mercer was trapped. The room was locked, his phone was gone, and he was constantly under the watchful eye of Giannelli's cameras. He hoped it wouldn't be too late before the Leaf Runners figured out how to help him. Too late for what? Giannelli was excited about his plan, so it must be something big. Wondering and hoping wasn't getting him anywhere, so he thought it best to get some sleep. The night was fitful, filled with nightmares from his previous trips to the past—the pain of disease, the pain of being eaten alive, the pain of torture, so much pain. The hours dragged on, but he must have slept because a knock at the door awakened him.

"Yes," he said with a start.

"Mr. Evans, your presence is required for breakfast in thirty minutes," said a refined voice.

The clock showed seven, and sunlight streamed through the lace curtain in front of the lone window to the room. He stood and peered out the window, blinded by the sunlight reflecting off the rippling ocean surface, then tested the latch to see if he could open it. The window swung open about six inches, enough to allow air in but not enough for a person to slip through. It wouldn't have mattered anyway, with eyes watching his every move.

As he turned toward the bathroom, Mercer noticed a pile of clothing lying on the desk where the empty food tray had been the night before. The clothes were his style and size; how presumptuous. He walked into the bathroom and wondered for a minute about whether he should shower under those watchful eyes. To hell with it. He needed a hot shower to start the day. The soothing water helped sharpen his mind, and he dressed in the new clothes. It was almost time to go, so he tried the door. Of course, it was locked. He sat at the desk and waited the fifty remaining seconds of his thirty minutes. The door opened right on time, and Mason waited impatiently in the doorway.

This time the guard walked through the house in front of Mercer instead of pulling him by the arm. Mason paced briskly to an outdoor patio overlooking a pool with a view of the ocean. A round outdoor dining table was adorned with a vase containing hibiscus flowers in various colors, formal ivory china, and silverware. Giannelli was seated on one chair, so Mercer sat in the chair opposite him.

"Good morning, Evans," Giannelli said. "I trust the service is to your liking?"

"Can we just get on with it?" snapped Mercer.

"Your sister's lover should be here shortly," jabbed Giannelli. Mercer knew this was an attempt by Giannelli to gain the upper hand, but thinking about Lizzy and Connor made his skin crawl. "Eat, enjoy a good breakfast. You have a busy day ahead of you."

Mercer ate the food, and when he was finished, he wished he hadn't. His stomach lurched as Connor stepped through a sliding glass door onto the patio, followed by a muscular man in a suit, and sauntered over to the table as a servant brought a chair.

Connor sat and looked at Mercer with a sly grin. Mercer was stone still for a few moments, then in a heartbeat, leaped toward Connor and connected with a right cross to his left cheek, almost knocking Connor off his chair. Before Mercer could land a second punch, his arms were pinned from behind, and he was roughly forced to sit back in his chair.

"You're a sadistic bastard!" Mercer screamed at Connor.

"Ooh, so touchy," sniped Connor, woozily sitting while holding a hand to his cheek.

Giannelli interrupted, "Since you two are already acquainted, we will dispense with further pleasantries. Obviously, we cannot ignore the possibility that you intend to kill each other. Of course, that would be detrimental to the mission, so we must find a way to prevent this…eventuality. Mason and Troy will each be assigned to one of you, and you will be in separate rooms during the mission. Should the mission fail due to one of you causing his ancestor to murder the other's before completion, both of you will be dispatched using a method similar to one my ancestors employed as they built their businesses on the island of Sicily. However, I see no need to carry the Sicilian Necktie to its ultimate conclusion for you, Connor. Your death will be enough. However, Evans will get the full treatment so that his Leaf Runner friends can appreciate the seriousness of the situation. Am I understood?"

Giannelli watched them both, waiting for their confirmation. Neither moved, staring at each other with their temples twitching.

"Am… I…understood," he said forcefully.

Connor said, "Yes."

Mercer nodded slowly.

"Excellent!" said Giannelli. "Now to the business at hand. It's time to go." After a short pause, he said to Connor, "Oh, and get some ice for that cheek. It's starting to swell."

Once the group left the patio and entered the house, Connor followed Troy while Mason led Mercer in the opposite direction. Mason pushed Mercer through an open doorway at the end of a long hallway lined with doors, then closed the heavy metal door behind him. A folding chair sat in the far corner, and a plush red recliner, dominating the small space, occupied the center of the room. A mirror nearly covered one wall, reminding Mercer of the kind of rooms police used to interrogate suspects in the movies. It was probably a one-way mirror, so someone would be watching him the entire time, as they had been since he arrived. The recliner was obviously for him, so he sat down and lay back, looking up at ceiling tiles filled with hundreds of small holes. Maybe he could pass the time counting them and avoid whatever Giannelli had in store.

His plan was short lived as a voice boomed over invisible speakers. "Okay, Evans," said a giddy Giannelli. "You will transfer to your ancestor, Cristoff Ritter, on October 15, 1517. Cristoff lived in Wittenberg, Germany, and worked as a stonemason, building and repairing government and university buildings and churches."

Mercer looked incredulous and said, "A stonemason? How is a stonemason going to help you, Giannelli?"

"Cristoff was fortunate to have lived in a time and place where he could affect history in the desired way. You see, there was a very famous man teaching at the University of Wittenberg at that time. Of course, he hadn't become famous yet. He was still an unknown as of this date. You are being sent to keep it that way. Should you and Connor effectively carry out the plan, the name Martin Luther will all but be forgotten in the annals of time."

"Martin Luther?" said Mercer. "Didn't he nail some document to the door of a church? A document that started…of course, the Protestant Reformation."

"Martin Luther, in sparking the Protestant Reformation, has done more to negatively affect the history of the church and its teachings than almost any other. Your mission will succeed, and the Reformation will never have happened."

"Do you have any idea what the impact of changing this piece of history might have on humankind? Have you thought this through? The negative consequences of a change like that could be devastating."

"I've analyzed the possibilities, and I see nothing but a bright future for man and religion after this is completed," said Giannelli with an air of satisfaction.

It was madness, thought Mercer.

"Exactly what do you want me to do?" asked Mercer.

"You will find out when you meet a man named Balthazar Himmler," said Giannelli.

Mercer paused as he pondered the name.

"Himmler," he said with sarcasm. "You're not serious."

"It so happens that Connor is in the same family tree as the famous Nazi leader, Heinrich Himmler. They have mutual ancestors, one to which Connor will transfer to execute this mission. You are to meet Himmler the morning after you transfer near the Castle Church of All Saints entrance at eight o'clock, the same church entrance to which Luther will nail his Ninety-Five Theses, should you fail," Giannelli ended dourly.

Mercer sincerely wanted to avoid having to do as Giannelli directed. But he could see no way to escape with his life. He would have to play things out and hope he could create an opportunity to sabotage this mission in a less-than-obvious manner. All that could be done now was to stall.

"Gianelli, have you considered that there might be other less violent ways to achieve your objectives? Maybe you could use the power of suggestion on some key figures to change some decisions they made way back when. Maybe you could influence someone to choose a different line of work to prevent them from being in a position to affect history the way they did."

"Save it, Evans. All of this has been carefully planned. I don't need any of your suggestions."

Realizing the inevitability of his situation, Mercer asked, "Is there any other information I need before I go?"

"Ah, so you grow eager, as do I. There are two considerations you must be aware of. First, you have less than two weeks to complete your task, and second, it is wise to minimize the impact of your actions on the life of your host. Unlike Rudolf, who was related to you through a sibling, Cristoff is your direct ancestor.

There are things you could do to change the direction of his life, or end it, which could fracture your ancestral tree and wipe you out of existence." Giannelli paused to let that sink in, then said, "It's time for you to transfer. We will speak next upon your return." The speaker clicked as Giannelli ended the discussion.

The holes in the ceiling melted into a gray background as the lights in the room were dimmed. Mercer kept his eyes open for a while to allow them to adjust to the low lighting. After about fifteen minutes of Mercer not making any attempt to transfer, Mason's deep voice came over the invisible speakers, "Evans, get a move on."

He'd wasted as much time as he dared. It was time to go. His eyes closed, and he relaxed, feeling for the ancestral pool that had become so familiar. He dove to the bottom, finding his name on the trunk, and searched for the branch of interest. The path to Cristoff was long and contained many different surnames, which females traditionally changed upon marriage. To reach the early sixteenth century, he traversed eighteen generations. Recalling Giannelli's warning, Mercer knew that a change this far back in time could impact his life today, but measuring such an impact would be impossible. The realization brought fear, and he yearned to have as little effect upon history as possible. Saving Charles Darwin had already made him realize some of the impacts his ability could have, but the farther up the ancestral tree he went and the farther in time he got from himself, the greater the burden he felt.

Mercer finally found the Ritter line, which ended with Cristoff's daughter, Gisela. He also noted that Cristoff's mother, Agnes, died on October 22, 1517. She was to die during Mercer's transference. He hesitated, then touched Cristoff's leaf, sliding the timeline to October 15, 1517. With trepidation, he rose to the ancestral pool's surface and into Cristoff's consciousness.

23

THE WELCOME COOL BREEZE OF Autumn danced across my face as I stood on the floorboard of the scaffolding. Laboring in the sun could make the chisel work seem to drag on for days, but today's comfortable weather gave me a reason to pause and enjoy the feeling of purpose and love I frequently felt while working with stone. The angel's wings I was chiseling were a testament to the beauty of the Creator, and my hands were guided by his as I created such images from hardened granite carved from the earth. The angels and other reliefs adorning the facade would remind those who approached this magnificent church of the solemnity and grace represented within its walls, as driven by his divine nature. I loved my work and the positive impact it had on others. At the end of this day, the coins I would take home were enough to buy food for my ailing mother and me for nearly a week. What a blessing!

Heinz was working on a Latin scroll a few scaffold columns to my right and yelled to me that the day was done and it was time for a beer at the brewhouse. I politely declined, saying that I had some other things which needed tending, but I might be able to join him the following week. In truth, I had no money for the luxury of beer and didn't want to admit as much to him. It would have been wonderful to enjoy a pint with my fellow stonemasons, but it was not practical and wouldn't be so until the job was completed and the balance of my pay was provided to me. The beer could wait.

After bidding my coworkers farewell, I walked along the cobblestone street past a group of upper-class gentlemen talking to a traveler of a similar caste. I overheard the traveler say, "And I was assured, after handing Tetzel my bag of gold, I could violate the Virgin Mary and still be pardoned for my sins. Such is the power of these indulgences that even horrific sin can be washed away if enough coin is paid to the church. Some have also paid for sins they have not yet committed, so I have heard."

The men around the traveler murmured in shock as I continued walking. Did my ears deceive me? How is it possible that a man can pay money to have the burden of sin removed from his soul rather than repent? Had I been able to read one, I would have gone to the nearest Bible to see where it is written that this should be so.

Having to make stops at both the bakery and the butcher to gather the food we needed for the next few days, I did not arrive at the house where my mother and I lived until well after dark. The meat needed to be placed in the cellar to keep it cool until we chose to prepare it, so I did not immediately check on her. As I approached her room, I could hear her moaning. I ran to her side and asked her how she was.

"I have had…better days, my son." Her breathing was shallow and labored. "I fear…there is not much time…left for me. This will be well…for you. I am just a burden…upon you."

"Oh, Mother," I said. "Please do not talk this way. You are no burden. I am proud to be able to provide for you and keep you company. Do not talk this way."

"It is well…my son. You honor me so…and you did the same for…your father before he…passed."

"It was, and is, my pleasure to do so, Mother. I will prepare our meal, and then I will help you eat. I will summon Dr. Ricard if needed. Please rest now and gather your breath."

After taking care of her bedpan, I hurriedly prepared pork chops, endive, and potatoes, then brought a tray of the food to her. She had been unable to leave her bed for weeks, and the sores on her backside were causing her considerable discomfort. I soothed the sores with cool, damp clothes whenever I could, but it was not enough. She did not complain; she only apologized to me for being a burden. She barely ate and only could take a few sips of water. However, she insisted that I do not call upon the doctor and that I should retire for the night because I had a full day of work again tomorrow. Begrudgingly, I agreed with her and went to bed, exhausted from another long day.

Fortunately, our neighbor, Ernestine, could check in on Mother during the day and ensure she had what she needed while I was away. Each day was much the same as the last, except for Sunday, which was the one day of the week I did not cut stone. Mother and I had no opportunity to socialize with others. On Sundays, the priest would come to the house to give Mother communion later in the day to ensure she could partake in the sacrament.

This night, sleep came quickly, as did the new day's dawn. As I did every morning, I arose at six to prepare breakfast and ensure that Mother was ready for the day. I was on my way to work at half past seven when I had the sudden urge to modify my route and make a stop at the Castle Church. The church was several blocks out of my way, a detour that would cause me to arrive late for work, should I choose to divert. However, my compulsion to take this detour was so intense I buried any concern and hastened in the direction of the church. Arriving at a quarter until eight, I found a bench near the main entrance to sit on for a few minutes while I pondered why I was here. The fatigue I experienced due to long days and little rest had me staring blankly into the street.

* * * * *

Mercer filled Cristoff's consciousness and waited for Connor to arrive. There was a steady stream of people entering and leaving the church, and he had no idea what this Himmler guy looked like. At two minutes before the hour, the well-dressed traveler Mercer had overheard the previous day approached and scoured the area, locking eyes with Mercer. Those eyes, and the man's mannerisms, were different than what he remembered from yesterday. The man walked toward him with an air of arrogance and a familiar icy glare. It had to be Connor in the body of Balthazar Himmler, a man much older than Cristoff and physically frail. Connor sat at the far end of Mercer's bench, looked forward, and avoided turning toward Mercer.

"Cristoff Ritter, I presume," he said out of the side of his mouth in a hoarse and gravelly voice. "I'm Balthazar Himmler."

"There's a shocker, Nazi bastard," muttered Mercer. Connor's temple spasmed and his body tensed. He didn't move or immediately respond, however.

"You're a liability," he said so only Mercer could hear. "It would be best if you'd never come."

"Great, now that we finally agree on something, what am I supposed to do?"

Glancing offhandedly at Mercer, Connor said, "You'll have the easy job. Luther lives in a place called the Black Monastery, which houses a cloister of black-robed monks of the Order of St. Augustine. He's allowed to live there because he teaches theology and biblical theory at the university. Are you following, or should I dumb things down for you?"

"Fascinating," Mercer said dryly.

"Luther was sick much of his life, and his gout started around the time he nailed his theses to that door." He pointed with his thumb over his shoulder toward the church entrance. "This means he often experiences significant pain and is likely to seek effective remedies to treat it. One therapy that was frequently used until the twentieth century was developed in Germany at the beginning of the sixteenth century, so it exists today but may be difficult for you to find. In our time, it is called tincture of opium, but in this time, it's called laudanum. Our basic plan is to create a fatal dose of laudanum and replace Luther's usual dose. Of course, we must do this without being caught."

"So we poison him then. Sounds simple enough."

"Well, poisoning happens to be a rather common occurrence during this time, so men of prominence take great precautions to prevent it. Also, members of communes have the resources to produce most of what they need to survive and do not usually require things to be purchased from merchants. In addition, as another form of self-preservation, they thoroughly search any visitor who enters their private living spaces to prevent harm from weapons or dangerous substances. This makes the task of introducing our little concoction very challenging. We will need all of the time available to us to prepare."

"I have a full-time job and a sick mother, ya know. I'll have little time to prepare anything," said Mercer.

"There's very little you need to do outside of your daily routine. Other than gathering a few items and performing a few tasks at key times, the rest will be up to me. So here is what you need to do…" Connor gave Mercer a list of items he needed to acquire, where to leave them, and when. Once this task was completed, Mercer would be given further instructions. "Otherwise, let Cristoff live as he normally would. See, I told you that you had the easy part." Connor stood and turned, walking in front of Mercer on the path. As he passed, and so only Mercer could hear, he whispered, "Cristoff dies if you don't do as I command."

Mercer seethed as he watched Connor hobble away. He was trapped and might have to sacrifice Cristoff to prevent this murder. However, Connor would still probably be able to complete his mission, leaving Cristoff's death all for naught. All Mercer could do was wait for an opportunity to upset the apple cart and prevent this perverse mission from being a success. It was time for him to recede and allow Cristoff to continue his day. Mercer would intercede again only when necessary to gather the items he needed for Connor.

* * * * *

I came out of the daze sitting on the bench near the church entrance. Had I not slept last night to be in such a state as to nearly fall asleep in the daylight seated on a bench for all who pass by to see? The clock tower showed a quarter past eight, and a ten-minute walk was required to get to my job at the Town Church of St. Mary's. I hurried as fast as my legs could carry me.

Over the next week, Mother's health deteriorated, along with the weather, and she had such difficulty breathing that she could only say single words when she spoke. Oddly, there were several strange occurrences as I walked about town the way I usually did to buy things at sundry shops and travel to and from my work site. In three different places on different days, I saw a man I vaguely remembered staring at me as I passed him. He was of high class and aged, and his movements were awkward, with a visible limp. The first occurrence was after I had stopped at the apothecary to collect some medicine for Mother. After seeing him, I found myself standing in the rain at the side of a building, daydreaming as he walked away from me. I had just completed business with a merchant in each instance—I am not sure why I had to stop at the glassmaker—when I saw the man. And each time, I remembered dazedly watching the man walking away from me after I seemed to black out for a moment. I do not believe I was unwell, but I do not remember seeing him approach me, only seeing him shuffle away.

After the last incident, it struck me that it must be the ghost of my father haunting me. The man had no resemblance to my father, but I had never seen a ghost before, so how could I know for sure? I surmised that he was indicating he was prepared to meet my mother in heaven since her time on the earth would soon end.

The following Monday brought the start of work on another job site, the Black Monastery. A new addition was to be built in line with the current main building, and some areas of the old building needed restoration. The monks intended to remain on the premises during construction, so we were to perform our work as discreetly as possible. They inspected our tools and equipment each day, patting us down to look for anything we might be trying to slip onto the site. The end of the workday was timed well with a stop in the incessant rain, so I left and headed for home. Due to the break in the weather, the streets were quite busy, and the bustle of people around me became a blur. Opposite my usual demeanor, I was too tired to look at their faces and greet them as I passed. As I walked through a park, I stopped to rest on a park bench. The man with the limp approached and stood before me.

* * * * *

Mercer invaded Cristoff's consciousness and said, "Isn't there a better way to meet? Cristoff is starting to freak out every time he sees you. He thinks you're the ghost of his father."

"Then you should remain in control instead of popping in and out like some fairy godmother," said Connor as he sat next to Mercer. "You'll place this bottle in the Black Monastery for me to locate and substitute when I visit, which is the morning after tomorrow. So you need to hide it tomorrow." Connor handed him a clear vial that couldn't have contained more than a couple of ounces of a brownish liquid, the poison they would use to kill Martin Luther.

"That's all there is?" said Mercer.

"That's all it takes," said Connor wearily. "Oh, and don't try to open it or switch it out with another one. I will know." There was no doubting him based on the threatening stare he gave Mercer. As Connor shakily stood and walked away, Mercer was sure he heard the word "idiot" muttered. He couldn't wait for this to all be over.

Trying to do it covertly so passersby could not see the vessel, he examined the bottle in his hands. It was hard to imagine how something so simple and small as this could profoundly affect the future. Mercer could see no apparent markings or indicators to identify that it had been tampered with. However, he wasn't about to call Connor's bluff on this one. Connor had probably applied his knowledge of physics to make his tamper detection invisible to the untrained eye. Of course, Mercer could accidentally break or lose the bottle, but that would be an obvious tactic, and he was confident there would be a plan B and even a C if needed. Those plans would, undoubtedly, entail more risk-taking on the part of Cristoff.

Mercer's next concern was hiding the bottle from Cristoff and the monks until he needed to place it where Connor could get it. He noticed that the monks only inspected the men in the morning when they arrived at work. There was no inspection during breaks, even if a man left the site, as he noted Heinz had done during the lunch break. For now, his best option was to stay in Cristoff's conscious until he arrived home and could hide the vial somewhere. He would figure out how to retrieve it in the morning before Cristoff went to work.

The distance from the Black Monastery to Cristoff's home was farther than the Town Church, and with the time added due to the stop in the park, Mercer arrived at the house after the setting of the late October sun. He immediately went to the kitchen and found a cupboard he hadn't recalled Cristoff opening. The cabinet was partially filled with books of various sizes, and in a small wooden box were decorative figurines which looked to be handmade. Mercer placed the vial at the bottom of the box and covered it with the figurines. He would be able to stop Cristoff from making this discovery at any time, but it would require much less focused observation doing it this way, and it would be safer for all. After everything was placed as it had been and the cupboard closed, he walked back to the entrance and receded, but not entirely, from Cristoff's consciousness.

* * * * *

Standing in the foyer of my house, I had no idea how I came to be there. The place was quiet and dark, and there suddenly was a voice that spoke. It seemed to come from every direction at once.

"Cristoff," said the voice.

"Hello, who is there," I said into the darkness.

I lit a lantern as quickly as I could and then searched for the source of the voice. I found no one, but the voice still spoke. It came from inside my head.

"Cristoff, do not be afraid." The voice was soothing. "There is nothing wrong with you. Your memory lapses occur not because of a problem with your mind but because I have interceded into your consciousness to fulfill a purpose. Know that my intercession should not bring you harm, but I will intercede again. It is best that you not know the nature of my intentions. In due time, I will reveal what I can. Now you must go to your mother's side. She is at peace."

I was shaken and unsure if the voice was that of God or the devil, but I immediately went to Mother's room to check on her. Upon entering, I noticed the space to be malodorous. She was lying in bed, and I approached her to attempt to roust her from her sleep. The shaking did nothing, and the coldness of her hand alarmed me. There was no response from her, no breathing, no muscle movement. Her hands and face felt like ice covering a frozen lake. The voice in my head had told me she was at peace. The voice knew that sometime during the day, Mother had died.

24

THE TEARS AND ANGUISH OF loss bubbled up inside of me and shattered my steely veneer with a suddenness for which I was unprepared. I broke down and sobbed at her bedside, memories of her at formative moments of my life rushing past in a blur of emotions. The image of her standing by my bedside, her face filled with concern and sadness, as I thought I was dying from the pox; of her smiling as we celebrated every one of my birthdays; the anger and bitterness she displayed when my sister, Gretel, left the house, never to return; the unrestrained grief she showed at Father's funeral. This woman had such a profound impact on my life that I didn't think I could put the loss of her behind me. Eventually, I would, for the most part.

Dr. Ricard arrived at the house over an hour later, after I had sent Ernestine to fetch him.

"She was laboring to breathe, as she had been doing for the past several days when I left her," said Ernestine in a hoarse voice. "I had to be out by three o'clock to run errands. That is the last…" She could not say more as sobs overtook her. I put my arm around her. Ernestine felt it was her fault Mother passed away alone since she was the last person to see her alive.

"It could not be helped, Ernestine," I consoled her. "She went as peacefully as anyone could. God rest her soul." The knot in my throat prevented me from saying anything more.

"I shall help you prepare the body for burial," said Dr. Ricard. "We must wash her and dress her in the clothes you intend her to be buried and then lay her in the parlor for viewing by her acquaintances tomorrow. In the morn, I will contact the priests of the Town Church to arrange her funeral."

Ernestine and I cleaned and dressed Mother under Dr. Ricard's guidance. Then I bid them both good night. Unable to sleep, I cleaned the bed and burned the bedding upon which she had laid for so long. Although fitful, sleep came eventually.

With the daylight, Ernestine arrived at the door, pressing to help prepare for visitors. I obliged her, and she began to gather some of Mother's favorite items from around the house to display near her during the viewing. I kept busy cleaning after I'd sent a message to my supervisor at the Black Monastery to explain my absence. Then Ernestine came to me with a puzzled look.

"Herr Cristoff," she said. "As I was arranging some of your mother's favorite figurines by her side in the parlor, I found this bottle marked 'laudanum.' I do not know why this would be in a box of figurines." She held a small bottle containing a dark brown liquid toward me. I reached for it…

* * * * *

Mercer quickly pushed into Cristoff's conscious mind. In his haste, he did not have complete control of Cristoff's body before he bumped the hand in which Ernestine held the bottle, causing her to lose her grasp. He watched as the bottle fell toward the stone floor and then shattered into dozens of pieces, spraying the poison in every direction. Ernestine let out a shriek.

"I am so sorry, Herr Cristoff," she said. "I shall clean this for you."

"No, Ernestine!" Mercer said, a bit too forcefully. Ernestine shrank from him. In a calmer voice, he said, "I apologize. I will take care of it. Check to see if there is any of the liquid on you. It might be harmful."

After checking herself, Ernestine went back to her decorating, and Mercer carefully cleaned up the broken pieces of the bottle and the spilled poison. Connor was never going to buy this story. Although Mercer was somewhat relieved that the poison had been destroyed, he expected Connor to adjust his plans. No doubt, those plans would become ever more daring and riskier as Connor would be wholly focused on his goal of killing Luther. Mercer had no way to communicate the problem to Connor before he visited Luther, where he planned to switch the bottles. Connor would be furious when he discovered there was no bottle of poison, which brought a wry smile to Mercer's lips.

Mercer receded from Cristoff's conscious mind, telling Cristoff that he'd had to intercede for a time. Agitation at his episodes of blacking out had lessened since Mercer spoke to him.

A casket was brought in during the morning, and Cristoff helped some men place his mother into it, positioning her body to evoke a sense she was at peace. Cristoff then greeted friends and extended family during the viewing of his mother. A couple of hours into the viewing, Mercer noted Dr. Ricard arriving at the home followed by a short, rotund man in the dark clothing of a monk or priest, his hair brown and tonsured. Cristoff approached the two men as Dr. Ricard said, "Father, this is Cristoff Ritter, son of the deceased."

The priest reached a hand out to Cristoff, who extended his own, and said, "Hello, my son. I am Father Martin Luther."

Mercer was dumbfounded as Cristoff stared into Martin Luther's eyes and shook his hand. He was in awe at meeting such a significant figure in history. Luther was a simple man. There was nothing visually special or appealing about him, yet a feeling of immense admiration overwhelmed Mercer. What an extraordinary and unbelievable experience! He instantly knew that Luther was a genuinely wonderful man, kind, warm, and caring. The enormity of Mercer's role in the history of Charles Darwin and now that of Martin Luther struck him. He knew he needed to do everything possible to prevent Connor from succeeding, whatever the consequences to himself and Cristoff. His focus was the safety of Martin Luther.

Luther said, "I am sorry for the loss of your mother. May God have mercy on her soul."

He made the sign of the cross with his right hand by touching his forehead, breast, left shoulder, then right shoulder.

"Thank you, Father," said Cristoff.

"I plan to perform the funeral ceremony for your mother tomorrow afternoon at the Town Church of St. Mary's. Is this to your satisfaction?" asked Luther politely.

"Yes, that will do just fine. Thank you for being so kind, Father," said Cristoff respectfully. Mercer badly wanted Cristoff to know how this man would impact history, but that was a bad idea.

Luther proceeded reverently to the deceased woman and quietly spoke words in Latin while moving his hand over her body, again in the sign of the cross. Then, he stood next to the casket, bowed his head, and placed one hand on its edge, moving his mouth quietly in prayer. After a few minutes, he lifted his head and walked back toward Cristoff with a slight smile.

Placing a hand on Cristoff's shoulder, he said, "Her soul shall be at peace and her body at rest soon, my son. I will await you at the Town Church in the morrow." With that, Luther and Dr. Ricard left the house.

The funeral came, and Cristoff provided his mother with a medium-class ceremony that would have bankrupted him had his mother not set aside money for her funeral arrangements. All in attendance were dressed in black as Martin Luther eloquently spoke of Cristoff's mother, Agnes, like he had known her for his entire life. Finally, she was laid to rest, and Cristoff returned home. A quiet stillness filled every corner of the home he had shared with her these last few years. He walked the house in a daze, clearly not knowing what he should do next now that she was gone. She had filled his time at home with her need for his care. Now his hands were idle, and he struggled to relax, feeling as though doing so would let her down somehow.

The next day, it was back to work for Cristoff. Due to his mother's death, he had been off the past two days and was eager to work with stone again, which would allow him to keep his mind off his sorrow.

Mercer was keenly aware that Connor could lurk around any corner, wanting to press his next plan into action, so he remained focused and on the lookout for trouble. Two days after the funeral, he was disappointed when he saw Himmler approaching from his right as he walked home from work through the park. Taking control, Mercer directed himself toward a bench under a tree in a more secluded area, feeling Himmler's presence several steps behind as he walked. He sat and was joined in short order by the man.

"Failure is not acceptable!" Connor fumed as spittle flew from the corners of his mouth. "I visited Luther yesterday evening. However, I wasn't expecting an empty cubbyhole where the laudanum should be. What a waste of time. We only have one day to complete this mission, or it *will* be a failure! He hangs his theses on the door tomorrow afternoon."

"How could I help it that Cristoff's mother died? He was kept busy the entire time with preparations for the funeral and receiving condolences from grieving friends of his mother. There was no way to get the bottle to you. What was I supposed to do in that situation?" Mercer shot back.

Ignoring Mercer, Connor said, "Poison is no longer an option. Tomorrow morning you will kill Luther in his cell at the monastery."

"What? That's your plan? Cristoff is not a murderer, and I will not let you make him one. I won't do it."

A knife was suddenly pressing its tip against the side of Cristoff's throat. Connor hissed, "Now isn't this a familiar situation, my ancestor with a knife at your ancestor's throat? So here is your choice, Mercer. Either I kill Cristoff right here and now, or you kill Luther tomorrow before he goes to the Castle Church."

"Either way, it's a death sentence for Cristoff."

"I don't care. It's too late to worry about collateral damage. Luther is going to die tomorrow. When I visited him, I was able to destroy the copy of the theses he made, so after you kill him, you'll need to burn the original to ensure there's no way for someone to resurrect the document. Do you understand?"

"Yes," muttered Mercer.

"Know this, after Luther is dead, your knuckle-dragging ancestor, Cristoff, will die at my hands if you don't take care of this business."

Connor stood and limped away hurriedly, placing his knife into an inner coat pocket. As Mercer continued his journey home, his mind searched for a way out. He came up with nothing.

After arriving at work the following morning, October 31, 1517, Mercer began searching for Martin Luther's cell to inform him about the imminent threat to his life. Not knowing where the room was, he asked one of the monks he encountered, "Pardon me, but could you please direct me to the cell of Father Martin Luther, please?"

"Luther, you say?" said the monk. "Well, you have missed him. He is at the university teaching classes this morning. I believe he plans to be back after midday. He mentioned something about a disputation and the Castle Church that he needed to tend to later this afternoon."

Mercer thanked the monk for his help and scouted the building for somewhere he would be able to see Luther enter. The north entrance was the one most frequented by the monks and was closed to the public, so he expected Luther would use it. He bided his time working some stone cornices in another area of the building until after the noon lunch was over, then placed himself near the entrance of interest with a few tools. Acting like he was performing renovation work on a corner of the structure, he observed all comers and goers through the entryway.

Several dozen people went through the area over the next couple of hours, but none were Martin Luther. As the clock struck three, Mercer worried that Luther may have used a different entrance or might not return to the monastery before making for the Castle Church. So he gathered his tools and hailed the first monk he could find.

"Pardon me, but I am looking for Father Martin Luther. Can you guide me to him?" Mercer asked.

"Luther will likely not return until nightfall," said the monk. "He is just finishing his day at the university and then has business at the Castle Church."

Mercer hoped he wasn't too late as he ran from the monastery toward the university building, two blocks away. The streets were laden with people, carriages, and wagons, all going about the day's business. It was quicker to run in the center of the road to avoid those moving at a slow walk near the buildings. It was also much more dangerous. From behind, he heard a shout as a horse and carriage galloped toward him, barely giving him enough time to step aside. Another carriage quickly approached from the opposite direction, and Mercer whirled around to avoid it like a pirouetting ballet dancer. In less than a minute, he was at the university and hailed a few students as they were leaving the building.

Breathless, Mercer asked, "Has anyone seen Father Martin Luther? Is he here?"

"Professor Luther went to the Castle Church with his assistant and some large rolls of paper," said a blond-haired, blue-eyed young man.

"How long ago?"

"He left maybe five minutes ago."

As Mercer ran toward the Castle Church, he yelled "Thank you!" over his shoulder and proceeded to dodge more carts, wagons, and carriages. It would take him fifteen minutes to reach the church if he walked unimpeded, but running in the street while dodging traffic should get him there in seven. The crowds of people continued to grow as he got closer to the church, and he was forced to slow his pace. Then he glimpsed Luther and another man holding rolls of paper and leading a small group of people twenty paces ahead. They were still several blocks from the church and paused at a street corner as a caravan of wagons passed along the cross street.

Mercer glanced around the crowd, trying to see if Himmler was anywhere near, then looked back toward Luther. In the small group with Luther was a woman wearing a shawl. She turned to look back, and he recognized her face as someone from Cristoff's memory. She was his estranged sister Gretel. For a moment, they locked eyes. She smiled a quick, knowing smile, then continued to scan the crowd as she stood with the group. What was she doing here with Martin Luther? Cristoff hadn't seen her for over a year and had no idea where she'd been. For her to appear at this moment was…improbable.

As he started to move toward Gretel, Mercer spotted Balthazar Himmler on the other side of the street, ready to cross toward Luther. Mercer ran out into the street and narrowly missed being rolled over by a wagon wheel as he grabbed Himmler's arm.

"Do not do this!" Mercer yelled.

Connor looked surprised as he turned to face Mercer. He seized Mercer and pulled him away from the center of the road until they stood in an alcove at the side of a building. His arm came out of his coat as he said, "So you'll make this easy for me, then. Since you're already here, I can take care of you first, something I should have done long ago."

Searing pain shot through Mercer's right leg, and he felt warm blood starting to soak through his pants. Connor pulled the knife out and hid it in his coat, leering at Mercer, who immediately covered the wound with his hand and pressed on it to staunch the flow of blood.

Connor quietly and quickly said, "Before you leave this body, there's something you need to know. Five years ago, Jimmy Evans tried to prevent us from achieving our goals, much as you are. He needed to be eliminated, so I killed your brother on that platform in Rome. I can't wait to do the same to you, Mercer."

Connor gave Mercer a satisfied smirk, turned, and headed across the street toward Martin Luther.

Mercer could feel Cristoff's body becoming numb as a pool of blood collected at his feet. Waves of nausea washed over him, and the feeling of faintness overwhelmed him. He slid down the wall to a sitting position, still holding his hand over the wound, when he heard a scream next to him. A woman saw his blood on the ground and cried out. As his ability to maintain Cristoff's conscious mind faded, more screams and a crunching sound came from the street. Before he passed out, he saw a wagon that had stopped in the middle of the intersection. Near one of its wheels was the hat Himmler had been wearing, upside down, wobbling around like a roly-poly doll. The hat was not empty. Himmler's head was still there, with the lower part of his face visible, although much of his chin was gone.

25

THE MAN WITH THE LIMP who had pulled Cristoff away a few moments ago was coming back across the busy street toward them. In the body of Gretel Ritter, Lizzy quickly scanned the crowd for Cristoff, but he was nowhere to be seen. The man's eyes were locked on Martin Luther as he pulled a bloody knife from inside his coat.

A woman pointed and yelled, "He has a knife!"

Heads all around them turned to look in the direction she pointed. He'd almost reached Martin Luther when Lizzy ran toward him, lowered her shoulder, and knocked him in the side. Having been so focused on his target, the man did not see her coming. He lost his balance and toppled into the street. The driver of a passing wagon stopped his horses abruptly when he saw the man fall, but it was too late as a narrow wheel rolled onto the man's neck, severing his head from his body.

A crowd quickly gathered around the scene. Martin Luther was ashen but went to the dead man and, bending over him, imparted last rites.

After verifying that the threat had passed, Lizzy searched the area for Cristoff but didn't see his face in the crowd. Then she retraced the dead man's steps toward where she'd last seen Cristoff. As she approached the other side of the street, a group was gathered along the side of a building. She pushed some aside as she tried to get to the focus of their attention. There sat Cristoff, eyes closed, leaning against the wall of a building with bright blood staining his right thigh and the ground beneath it.

"Can someone call for a doctor, please? Is there a healer close? This man will die without immediate medical attention," she said as she knelt and applied pressure to the bleeding wound. He'd lost a lot of blood.

"Cristoff. Cristoff! Speak to me!" she yelled. There was no response.

After a minute that seemed like an hour, a portly well-dressed man with a round red face and silver-white hair came loping up to her, out of breath, and said, "I am a surgeon from the university. I might be able to help this man. We need to get him to the infirmary at the monastery immediately. Young lady, please continue doing as you are and put pressure on the wound as we transport him. Do not stop applying the pressure until I tell you."

Several men lifted Cristoff and placed him in a wagon as Lizzy continued to hold the wound. Minutes later, the bumpy ride ended at the Black Monastery, and some of the monks came out to rush Cristoff to the infirmary. As the doctor left the wagon with Cristoff, Lizzy stopped him and said, "Doctor, his name is Cristoff Ritter. I am his sister, Gretel. May I attend the surgery and remain with him here during his recovery?"

The doctor froze, dumbfounded, and said, "Young lady, the last thing we need now is a woman swooning in the midst of a delicate procedure."

"Then can I stay with him after you are finished?" she pressed.

The doctor thought for a moment and then reluctantly said, "You may wait here until someone comes out to inform you at the conclusion of the surgery. Now I must go. Your brother's injuries need immediate attention."

Lizzy sat on a nearby park bench, her mind reviewing the events of the previous twelve minutes. Everything happened so fast. She barely had time to react when she saw the man with the knife coming toward Martin Luther. Another couple of seconds, and he would've plunged the knife deep into Luther's body. She hadn't intended to push the man hard enough for him to fall in front of the wagon, but she'd surprised him, and his balance must have been poor, to begin with, given that his limp was pronounced. He…just…tumbled into the path of the wheel. All she could do after was to search for the face she'd seen in the crowd, as recognized by Gretel. Cristoff was there, which meant Mercer probably was, too.

Gretel's body was exhausted after traveling from Dresden over the last seven days, barely making it in time to get to Luther before the attempt on his life. At the beginning of her journey, the poor weather added days of delay that Aniyah hadn't accounted for when she timed Lizzy's transfer to Gretel. Aniyah had worked with Lizzy on honing her Leaf Runner abilities. She planned to transfer to Gretel after a good night's sleep at the new headquarters for the Leaf Runners.

Aniyah was very helpful, but she was also direct. The dangerous mission Lizzy was about to embark on, the lack of modern conveniences during the early sixteenth century, and the diminished standing of women would be challenging for her to deal with, Aniyah had said. She preferred having more time to prepare Lizzy, but Mercer was in danger, and they had to work fast. Although Lizzy had always been a quick study, the combined physical and mental fatigue made the situation challenging. Aniyah was right; this was harder than anything she had ever done before.

She waited in the area near the entrance to the monastery for hours, and it was well after dark when the surgeon finally appeared at the doorway with a worn look. She ran to him and asked, "How is Cristoff? Will he live?"

"He is resting now," said the surgeon. "I shall not know whether he will live until tomorrow. He lost a great deal of blood. I have given him water and liniments to prevent festering. It will be a good sign if he makes it through the night. He is strong, which will improve his likelihood of survival."

"Can I stay with him tonight?"

The chubby man grimaced, highlighting the skinfolds on his forehead and chin and making his face look like a ripe European cantaloupe. "Although highly unusual, in this situation, the monks have agreed for you to remain on the premises, although with restrictions, throughout the night," said the surgeon.

She thanked him and followed a waiting monk into the monastery, where few women were allowed to go. As the two walked through the stone-walled hallways, their shadows in the flickering torchlight reminded Lizzy of those projected on distant trees by campers sitting around a fire pit. The last time she went camping was in Maine with her father and Mercer half a decade ago. Why this particular thought occurred to her now, she didn't know.

At the end of the long hall was a door that opened into a room lit by a dozen torches placed in sconces on the walls. A half dozen beds, only two of which were occupied, were spaced evenly along the longer walls of the room. Cristoff was lying on a bed at the far end of one wall, unmoving, with a nearly imperceptible rising and lowering of his chest as he breathed. Lizzy went to him and surveyed his condition. His face and hands showed a deathlike pallor. He'd lost much blood, indeed. An earthen jar filled with water stood on a small table near the head of the bed, and a small three-legged stool had been brought for Lizzy to sit on. It would be uncomfortable, but luxury was not a thing to be found in a monastery.

The monk told her she was welcome to lay on the middle cot if she became tired and needed sleep and that a monk would always be present in the room and must always accompany her. Lack of privacy was a small price to pay for being allowed to stay with Mercer. The nearness of death faced by Cristoff made it possible Mercer would be unable to remain. She hoped he was still present and hadn't been forced to return to his own body. Unfortunately, she could not be sure where he was until Cristoff either passed on or awoke, so she would not leave until one of those two things happened.

Humming a bedtime song sung to her by her father and Jimmy when she was a small girl, Lizzy sat on the stool and watched Cristoff as the hours passed. Nearly falling at one point, she thought it best to lie down and sleep rather than hurt herself by falling off the stool. Cristoff's condition hadn't changed since she arrived, so a little sleep wouldn't cause her to miss anything important.

Sleep came quickly, and so did dreams. While occupying another person's body, dreams took on a new dimension. Because the conscious mind is vacant during sleep, Lizzy's dreams were jumbled together with Gretel's. Images from her life and childhood were intermingled with images of a stone house at the edge of a meadow near a small barnyard containing a cow and two pigs. A girl and a boy ran through the field as the wildflowers of springtime filled the panorama surrounding them. They laughed and played as they twirled themselves around, reminding Lizzy of an old movie she used to watch around Christmas time.

A light tug on her arm jolted her out of the dream, and she quickly filled the conscious void before Gretel could do so. Her eyes opened to see a monk staring down at her. The place was strange, at first, until she began to recall where she was and why. She sat upright and looked toward Cristoff's bed. The absence of movement the night before was gone, replaced by a man writhing in the pain of a potentially mortal wound and the aftermath of the work of an early sixteenth-century surgeon. Cristoff was very uncomfortable, and a monk was trying to get him to swallow some dark brown liquid from a small vial. Cristoff's eyes were still closed, and he was mumbling something incomprehensible. She left the cot she had slept in and went to his side, noticing more light in the room. The sun was up, and morning had arrived, but she had no idea what time it was. Gretel's exhausted body slept soundly throughout the night and well into the morning.

Cristoff was trying to speak, so she bent down to him to listen. "Gr…greh…g…," he stammered.

"Cristoff, it's me, Gretel. I'm here, Cristoff. You're going to be okay," she said quietly in his ear. She looked at him, and his eyelids fluttered open. It took several seconds for his eyes to focus on her, then he tried to sit up, and his eyes slammed shut as he grimaced in pain and laid back down. When the pain finally subsided, he opened his eyes again and focused on her.

"Gretel, why are you here?" he asked. "I… I saw you in the street. You were there… Why?"

"Cristoff, I came to help," she said. "I knew you needed me, so I came. How do you feel?"

He licked his lips a few times, and she gently poured some water from the jar onto them. He indicated he wanted to drink, and she held the jar so he could sip from it. Then he said, "The pain is terrible. It feels worse than when the knife was there. It hurts so bad." He closed his eyes for a few seconds to recover and said, "Gretel, how did you know I needed you?"

"I've learned that brothers need sisters as much as sisters need brothers," she said. Then she bent down to him and whispered so only he could hear, "Help is on the way, Mercer."

Cristoff's eyes grew as wide as dinner plates. "Mer…but how did…"

"Shhhh," she hushed him, trying to calm him. Then she whispered, "Mercer, it's me, Lizzy. I'm a Leaf Runner like you. I came to help you stop the murder of Martin Luther. Aniyah taught me what I needed to know to be able to come and help. So I traveled for the past week from Dresden to get here."

She backed away and smiled as he looked up at her, tears filling his eyes. His lips and mouth moved, but he could produce no words; the emotions were too strong. Finally, he mustered enough control to say, "Thank you, I love you."

The tears she was holding back rolled down her cheeks, and she couldn't suppress a couple of sobs. However, she quickly regained composure and said, "I wasn't sure if you'd still be here. I was worried you'd be gone when Cristoff woke up." She resumed a normal speaking voice. "I must tell you that Luther is well and completed his undertaking yesterday. The man who tried to kill him was killed as a wagon ran him over in the street."

Mercer looked relieved and relaxed as much as the pain would allow. The color of his skin was changing from pasty white to rosy. The monks brought him some bread to eat, which he did tentatively at first. Then he told her of the recent passing of their mother and her funeral, which was presided over by Martin Luther.

Speaking to the monk nearby, Mercer said, "My sister and I have much to discuss, and we would like some privacy, please."

Obligingly, the monk went to the other side of the room to tend the other patient and was well out of earshot. Mercer said quietly, "I think we should return after allowing Cristoff and Gretel to fill the void. They need to be made aware of their situation. Then, maybe they can reconcile their differences. But we first need to speak." He paused, double-checking to make sure they could not be overheard. "I am being held prisoner in the mansion of Professor Lazarro Giannelli and forced to use my abilities to assist him in changing history. Lizzy, these are dangerous people who need to be stopped."

"I know," said Lizzy. "We weren't sure where you're being held, but Ned Lamb is one of them."

"What? Ned Lamb? But he's a...," said Mercer with a mystified expression.

"He's actually a double agent. He infiltrated God's Left Hand and is working with the Leaf Runners to help bring them down. He was the one who told me the target was Martin Luther before I was traded for you. He also told me he would protect you. But I don't know where he is right now. Nigel and Aniyah are preparing to rescue you once we know your location."

"Wow, there's so much to wrap my head around. I can't believe that you...and Ned...and Connor," he trailed off.

"Wait, Connor?" she said, her eyes drilling into Mercer. "What do you mean, Connor?"

"Well, I'm sorry to have to be the one to tell you this, sis, but Connor is not a good guy. He's part of God's Left Hand. He has been all along." Mercer winced in pain as he tried to get to a sitting position, so Lizzy helped him get comfortable as he continued, "He was Lutomir, the guy who ruthlessly tortured John Freeman in Korea, eventually having him killed. During my first real mission as a Leaf Runner, he was Marine Clay Middleton of the Royal Marines. He almost killed Charles Darwin on the HMS *Beagle*."

As Mercer spoke, Lizzy went pale. She said, "I had no idea..."

"Connor used you to get to me. He probably doesn't know you're a Leaf Runner. Hell, I didn't even know! Anyway, he's with me at Giannelli's, and I think he plans to kill me as soon as he can get to me. Lizzy, when I get back, all hell is going to break loose. I'll need all of the help the Leaf Runners can give me."

"I'll tell Aniyah everything you told me as soon as I get back." She paused, trying to think of something more to say, but there was nothing. "So I guess we'd better go," she said, fumbling for words. She bit her lip, trying not to let her emotions overcome her. If they didn't reach him in time, she would never be able to speak to Mercer again.

"Lizzy, just do what Aniyah and Nigel tell you to and help them as best you can. We'll find a way out of this." Now it was Mercer's turn to get choked up. "You… I want you to know I love you, and I'm sorry I don't ever tell you… You're amazing, and I'm proud to be your brother."

After a pause, Mercer chuckled and said, "Look what you did. I was here for two weeks and still couldn't stop Balthazar Himmler. Without you, Martin Luther would've been killed."

"Balthazar Himmler? Was that the man I pushed into the wagon?" she said.

"Yes, he stabbed me and almost got to Luther. He was also an ancestor to none other than Heinrich Himmler."

"That figures," said Lizzy.

"He was under Connor's control until that wagon decapitated him, but you haven't heard the worst part yet."

"The worst part. You mean the part about Connor being a murderer isn't the worst part?" she said apprehensively.

"Lizzy, Connor told me he killed our brother, Jimmy."

26

THE REUNION OF CRISTOFF AND Gretel got off to a rocky start. Both were disoriented and confused about where they were and how they got there. As they spoke, Mercer gently pushed vital bits of information into Cristoff's consciousness that helped him piece together the current situation. Mercer thought Lizzy did the same for Gretel because they eventually talked cordially about their mother and their lives since Gretel had left. Mercer felt relieved as the siblings converged on similar emotional places of forgiveness and a willingness to move on. It was time to go.

He dove for the bottom of the pool and found Cristoff's leaf. Nothing had changed; Gisela was still the connection between his family and Cristoff. But he did notice a change on Gretel's leaf. The date of her death changed from 1531 to 1575. Gretel lived a much longer life and started six new branches on the tree, one for each of her children. Mercer and Lizzy's involvement had changed the course of Gretel's life.

After reaching his name on the trunk and rising to the pool's surface, he was aware of another presence. It wasn't a physical presence, but it was comforting and welcoming and had other characteristics with which he was familiar. He felt a bond like that between siblings, but how was it that Lizzy felt so close to him?

He opened his eyes to the same dim room as before he journeyed to Cristoff's body. The drab brown ceiling with its little black dots was still above him. He lifted his head and searched the room, not seeing anyone but knowing that Mason was probably watching him from the viewing room on the other side of the one-way glass.

Mercer leaned forward to get out of the chair as the lights went out and the room plunged into darkness. All sounds ceased, including the quiet hum of the ventilation fan he hadn't noticed until it stopped. A long beep sounded as emergency lights lit the room seconds later. After a pause, the beep repeated.

Mason burst into the room, bellowing, "Someone's cut the power to the building. We need to leave now."

Mercer didn't hesitate, hopping out of the chair and dashing over to Mason, who led the way out of the room and into the hallway, partially lit by emergency lighting. With Mercer a few steps behind, Mason continued forward until he reached the large main living room, where he stopped in front of a crumpled figure lying on the floor. He bent down and turned over the body of Troy, the side of whose head had been smashed in by something, a gruesome sight even in the low light. Mason felt for a pulse, shook his head, then opened Troy's jacket to examine the gun holster strapped to his side.

Mason said, "Someone took his gun."

Mason's gaze swept the room as the beeps continued sounding from different locations at different times. He jerked as Mercer heard two loud popping noises, then fell forward face-first onto the floor, not attempting to catch himself. A pool of blood quickly covered the floor around Mason's head, so Mercer ran back down the hallway of doors, trying each as he went hoping to find one unlocked. He knew that if he were forced into the room he had been in at the end of the hall, there was no way out.

At last, a door opened, and he dove inside to another loud pop as splinters of wood showered him. He pushed the door to close it, but the damaged door was jammed. Mercer was on stairs heading downward. There were lights, but he could only see a short distance like he was inside a cave with only a match for light. He was pressing forward through the dark passageways of the lower level and away from the stairs when a crash came from the door at the top of the stairs.

"Mercer, I know you're down there. There's no way out," said Connor eerily as he descended the stairs. Mercer kept moving and feeling his way along, hoping he wouldn't run into something or make a noise that would expose his position to Connor. After zigzagging through the hallway, he found himself in a long straight corridor with only one dim emergency light and a large metal door at the far end. Backtracking would be suicide, so he ran for the door and tried to open it. Although the handle turned easily, the door didn't budge. He pushed to no avail, then prepared to kick it. As he wound up and started moving his leg forward, the sight of a sliding latch at the bottom of the door brought his leg to a halt before his foot connected. He caught his balance and reached down to release the latch. It moved effortlessly out of the floor, so he checked the door for other latches and found one at the top. After releasing the top latch, the door opened into a garage with a concrete floor lit naturally by windows along the top of the garage door panels. As he closed the door, it was wrenched from his hand by a bullet that struck it and ricocheted past Mercer's left shoulder, barely missing him.

He slammed the door shut and dashed into the garage. A quick scan revealed several expensive sports cars parked there, with at least one red Ferrari and a yellow Lamborghini. Why God's Left Hand needed sports cars was lost on Mercer. Along a wall to his left was a short run of stairs leading up to another door, which he raced toward as fast as he could, climbed the stairs, and opened the door. A bullet found its mark as Mercer was knocked forward into a mudroom entry area on the main floor of the house and fell onto his stomach, crying out. His left shoulder blazed from the wound as he rolled onto his back and closed the door by kicking it with his feet. He crawled over and reached up to the lock and deadbolt with his right hand, turning them both to secure the door.

Mercer sat upright and touched the area around his left shoulder. With the light that came into the mudroom through the kitchen window, he could see dark blood coming from the wound, but the small amount eased Mercer's concern about the extent of the damage. He was trying to catch his breath when the knob clicked as it was being turned from the other side. Connor pounded on the door and yelled as Mercer rose to his feet and moved away from it. The searing pain in his shoulder was letting up only slightly, and he didn't dare try to use his arm. A bullet pierced the mudroom door as Mercer sprinted toward the main living room. Then another shot, and another. The pounding on the door continued, so Mercer moved quickly through the house toward the front entryway. As he approached it in the dim light, a shadow loomed in front of him. The way was blocked by a figure holding a long-barreled shotgun pointed at Mercer's chest.

"Evans, I told you, you would die if you interfered," hissed Giannelli. "Connor was right about you. It was a mistake to include you. I thought things would be more difficult without you and your ancestors, but he was right. We would have been successful without you. I cannot allow you to interfere again."

"I didn't interfere or sabotage anything," said Mercer, technically not lying but mostly stalling for time.

"Now, now," said Giannelli. "Do you really expect me to believe that? How is it that the mission failed, then?"

"Well, Connor fell in the path of a wagon and was killed as he went after Luther with a knife."

"Stabbing Luther was not the plan. He must have needed to improvise because of your interference."

"The vial of poison I was given to place in the monastery was accidentally destroyed," said Mercer.

"Incompetence, interference, it doesn't matter. You are no longer needed. I doubt, given your heritage, that you could help with our next mission, anyway."

"Next mission?"

"Yes, Evans, the next mission," Giannelli said. Then his face twisted grotesquely with a look of abject hate and he said, "Imagine, if you would, a world without Islam, a world without the centuries of death and destruction carried out in its name. The problem can easily be remedied by removing one man, the Prophet Muhammad of Mecca."

Arrogance oozed from him as he spoke, "I tell you this because I want you to know what is coming, what will happen to the world after you leave it. We serve God as we continue our quest to…adjust the world. Your death is simply another of these adjustments. I would wish you farewell, but it would be a lie. So instead, rot in hell, Evans!"

Mercer dove to his right behind a couch as the shotgun thundered through the house. A large hole appeared in the back of the sofa just behind where he lay, the slug missing his foot by an inch and knocking over a large vase as it tore up the floor in front of it.

His shoulder burned as he scooted away from Giannelli behind the couch and other furniture. Mercer moved as fast as possible while Gianelli reloaded his shotgun, the beeping tones of the emergency lights creating a dissonance with the ringing in his ears from the blast of the gun. He turned to see Giannelli appear behind the couch with the gun raised and aimed at Mercer's chest.

Suddenly light streamed into the entryway from the front door and exposed specks of dust that casually floated on invisible waves of air. Another loud boom startled Mercer. The beams of light reflected off Giannelli as his body shook from the blast, but Mercer didn't see a flash come from his shotgun. Mercer was paralyzed as he watched Giannelli lower the shotgun barrel toward the floor like he was too weak to hold it. The blank mask of death appeared on Giannelli's face as he swayed for a moment, then his lifeless body fell forward and crashed at Mercer's feet.

Mercer scrambled to stand as shadows moved in the light coming through the open front door. Ready to dive behind another piece of furniture, Mercer froze as he recognized the man who had entered holding a pistol.

"Ned?" he said.

"Mercer, you all right?" said Ned. He walked over to Mercer while giving him the once-over and said, "You're bleeding. We need to get you to a hospital."

"Jesus, Ned! What took you so long?" Mercer said with a thin smile on his face.

Ned laughed. During his life, Mercer had never been so happy to see someone. He also never would have guessed Ned would be that person. "God, Ned, it's good to see you! Giannelli was just about to—"

"It's okay, Mercer. I told Lizzy that I would take care of you. Things will be fine. More help should be here soon," Ned said.

"Lizzy," muttered Mercer to himself as he still felt her presence.

"She's pretty amazing, Mercer," said Ned. "I really put her through hell, and I feel horrible about it. But even after her traumatic experience, she gave my message to Nigel. When I apologized to her, she was very gracious. I don't think I would've been."

Mercer nodded knowingly and said, "Yes, she is amazing. And thanks for saving my life, Ned. You are a surprising man. I had no idea…"

"That's okay, Mercer. I'm sure I'll find a way for you to repay me at work," said Ned with a wink and a smile.

"Great. I'm looking forward—" Mercer started to say.

A shadow came from the direction of the entryway behind Ned, who noticed the movement and stepped to his left, placing himself between Mercer and the doorway. As Ned looked over his shoulder to see who it was, two gunshots rang out. Ned turned back toward Mercer with surprise as his hand went up to his chest.

"Oh no," gasped Ned. Bright blood had already engulfed his hand, and his face turned ashen. "I'm sorry, Mercer. I promised…" He stumbled as Mercer grabbed him.

Connor was standing near the door and pointing his gun at Mercer. "I never did trust him. I should've known he was the rat we've been looking for. Well, our rodent problem has been solved."

Ned's weight was too much for Mercer, so he lowered himself and Ned's lifeless frame to the floor and sat there, waiting for the fatal shot from Connor.

"Lizzy's next," said Connor as he pulled the trigger with a smirk.

Mercer blinked when he heard the click, but there was no loud pop. The gun was empty. Connor's look of surprise imprinted on Mercer's mind, and time stood still as they stared at each other. Mercer finally looked down and noticed the butt of Ned's pistol sticking out from under his left shoulder, so he grabbed it and brought it to bear on Connor. Seeing Mercer's movement and the gun coming up, Connor ran as Mercer fired. He'd moved enough for the projectile to miss him and bury itself into the wall harmlessly. Connor ran out the front door.

Mercer wasn't sure if he'd hit Connor. He knew there was nothing he could do to help Ned. Ned was already dead. Shaken, Mercer took a few seconds to regain his composure. Instead of chasing after Connor, Mercer stood and approached the door slowly, uncertain whether Connor had obtained another weapon. He exited the front of the house, looked in all directions, and gave himself protective cover using the building's architecture and landscape plantings as he moved. Not sure which way Connor had gone after exiting the house and seeing no movement, Mercer walked around the house toward the driveway.

The well-manicured grounds showed no signs of recent foot traffic. Mercer followed an inlaid stone path to the asphalt driveway and looked toward the driveway entrance at the road. But there was still no sound or movement of any kind. Even the street seemed to be holding its breath, waiting for something to happen.

Mercer turned and cautiously walked down the driveway toward the garage, which was not visible because it was tucked behind the house. As the garage came into view, he saw a slight movement inside. One of the bay doors, which were both closed when he passed through the garage earlier, was now open, and he was sure something had moved inside as he came near. He raised the gun and froze, watching to see if he could sense more movement. Then, in the distance, a siren blared.

Heart racing, Mercer approached the garage door and scanned the array of supercars, looking for anything out of place. He stepped across the garage door's threshold as a shadow moved on his left. Because of adrenaline and reflexes, the pistol fired before he could take proper aim at the figure rushing toward him. Connor's momentum plowed into Mercer full force, knocking them to the concrete floor. The gun dislodged from Mercer's hand and skidded across the floor as he hit the ground, disappearing underneath the Lamborghini.

Mercer had fallen onto his injured shoulder, and the searing pain overwhelmed all other senses. He lay staring up at the ceiling, trying to fight for control. Connor didn't move and was lying face-down on the garage floor. Unsure if he'd struck Connor, Mercer pulled himself up to a sitting position. Then Connor, who had a large gash on his skull, groaned and moved his arms slightly. He was coming to, and Mercer had to move quickly.

Bracing his body using his good arm, Mercer stood. He staggered from the garage and gradually picked up speed as his balance returned. Soon he was running down a path in the back of the house toward a small breakwater that extended a dozen yards into the ocean. Beside the breakwater stood a matrix of crumbling pilings from an old dock. Mercer surveyed the area for some way to escape the fenced yard. He spotted a canal large enough for a boat to pass through, but a retaining wall and some foliage obscured its source. Following a path around the retaining wall, he discovered a dock with a large boathouse that extended out into a lagoon.

From a distance, he heard Connor yell, "Evans! Where are you, Evans!"

Mercer entered the unlocked boathouse and found a long black-and-red cigar boat resting on a boat lift. The boat had five engines mounted to its stern, and keys were in the ignition. He lowered the craft into the water with the electric lift control, climbed in, and started the engines. Then he throttled them up, launching the vessel out into the lagoon. Immediately there was a terrible grinding sound, and the boat shook. He quickly brought the engines back to idle because the props had dug into the shallow canal when the boat reared. Mercer guided the boat slowly through the channel to prevent further damage to the props.

As the bow reached the end of the retaining wall where Mercer had first seen the boathouse, Connor suddenly appeared and leaped toward the boat. Mercer gunned the throttle. The motorboat reared up, and the props dug into the canal's silty soil. As the vessel lurched forward, mud and water spewed into the air like a fountain. Connor's torso landed inside the cockpit next to Mercer as his legs dangled precariously alongside the hull.

Mercer could barely control the craft as it careened toward the rocky breakwater. Then, just as the boat looked like it would dash itself against the rocks, he jerked the wheel to the right, but not before one of Connor's legs was crushed between the boat and a rocky outcropping. The impact veered the boat toward open water and catapulted Connor's lower half through the air and into the cockpit.

Connor screamed as he landed, his left leg bloody and twisted, and his face ashen. His eyes were dazed, and his mouth was open as Mercer glanced at him. Mercer became focused on controlling the boat, steering so he could avoid the rocks, and didn't see the fist coming at the side of his head. The punch nearly knocked Mercer out of the boat, only his tight grip on the steering wheel preventing him from going overboard. However, the wheel's sudden movement veered the vessel sharply, wrenching the wheel from Mercer's hands. Both men were tossed around in the cockpit.

With no one at the helm, the boat straightened itself at full throttle and headed for the open ocean within a few seconds. Mercer and Connor traded multiple punches as the craft gained speed. Connor was strong but passed out when Mercer fell on his mangled leg. He rolled Connor to the back of the cockpit and regained control of the boat.

A black helicopter buzzed past them as Mercer tried to get his bearings and find somewhere to dock the boat. The aircraft returned, sliding sideways and matching his speed, and a familiar figure waved at him from the open doorway. Aniyah wore tactical gear and pointed him toward the entrance to a bay a mile or so up the shore. He raised his hand and waved, turning the boat toward the bay.

Once again, Mercer didn't see the arm sweep his feet out from underneath him. The next thing he knew, he was lying on his back.

Connor delivered a barrage of blows to his neck and face. The driverless boat took a new heading back toward the open ocean. The vessel had picked up considerable speed and slammed against the choppy water with significant force. Connor lost his balance on the unstable platform and fell away from Mercer, which gave Mercer a brief moment to collect himself and face Connor.

The two fought while hurtling in an out-of-control cigar boat over choppy ocean waves at more than sixty knots. Mercer attempted to inflict more damage on Connors's leg, but Connor quickly adapted to this tactic. Connor pulled Mercer off balance and pinned him between two revving outboard motors at the stern. Mercer's hands and legs were trapped, and his arm was bent such that his wounded shoulder burned in agony. He cried out in pain and couldn't move.

"You're a tough person to kill, Evans," said Connor, who somehow sneered through his puffy lips and cheeks. "Harder than other members of your family. But I've had enough of you."

Connor took one of the anchor ropes and looped it around Mercer's neck and shoulder. If Connor threw him from the boat at this speed, Mercer would get dragged by his neck and be hanged. Mercer was out of options. As Connor started to push Mercer off the rear of the boat, Mercer looked up to the sky where the black helicopter stood out starkly against the deep blue autumn sky. Aniyah stood in the aircraft's open door and kicked her right leg out. Mercer couldn't comprehend this gesture and felt his body sliding slowly off the stern.

But another presence had his attention. This presence conveyed a jumble of thoughts, words, and images. To anyone other than Mercer, these would seem random. But Mercer knew they meant Connor had looped the secondary anchor line around himself while working on Mercer. If Mercer wrapped his right leg around Connor's mangled left leg to inflict severe pain, Mercer could twist out from underneath him and use the momentum to flip Connor over the back of the boat. A golden face surrounded by long windblown dark hair appeared through the helicopter doorway over Aniyah's shoulder. Lizzy!

She was right. While basking in his triumph, Connor had forgotten to defend his damaged leg. Mercer's head was nearing the spray of the prop wash, and he would be dead in seconds. Summoning his courage and strength for one last attempt to free himself, he wrapped his right leg around Connor's left and felt the bones crunching as he tightened. Connor reared up and bent to reach for the cause of his anguish. This gave Mercer enough freedom to twist to his right and slide out from underneath Connor. Bracing against one of the outboard engine cowlings, he used both legs to flip Connor's lower half through the air. Connor tumbled backward over the outboard engines and into the water. A rope suddenly became taught, and one of the engines bogged down as if under a significant load.

Mercer freed himself from the rope looped around his neck and turned to see one of the engines bobbing up and down and smoking, bucking for all it was worth against something lodged in its prop. Mercer hit the kill switch, and the engines immediately slowed and quieted as the boat came off its plane and started to drift. There was no sign of Connor other than a bloody trail of chum which followed the boat for about thirty yards.

— **27** —

THE EIGHT-AND-A-HALF-HOUR FLIGHT TO ROME seemed like an eternity. All her life, Lizzy couldn't sleep on car or plane rides. A three-hundred-pound man sat beside her and snored for about six of those hours while Mercer slept angelically on her other side after finishing his in-flight movie. As the plane arrived at the gate, she wondered why she hadn't woken Mercer and made him switch seats with her, but it was too late now. Aniyah, seated in business class, was waiting for them as they entered the terminal from the gangway.

As they began the walk to baggage claim, Mercer exclaimed, "I can't wait to get out there and tour this place!"

"I know some places you guys will love to check out," Aniyah chirped.

"Are you kidding? I'm exhausted. You slept like a baby, Mercer. And I'm sure you did too, Ms. Business Class. I didn't sleep a wink," said Lizzy.

Mercer and Aniyah gave each other a cautious glance.

"You can't crash yet. The quickest way to get over jet lag is to stay awake until you'd normally go to bed," stated Mercer.

"Then can we at least have something to eat before walking around?" she pleaded. "The meal on the airplane was dry and tasteless. I want some good Italian food."

"You're speaking my language, sis," said Mercer.

"I also know some great spots to eat that aren't far from our hotel," Aniyah offered thoughtfully.

The purpose of this trip was to transport Jimmy's remains back to the United States. The bureaucratic red tape Lizzy and Mercer waded through to get to this point had been daunting. Although the DNA matches were indisputable—results from Lizzy's and Mercer's tests verified that the remains in question were their brother—getting Jimmy home would be tricky. As they understood, cremation was the best way to simplify and stream-line the paperwork and transportation logistics. Because Jimmy had never been positively identified by the Italian authorities, their first task was to get a proper death certificate. Lizzy didn't look forward to the process, but she knew it was well worth the time and effort to bring Jimmy back home, where they could give him the memorial he deserved.

They retrieved their luggage, hopped into a cramped taxi, and braved the white-knuckle ride to their hotel. Within a fifteen-min-ute walk of the Vatican, Lizzy and Mercer shared a two-bedroom suite that overlooked the River Tiber and had a beautiful view of Castel Sant'Angelo, which sprawled along the other side of the river. Aniyah's room was a few doors down the hallway from theirs. There were plenty of places to eat in the historic Ponte neighborhood, and Aniyah guided them to a lovely little bistro with comfortable outdoor seating.

They discussed their plans for the next day while savoring a delicious meal.

"What time are we supposed to meet…oh, what's-his-name at the Vatican?" yawned Lizzy. The fatigue had caught up to her.

"His name is Dino Bianchi. Well, I didn't know how long it would take to get everything done at the police station tomorrow, so I requested the latest appointment possible, four o'clock," said Mercer.

"And who's Dino Bianchi again?"

Aniyah answered, "The Leaf Runners didn't know Jimmy was here when he disappeared. Nigel didn't know until Mercer told him what Connor said. Once he knew where to look, Nigel tracked down Dino, who was actually born and raised in New York, where he befriended Jimmy. Shortly after, Dino moved to Rome to work on his doctoral dissertation. Besides the local police, he's our best hope of learning about the circumstances surrounding Jimmy's death."

Blankly, Lizzy said, "Uh-huh."

"I'm sorry, Lizzy," said Mercer. "I know you're dead tired, but you need to push through for another hour or so before crashing."

She frowned and said, "Sure."

Mercer chuckled. "I also know that I'm annoying the hell out of you."

When Lizzy discovered she was a Leaf Runner, she also found a sixth sense. She and Mercer had a connection. They could communicate at a rudimentary level and, at times, could sense what the other was thinking, which was cool but could also be a pain in the ass. At the moment, he was amused by her annoyance.

"The fact that you're finding me funny is not helping, Mercer."

"I know, I know, and I'm sorry Lizzy," Mercer said ashamedly.

They quietly finished their meals and a nice bottle of Chianti, then walked back to their hotel. Lizzy was so exhausted she could barely climb the stairs to the suite and was asleep before her head hit the pillow.

* * * * *

A knock at the door woke Mercer from a sound sleep, and he rolled over in bed. Beams of sunlight sliced through the sheer curtains in the hotel room and splashed across his face. The brightness of the day surprised him until he glanced at his watch and saw the time was half past eight. They needed to be at the police station by nine thirty for their appointment. He ran to the main door wearing only his boxers and opened it without thinking. Standing before him was the closest thing to an angel that Mercer could imagine, and he stared, frozen in place. Aniyah's startled look quickly turned into embarrassment, and she gracefully turned her face away from him. Mercer finally realized he was standing in front of her, nearly naked, and fumbled for words.

"Um…ahh…shit. We're going to be late if we don't get moving. Can you wake Lizzy?" he said as he turned and nearly sprinted back to his bedroom.

The two months since Ned's death had been a whirlwind of activity, what with his funeral, tracking down information about Jimmy's death, and planning the trip to Rome. Mercer still worked for Highbridge doing his "day job," as he thought of it. He hadn't visited his ancestral tree since, and he had barely spent time with the Leaf Runners, including Aniyah. He'd been anticipating this journey for many reasons, not the least because Aniyah was with them.

He hurriedly dressed and exited his bedroom, finding Aniyah sitting on a sofa waiting patiently. Uneasily, they made small talk until Lizzy appeared, refreshed and renewed from a whole night of peaceful sleep. The trio grabbed some coffee and cornetti before making the seven-minute walk across the river and around the castle to the police station.

Bounced between departments as different aspects of paperwork and proof of identification were required, they didn't meet with the investigator until after two o'clock. Inspector Isabella Fiore addressed them as Lizzy and Aniyah sat in the uncomfortable chairs in front of her desk while Mercer stood behind them.

"Your brother was found by a man whose dog had gotten away from him while on a walk. He followed his pet into the woods, where the animal had discovered the remains. Jimmy had no identification or papers, no jewelry, and—I'm sorry to have to say this but—his body was badly decomposed. Our medical examiner determined that his fingerprints had been removed, leaving only DNA to identify him. Unfortunately, his DNA did not match anything in our databases, and Interpol searches turned up empty. So everything was moved to our cold case files. The only item of interest found with him was this smudged rubbing of a pendant or broach. He had placed the paper inside a plastic bag and swallowed it."

She handed them an evidence bag containing a piece of paper with an image from a partial pencil rubbing. Assuming the whole picture was round, only about a quarter of the image was visible, as water or something smudged the remaining paper, making it indecipherable.

"The words you see around the edge are Latin, '…um est in me ipso,'" she said. "It says, 'something is within me.' We do not know the 'something' because everything before is missing."

Investigator Fiore gave them a copy of the piece of paper, and they bid her farewell. All three were famished, but lunchtime had passed, and dinner was still hours away. They bought sandwiches from a food vendor and ate on the walk to the Vatican, where they were to meet with Dino Bianchi.

Ned had been on Mercer's mind throughout the day as they waited and walked. He'd saved Mercer's life, and this fact clung to Mercer like velcro. The act was such a shock to Mercer, and he felt robbed of the chance to be able to make it up to Ned. The honor he felt when Ned's family asked him to give the eulogy at the funeral added more to the debt he owed the man. Mercer thought his words seemed hollow and unable to convey his genuine gratitude, his full measure of respect and admiration for Ned and his actions. Yet those words were moving to the people who were in attendance. Ned's friends and relatives, other than the Leaf Runners and those few present from Highbridge, had no idea who Mercer was and why he spoke so eloquently of Ned. After the funeral, all present knew the true bond between the two men and the deep-seated respect Mercer felt for Ned.

Per the communique from Dino, they were to enter Vatican City at Saint Anne's Gate, where special passes were awaiting them. When they arrived at the gate, they provided their identification papers to a member of the Swiss Guard, who wore a colorful blue, orange, yellow, and red striped uniform and had a black beret resting at an angle on his head. The guard contacted Dino using a telephone inside the guard station. Dino, clean-cut, in a suit, and about thirty years old, arrived within ten minutes and greeted them warmly.

As he led them toward the city's interior, Dino said, "I'm very pleased to meet relatives of Jimmy. He was one of the first

Leaf Runners and a great mentor of mine. Jimmy was my trainer. He helped identify others with the ability and worked to create the Leaf Runner organization. However, after a few harrowing experiences, I vowed never to use this ability as I believe it is dangerous to tamper with history."

Dino pulled an object from an inside suit pocket and held out his hand for them to see.

"Hey," exclaimed Mercer. "That's the Evans family crest. It's just like the one Uncle Stephen gave me."

"Jimmy told me to be careful who you trust. He handed this to me as he told me I was one of the few people he *did* trust," said Dino.

"Trust," murmured Mercer. *Is that why his uncle sent the crest?*

Dino continued to provide his oral history of the Leaf Runners, emphasizing Jimmy's contributions. He led them through the Apostolic Library with its pristine checkerboard marble floor, gilded molding and trim, and beautiful ornate frescoes. They eventually arrived in an area with several offices called the Librarian's Room. Dino invited them to sit in a small conference area where their discussion would be private.

"Why was Jimmy here, in Rome?" asked Lizzy after they were seated.

Dino hesitated, then said, "No one knew where Jimmy was. Not until you discovered he was killed here. Jimmy…well, I can only guess he must have come to Rome to investigate the group we now know as God's Left Hand. The Leaf Runners knew that history was being modified by collectively observing changes in our ancestral trees. These were changes that could only have been brought about by someone with the abilities of a Leaf Runner. We didn't know at the time that someone with a great deal of money had assembled this group and was developing their skills."

"That someone was Professor Lazzaro Giannelli, a physicist at New York University. He's no longer a problem," said Mercer. After a brief pause, he said, "Here, we have something to show you. The only thing found on his body was a paper with this partial rubbing of a broach or pendant." Mercer pulled the copy of the rubbing from his coat pocket and handed it to Dino.

Dino studied it quizzically, then raised his eyebrows and said, "This is not a broach. I've seen this before. It is a Roman coin that looks like one we have here in our archives. Let me show you." He went to a computer terminal and, after typing something into the keyboard and making a few clicks of the mouse, turned the monitor so they could see a picture of an ancient coin. The rubbing was an exact match for a portion of the coin.

"'Futurum est in me ipso,'" said Lizzy. "The future is within me?"

"Correct," said Dino. He thought for a second and then said, "Well, as Jimmy uncovered more about who God's Left Hand was and what they were doing, he put himself in danger. He knew this was so because I recall the last thing he said to me before he disappeared. He wanted me to make sure I remembered what he said if I didn't see him again. But his words seemed like a little thing at the time, so I never thought about it further. Maybe it is important…" He trailed off.

"What is important?" asked Lizzy after waiting a few seconds for Dino to finish.

Dino jumped slightly in surprise, then looked intently at Lizzy as he continued, "Jimmy told me, 'They're looking to the future.'"

Lizzy and Mercer looked at each other, bewildered. Both had the same thought.

Lizzy said absently, "Is that all there is? Dino, was there anything else he said to you?"

Dino shrugged his shoulders, shook his head, and said, "Nothing. I am sorry."

* * * * *

Mercer had barely spoken a word since they left the Vatican. As the three sat at the outdoor table and ate, it was like he was somewhere else. He hardly acknowledged their presence. Yet even in the darkening evening, Aniyah could see the lines of stress on his face and the tenseness in his body.

"Is everything okay, Mercer?" Aniyah asked. Lizzy gave her a sideways glance and shook her head slightly.

Mercer grunted and said, "I need some time. I'll see you two later."

With that, he stood and left, heading toward the river.

After Mercer was out of earshot, Aniyah said, "Lizzy, what was that all about?"

"He's worried and confused," said Lizzy.

"Worried about what?"

Lizzy said, "He was hoping for closure today. But instead, we have more questions. Right now, he's struggling with who he is and what he's become. In some ways, he wants everything to go back to normal, the way things used to be."

"How do you know? I've been with you two all day, and he's barely spoken a word."

Lizzy thought for a few seconds before confiding, "Mercer and I discovered something about ourselves, something no one else knows."

Aniyah stiffened and leaned toward Lizzy.

"What?" Aniyah drew the word out as if digging for some juicy gossip.

"Mercer and I have a…connection. We each have a sense of what the other is thinking and feeling."

"Like you're…telepathic?"

"No, I wouldn't say that. It's more like intuition or a sixth sense. It's not like we can read each other's minds or anything. But I can tell if he's happy or sad or if he's in danger."

"Incredible," said Aniyah in disbelief.

"I know my brother. Whenever he gets this way, he disappears for months on end. He withdraws from his family and tries to go it alone. What he needs right now is someone to talk to."

"Huh? But you just said—"

"Mercer's frightened and doesn't want anyone to see him this way. I never knew that before. I just thought he didn't want anything to do with me, so I left him alone." Then Lizzy murmured, "That was a mistake."

"So why don't you go to him now?"

Lizzy smiled weakly and said, "I *am* with him, in a way. But he needs something more. He needs to matter to someone else, someone who isn't family."

Aniyah turned her head and looked over her shoulder in the direction Mercer had gone.

* * * * *

Mercer was lost in thought while standing on the Ponte Flamingo bridge and looking down the River Tiber as the city lights reflected off its rippling surface. Filled with doubt and regret, he wondered if he could do what Dino had done. Could he vow never to use his ability? Should he?

Suddenly, someone was standing beside him, and he jumped in alarm.

Aniyah smiled and said, "I'm sorry. I didn't mean to scare you."

Flushed, Mercer said, "Oh, it's okay." Then, after a short pause, he said, "I was just standing here thinking."

Aniyah sighed and said, "It's a noble thing, what Dino did."

Surprised, Mercer said, "What? How did you know…?"

"You've been…preoccupied ever since we met him. You lost your brother. You lost a friend. Lizzy was in danger, and you could've lost her. You even almost lost your own life. And for what? So you could be some sort of time cop?"

He considered her words for a moment, then said, "Aniyah, I don't know if I can do this. I thought I needed to protect Lizzy. Instead, she protected me. She's all in on being a Leaf Runner. But I just don't know. I mean, is this what I'm supposed to do? Can I choose not to? Is it even up to me?"

"Yes, it's up to you. No one can force you to do anything. But walking away won't make you, or Lizzy, any safer. As long as we have the ability, we'll be targets because of what we're capable of, because we're Leaf Runners. You saved Charles Darwin. You and Lizzy saved Martin Luther. These are not small things. You helped to preserve history. These important historical figures weren't the first to be threatened, and they won't be the last. Ned knew it. And so do you."

She smiled. He looked into her eyes and saw intensity and sincerity. Of course, she was right. Everything she said was right. But that didn't make it any easier.

Her smile widened to reveal a beautiful grin. Then she moved closer to him and offered flirtatiously, "Oh, and I knew you were thinking about Dino because Lizzy told me. She told me about the...bond between you two."

"Of course," he said, shaking his head. He continued, "But you're right. I owe it to Ned. I owe it to Jimmy. I owe it to the millions throughout history who might not be here or might not be free if we don't protect them."

"I couldn't agree more," she said.

He turned and stared at the river for a moment as the emotions came to a boil within, finally saying with resolve, "It *is* my choice, and I choose to be the best I can be, whether that be a fund manager, a Leaf Runner, a friend, a brother..."

Choked up with emotion, he struggled to finish his words. Then he pivoted toward her and, in a shaky voice, said, "...or a man."

Aniyah tensed as Mercer swept her into his arms, her smiling face jolted into a mask of surprise. Her eyes locked onto his, then trembled, holding his stare as though an epic battle waged behind them. His grip was gentle yet unyielding as he pressed into her, lips inching ever closer. Mercer stopped moving toward her, wondering if his advance had been some great mistake, a tragically irreversible impulse. It seemed an eternity as he contemplated what to do. Just as he was about to release her and turn away in embarrassment, the alarm in her expression softened, as did her body. Then she tilted her head and aggressively pressed her lips into his. The world and all its troubles ebbed away from conscious thought as they kissed in a blaze of passion, bathed in the glow of the rising full moon as it reflected off the undulating waters of the River Tiber.

About the Author

John C. Stroebel was born and raised in the Driftless Area in Wisconsin and spent many summers baling hay on local farms in the hills around his small town. Since he could walk, he loved taking things apart to see how they worked and learning how to piece them back together. This passion eventually resulted in his graduating with an electrical engineering degree from the University of Minnesota. In 1987, he began designing implantable medical devices and has since amassed more than three-dozen patents in the field. His contributions have directly impacted the lives of millions of people worldwide.

John and his wife, Sue, have been married for over thirty years. While raising four children and fostering many more, John never lost that passion: taking things apart and putting them back together again. As COVID forced many to work from home, John took the opportunity to rework his lifelong interest. Instead of tinkering with electronics, John began dissecting and reassembling thoughts into words and words into stories. With the long days at home and a gentle nudge from his wife, John pieced together what would soon become *Leaf Runner*, his first full-length novel.

www.ingramcontent.com/pod-product-compliance
Lightning Source LLC
Chambersburg PA
CBHW051109300726
48981CB00001B/66